Suddenly, Kady shivered; he stepped toward her.

He liked being here with Kady, standing in the outdoors, far away from the burden of his memories, the strangling ties of his job. Standing before this beautiful vista of sand and surf, beside an equally beautiful and fascinating woman, almost felt surreal.

Kady rubbed her hands up and down her bare arms.

"Are you cold?"

"Yes. I should have grabbed my wrap before we came outside."

Dylan shrugged out of his jacket and placed it over her shoulders. She took the lapels in her hands and drew the coat around her.

"Better?"

She met his gaze. "Much."

They continued to stare at each other. Dylan was so drawn to this woman, he should be fighting it. It wasn't safe for either of them, and yet...he slid his arm around her waist. When she didn't move away, he pulled her closer.

Dear Reader,

Who doesn't love flowers? Or weddings? How about a mystery thrown in for good measure?

The Bridal Bouquet, the fourth installment in The Business of Weddings series, has all of the above, along with two strong-willed characters out to achieve their goals. Problem is, their goals don't include love so, of course, they can't help falling for each other.

Kady Lawrence has a lot to prove if she wants to take over the family floral shop. Attending the annual floral convention and winning the wedding bouquet competition is all part of her plan, that is until DEA special agent Dylan Matthews walks into her life.

Dylan has an old score to settle and the criminal in question is hiding out near Cypress Pointe. How to catch him? Pose undercover at the floral convention to gather information about the town and its people. Sounds easy enough. But bad guys have a way of changing the rules. Soon Dylan finds himself protecting Kady, and as danger escalates, love blossoms.

Welcome back to Cypress Pointe. For a small town, there always seems to be something exciting going on! You'll catch up with characters from my previous books and find out if any wedding bells will chime in the future. After all, this is the business of weddings.

Tara Randel

HEARTWARMING

The Bridal Bouquet

———

USA TODAY Bestselling Author

Tara Randel

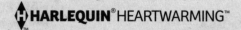

H HARLEQUIN®HEARTWARMING™

Recycling programs
for this product may
not exist in your area.

ISBN-13: 978-0-373-36793-1

The Bridal Bouquet

Copyright © 2016 by Tara Spicer

All rights reserved. Except for use in any review, the reproduction or utilization of this work in whole or in part in any form by any electronic, mechanical or other means, now known or hereinafter invented, including xerography, photocopying and recording, or in any information storage or retrieval system, is forbidden without the written permission of the publisher, Harlequin Enterprises Limited, 225 Duncan Mill Road, Don Mills, Ontario M3B 3K9, Canada.

This is a work of fiction. Names, characters, places and incidents are either the product of the author's imagination or are used fictitiously, and any resemblance to actual persons, living or dead, business establishments, events or locales is entirely coincidental.

This edition published by arrangement with Harlequin Books S.A.

For questions and comments about the quality of this book, please contact us at CustomerService@Harlequin.com.

® and TM are trademarks of Harlequin Enterprises Limited or its corporate affiliates. Trademarks indicated with ® are registered in the United States Patent and Trademark Office, the Canadian Intellectual Property Office and in other countries.

Printed in U.S.A.

Tara Randel is an award-winning, *USA TODAY* bestselling author of eleven novels. Family values, a bit of mystery and, of course, love and romance are her favorite themes, because she believes love is the greatest gift of all. Tara lives on the West Coast of Florida, where gorgeous sunsets and beautiful weather inspire the creation of heartwarming stories. This is her fourth book for Harlequin Heartwarming. Visit Tara at tararandel.com. Like her on Facebook at Tara Randel Books.

Books by Tara Randel

Harlequin Heartwarming

Honeysuckle Bride
Magnolia Bride
Orange Blossom Brides

To my wonderful friends Tiffany and Christian.

Thanks for the inspiration, Christian.
Your stories really lit a fire under me.

CHAPTER ONE

K ADY L AWRENCE DODGED the raucous wedding party eagerly heading for the reception-bound vehicles idling in the parking lot. Now that the photographer was concentrating solely on romantic bride-and-groom shots, Kady could transport the floral arrangements from the beach ceremony to the Grand Cypress Hotel ballroom.

Her feet sank into the cool, smooth sand, her flats keeping a minimum of the sugary grains from shifting into her shoes and tickling her toes. The sun shone bright on this seasonally cool January day, making this postcard-perfect weather in Cypress Pointe, Florida. The azure-blue sky played backdrop to fluffy, scuttling clouds above. A bride's dream come true, she thought. She glimpsed the couple staring into each other's eyes, the crystalline waters of the Gulf of Mexico a stunning vista in the background.

A brisk wind had whipped through during

the ceremony, rustling the skirts of the bridesmaids' dresses. But the bride lifted her face
to the sky and laughed, welcoming the heady
bluster with unbridled delight. The air settled
after the brief swirl, but the gulf waters continued to churn, a vivid reminder of the natu-
ral elements surrounding them.

While the couple laughed and enjoyed their
special day, Kady's thoughts ran more along
the lines of asking the photographer if she
could place some of his wedding prints on display in her family's flower shop. She had three
goals in life—number one, to make The Lavish Lily *the* one-stop floral shop for brides and
all bridal-related events. Working with fellow
wedding professionals could only propel her
dream forward.

Her other goals fed off the first—upgrade
the family flower shop and win the wedding-
bouquet category at the annual florist convention this year. Goals she was determined to
fulfill, no matter what roadblocks stood in her
way.

The late morning ceremony had been per-
formed on a wide wooden platform situated directly on the beach, with rows of bow-festooned
chairs lined up for the guests. On either end of
the platform were waist-high white pillars, a

beautiful flower arrangement placed on each for the ceremony.

Kady approached the first arrangement, sinking her nose into the fragrant collection. She adored the scent of fresh flowers, never tiring of the sweet aroma that touched her soul. Instead of going with a dozen traditional red roses, the bride had requested all white to go with her lovely gown, which was complemented by a red waist sash. Kady had designed a combination of gardenias, snow-white dahlias and white larkspur for height. Baby's breath was nestled throughout, the arrangement set in crystal containers and each accented with a bright red bow. Quite stunning, if she did say so herself.

"Kady," Nellie, the bride, called out as her new husband took her hand to help her step from the platform onto the red aisle runner. "The flowers are gorgeous. I didn't think you'd be able to create exactly what I wanted."

Why did everyone doubt her? She prided herself on being a competent floral designer and took each and every arrangement to heart. She knew from the beginning which flowers would please the bride and her mother, then sold them on her vision.

"Wait until you get to the reception."

Nellie beamed. "We're headed there now. See you there."

Kady nodded. "Just let me get these arrangements into the van. I'm delivering them myself."

"You are staying for the party, aren't you?"

Kady had been surprised at the impromptu invitation the last time she'd met with the bride. Normally she placed the flowers and other reception decor the bride had ordered, then left. But when Nellie asked her to join in the reception, she'd been honored.

"Thanks. That's so nice of you but I've just got a lot on my plate right now."

"I have a bunch of single cousins…" The bride left her suggestion open-ended, trying to wheedle Kady into changing her mind.

"I'm not in the market for a guy." Too many things to focus on at the moment, like pouring her time and energy into marketing the shop to brides. She had future weddings lined up and needed to prove to her parents that birthdays and funerals weren't the only ways to sustain their business.

Besides, she wasn't dressed for the occasion, even though she always looked appropriate when making a delivery. Today, she'd matched a fitted coral blouse with a flowing, patterned skirt. Pretty, but definitely not wedding attire. She'd pulled her shoulder-length hair into a ponytail to keep it out of the way while she worked.

"Come on. Every girl dreams of her special day," the bride teased.

"Not me."

Kady had never jumped on the crazy-bride bandwagon. Not after falling for a guy and having had him stomp on her heart. Instead, she was content to design flowers and hope her parents someday saw the talented woman she had grown into, rather than the aimless youth she'd once been.

"Let's go, babe," Dean, the groom, said. Nellie waved and the couple headed for their limousine.

It took three trips and fifteen minutes for Kady to get the flowers and pillars secured in the van before she set off for the reception. As she drove, she reviewed her mental checklist. She'd placed centerpieces and additional arrangements around the ballroom in advance of everyone arriving. The extra bridal bouquet, to be tossed into the group of single women at some point during the party, was waiting on a side table. Kady had even come up with what she dubbed a bouquet-docking station, a safe place for the bride and attendants to store their bouquets so they didn't get lost or ruined during the reception. Satisfied, Kady stepped on the gas. The sooner she delivered these ceremony flowers, the sooner she'd be done.

She'd just parked in the hotel lot when her cell phone rang. She swiped the screen and frowned. Her brother's number.

"Hey, Will."

"What time will you be back at the shop?" Right to the point, as always.

Kady held back a groan. Her older brother, the "doer of no wrong," checking in on her. She was thirty years old, for Pete's sake. When would her family stop thinking of her as a screwup? Okay, so years ago she'd gotten sidetracked and forgotten to take the work van to get an oil change. And yeah, yeah, the engine had blown. And yes, she'd botched a big order from the wholesaler one time when she'd been in her Save the Manatee phase and spent more time gathering names on petitions than doing inventory.

Always curious by nature, her mind switched gears with each new adventure calling her name. The more unique the challenge, the more Kady embraced it and stored away the experience, sure she'd later use the knowledge she'd gained.

Her parents, spending long hours running the flower shop, were either too busy or frustrated to redirect their inquisitive daughter. Especially when Kady's behavior continued well into her twenties.

It wasn't until she'd gone to live with her beloved aunt Cynthia, after her parents had thrown up their hands at her behavior, that Kady began to focus. Her aunt, who designed and handmade her own jewelry, stumbled upon the artistic nature in her and began to tap into Kady's energies. She encouraged Kady to assist her and Kady quickly realized she loved being creative. Her openness to so many different ideas made her excel at designing. And renewed her love for the floral shop. Merging her two passions together, she decided, The Lavish Lily would become her destiny.

For three years now she'd been full-time at the shop. She'd slowly taken over designing duties, making most of the deliveries and manning the front counter. No mishaps. No mistakes. So what if it had taken her a while to figure out what she wanted to do with her talent and abilities, traveling down a twisty, turning path instead of being on the straight and narrow. She'd made it here, finding purpose in her life. Why couldn't her family credit the change in her?

"I'm at the hotel. Let me get the delivery inside, make sure everything else is in place. Then I'll be there."

"How long?"

"Not sure. I'll call you when I leave."

"We're waiting."

Kady grimaced as she ended the call. She hated these family meetings. No good ever came from them, especially for her. Her parents had been acting oddly lately and Will, an accountant who didn't have the least interest in flowers, was hanging around the shop all the time. Yes, he had a share in the family business, but he'd never been involved with the day-to-day running of it. And had even been MIA for a long while. Why show up now?

She'd ignored their abrupt silences whenever she walked into the place, tried not to speculate why, lately, she alone worked the long hours filling wedding orders. Something was up, and by her brother's hounding, she figured it would be revealed this afternoon.

Brushing off the useless foreboding, she went to the back of the van to remove the first arrangement. Will would do what he wanted and her parents would be fine with it. All she could do was concentrate on getting new customers, brides specifically, and grow the business. Then maybe her parents would look at her with pride, like they did at Will.

Loud chatter spilled from the banquet room as Kady entered. The place was filled with milling guests congratulating the newly married couple. A few restless children raced around the dance floor, ignoring their mother's sharp tones imploring them to calm down. The DJ played soft music while people mingled. Lunch would be served soon if the delicious aromas wafting from the kitchen were any indication. Her tummy growling, Kady went about her job, blending in, while checking one last time to make sure all the arrangements she'd placed earlier were in good shape.

At the center of each table, white pillar candles flickered in tall hurricane glasses. The same floral theme—simple white flowers cascading around the glass—made a dramatic effect against the deep red table linen. The menu, printed in raised gold script, rested upon milk-white plates. The crystal glasses sported gold rims. The utensils, wrapped in a red napkin circled with a white-and-gold ring, tied the table ensemble together.

Subdued and elegant. Just what the bride dreamed of. Exactly what the wedding planner and Kady had delivered.

On her last trip with the final arrangement, Kady made her way around the far wall intent on the gift table. Only a few steps from her destination, she was suddenly under siege by a half-dozen playing children. She went into football mode, dodging first to the left, then to the right, spinning to avoid a rushing child as she held on tightly to the container of flowers. After evading the possible disaster, she grinned, impressed by her running-back skills. Who knew she was so light on her feet? The path clear now, she moved forward until she stepped on an abandoned toy left behind by one of the kids. Her ankle turned. Bracing herself, she securely locked her arms around the crystal container, holding on for dear life. But instead of going down, strong hands gripped her upper arms and kept her from falling.

Relieved, she looked over her shoulder, glimpsing the most unusual pair of blue eyes she'd ever seen. Actually, blue wasn't entirely correct. A hint of silver turned them an unusual shade of metallic gray. The man's somber expression matched the concern she read there and his very handsome face garnered her full attention.

"Steady there." His husky voice spoke close to her ear, sending shivers over her skin.

Rattled, she set down the flowers and turned to face her rescuer. "Thanks. That could have been a disaster."

"Then it's a good thing I happened to be nearby." A half grin curved his lips.

Kady's heart thumped in her chest. Talk about fantastic timing. She sneaked a peek at him. Yeah, she was going with not spilling the flowers to explain her racing pulse.

Mr. Awesome Eyes narrowed said eyes and stared down at one of the boys, perhaps the ringleader. "You should take the kids outside, Mikey. Otherwise I might have to get your daddy after you."

Mikey paled before nodding. "I will. Please don't tell Dad."

"Then quit running around when your mother asked you to stop."

The inherent command in his deep tone brooked no disobedience. Something told her she wouldn't want to get on the wrong side of this man.

The youngster rounded up the remaining children and they scurried out to the pool area before heading off the patio to a wide mani-cured lawn at the side of the hotel. Plenty of free space to run unchecked out there.

The stranger focused on her. "Bored kids

and distracted parents. Not the best combination at a wedding reception."

"No." She knew she should leave now, get back to the shop, but her feet seemed rooted to the spot. His cologne enveloped her. She tried to sort out the elements in the spicy fragrance like she always did when defining new scents, but his nearness made her jittery. Tucking an errant strand of hair behind her ear, she tried not to squirm.

The stranger stuck out his hand. "Dylan."

She accepted his warm, strong grip, surprised by a zing of awareness. "Kady."

He held on to her hand a few seconds longer than necessary. In that time, she noticed more about him. Tall. Hair razor-cut. Military? Even with the short look, she noticed a hint of gray peppering his temples. Tanned olive skin, as though he spent many hours outdoors. He filled the black suit paired with a charcoal shirt and red tie to perfection, his broad shoulders straight, his lean build steady.

She gulped. "I should probably go."

"You just got here."

"Only to deliver the flowers."

He tilted his head, his strange-colored eyes regarding her with unwavering scrutiny. "You're the most fascinating person at this party."

Fascinating? That was new. Why not throw *sublime* into that description, she thought, and hid a laugh. Still, she'd take it. Compliments had been few and far between lately.

"Um, thanks. I think."

"The way you saved those flowers? Classic football move. You got my attention right away."

He grinned, his serious expression lifting. Her breath caught at the transformation. When somber, he was handsome. Grinning, he was downright gorgeous. Okay, who was she kidding? She was way out of her element right now.

Before she could remind him she'd saved the flowers thanks to him, he was speaking again.

"I was debating a cheesy line about how your beauty struck me from across the room. Guess you're a bit too savvy than to fall for that."

"Yeah. Every woman hates to be called beautiful."

He chuckled. "In that case, it's true. I did notice you as soon as you came through the door."

"It was either that or the commotion from the kids."

"Nah. I really did notice you."

What should she say now? She felt her face

flush and hoped beyond measure her cheeks didn't light up like a neon sign flashing her guilty pleasure. How often did a good-looking guy notice her from across the room? Ah… never?

"Despite your line, I am glad you were here when I tripped."

"I live to serve."

She half expected a formal bow, like the staid British lords she read about in Regency novels. "So… I need to get going."

"You can't stay a few more minutes?"

She wanted to. More than anything. "I'm busy. Besides, this looks like a family reunion as well as a reception. I don't want to over-step."

"To be honest, that's kind of why I'd like you to stay. My cousin is the bride, so yeah, this is a reunion. I haven't seen most of my relatives for a few years and I'm all talked out. If my grandmother asks me one more time when I'm getting married, then points me to one of my cousin's single friends, I may lose it."

"Gee, that's tough. Dealing with people who love you."

He had the grace to smile disparagingly. "I'm a rotten grandson."

They both chuckled. Despite his complaining, she heard the affection in his tone for his grandmother. "So why haven't you seen your family in a while, if you don't mind my asking?"

"My job, mostly."

A waiter passed by, carrying a tray of sparkling champagne in crystal flutes. When he stopped, Dylan removed two, handing one to Kady.

"Oh, no. I shouldn't. I'm working."

"How about a quick toast. To new friends." He clinked his glass to hers.

"To new friends," she agreed.

She took a sip, noticing Dylan did the same. She was glad to see he didn't knock it back like some of the party animals she'd run across at other receptions.

They stood in awkward silence. Finally, Kady placed her glass on the table beside her. "So, it was nice meeting you."

"Maybe we'll run into each other?"

"Are you staying in Cypress Pointe long?"

"Depends on the coin toss."

"Excuse me?"

His mouth curved at the corners. "Inside family joke. Sorry."

She opened her mouth to ask him to elaborate, when an older gentleman approached

Dylan and started a conversation. Boxed into the corner, she couldn't leave until one of the men moved. After a few long minutes of trying not to eavesdrop, she cleared her throat. Dylan glanced her way.

"Uncle Frank, give me a few?"

Uncle Frank looked at Kady, then back to Dylan, and winked. "Sure, son."

Dylan slanted her an amused glance. "See."

"I get it now. Is your entire family comprised of matchmakers?"

"Yep. And I have three brothers who are also single. We try to stay low-key during family events. Keeps the meddlers from focusing on us."

"So you're saying *I* actually rescued *you*?"

His stunning eyes widened in surprise. "Yes, I'd say you had."

"Rescuer *and* floral designer." She pantomimed a motion of wiping her hands. "My work is done here."

Dylan laughed, his eyes filled with…admiration?

"Sure I can't convince you to stick around?"

"Sorry. I have a meeting I can't miss."

"Too bad. With you, this reception might have been fun."

"Thanks for the compliment."

At his wink, her heart thumped.
"Anytime."

DYLAN MATTHEWS WATCHED Kady as she weaved
through the crowd, stopped to hug the bride
and then exited through the same doors she'd
first walked through. He wasn't kidding when
he dropped the line about noticing her from
across the room. She'd caught his eye at first
glance and he was immediately fascinated.

Was it because the light draped her just the
right way when she'd entered the room? What
else explained how his gaze lit on her pretty
face? He rubbed a hand over his cleanly shaven
jaw. He'd been cooped up far too long. That
would explain the unusually poetic notions
rummaging around in his head.

As she'd drawn closer, he noticed she was
tall, not as tall as his six feet, but it wouldn't
take much effort for their eyes to meet. Her
brown hair was pulled into a ponytail, with
little fly-away strands framing her face. She'd
smiled, her cheeks flushed as she went about
her business.

When he'd braced her arms with his hands
to keep her from falling, he'd caught a whiff of
something fruity as he pulled her close. Raspberry? Her expression, when she turned, was

shaken but grateful. Then he got up close to her honey-brown eyes. A jolt seared his gut and he hesitated letting go of the connection.

When was the last time he'd recognized such a buzz of attraction? A long time, if he was honest. And he always tried to be honest with himself—good, bad or otherwise.

Best of all, she traded quips like a pro. Didn't miss a beat. Had to be the best quality about her. After talking with her, he realized he'd enjoyed every minute.

Something he hadn't experienced in quite a while.

With a sigh, he set down his glass beside Kady's. Too bad she took off. He would have liked to get to know her better. Her good humor had lifted some of the darkness that hung over him.

Before he had a chance to dwell on the past, his older brother, Derrick, joined him.

"Mom's worried about you."

"When is she not worried?" Dylan countered.

"When we're all at home under her roof where she can keep an eye on us."

"She does realize we're grown men, right?"

"She's a mother. According to her, we'll always be her babies."

Dylan shuddered. "Heaven save us."

"I saw you talking to a woman. Did Gram send her over?"

"No."

"You scare her off with your brooding Heathcliff imitation?"

"No, she had to work. She's the florist who supplied the flowers for the wedding."

"Huh. Nice job."

"Since when do you notice flowers?"

"Since I'm trying to be evolved." Derrick looked to the closest table where Kady had left an arrangement. "Hey, these are pretty."

Dylan laughed. "Evolved, hmm?"

"Complaints from the last two women I dated."

"And you're listening to their suggestions? After they dumped you? I'm impressed."

Derrick shrugged his shoulders as if brushing off Dylan's jab. "So how are you doing? Leg okay?"

At the mention of his injury, Dylan reached down and rubbed the back of his thigh where the exit wound still seemed raw. The gunshot damage had taken longer to heal than he'd hoped. On the bullet's journey through his thigh, it nicked the femur and splintered the bone. Multiple surgeries removed the fragments. Repairing structural damage had laid him up. Not that he was complaining. If the bullet had hit his femoral artery, it would have been lights out. Physical therapy had finished two weeks ago, but the ache still haunted him.

Besides the physical pain, there was the emotional as well. A constant reminder of whom he'd lost. A partner and a good friend. The grim reality Kady had eclipsed a few minutes ago returned with a vengeance. The constant enemy who never left his soul.

"I'm fine."

"Not true. I saw you favoring your leg when we walked into the hotel. Too much activity today?"

"Since when is sitting at the beach and walking into a building too much activity?"

"When you're recovering from a gunshot wound."

"I'm fine," he repeated through clenched teeth.

Derrick held his hand up in defense. "Hey, man. If you say so."

He wasn't fine. Not by a long shot. But he wouldn't burden Derrick, or his other brothers, and especially not his mother, with his problems. The burden and the guilt were his and his alone to carry.

When Dylan started as a special agent for the DEA ten years ago, he'd gotten into a few tight spots. Some moments had even been dangerous, since he went after guys who would rather shoot first and run later. He was relentless when pursuing dealers who put drugs on the streets. His good fortune finally came to an end when he ticked off the wrong guy.

He and his partner, Eddie, had spent many months in Miami planning to cut off the pipeline of a major dealer who didn't appreciate them gumming up his operation. Esposa was an especially tenacious criminal, moving operations whenever he and Eddie got a lead on his location. They'd played cat and mouse for so long, Dylan wasn't sure if he'd ever arrest this guy. He made headway by securing an informant within Esposa's organization. Every time the creep turned around, Dylan was right on him. But with that success, Dylan had made an enemy—an enemy who wanted him out of the picture permanently. Here Dylan was still breathing, while Eddie's wife and son grieved the man they'd loved.

Six months. Six long, hard months recovering from the wound. He had survived. Eddie had taken a fatal bullet. The shot meant for Dylan. Nothing could make him forget that fact. And nothing would stop him until the shooter paid.

Except that he was on desk duty at the division office for the foreseeable future. He was only thirty-five. Was his career over?

His jaw tensed as he thought about his fate, when his brother interrupted.

"Heads up, bro. I overheard Mom talking to Aunt Betty."

Derrick stared at Dylan, waiting. His brother loved to draw out a moment.

"And?"

"The florist convention is next week."

Dread immediately gripped Dylan. "How did we not know this?"

"Because Mom lulled us into a false sense of complacency. Since she hasn't mentioned it, our guards were down," Derrick replied. "She's sneaky like that."

Jasmine Matthews loved her boys. Enough to guilt or con them into doing her bidding and not feeling the least bit of remorse.

"To make matters worse, the convention is at this very hotel. I'm sure her evil plan is to get one of us to agree to stay since we already have rooms here."

For a man who didn't panic over much,

Dylan's fight-or-flight response kicked in. "We gotta get out of this."

Every year since their father died, their mother guilted her sons into attending the convention with her. Since she usually won some award, she claimed she needed a date to the banquet. Dylan had lucked out of this duty for five years now, but he was on borrowed time.

Belatedly he understood why his mother hadn't made a fuss about not supplying the flowers for his cousin's wedding. For the most part, she created arrangements for all the family affairs. He assumed she hadn't done so this time because of the distance, since she lived in Cocoa Beach, on the other side of the state from Cypress Pointe. Although a very capable woman, she would have had to work with a local florist due to the logistics of the ceremony and reception. Now he realized she had a much greater goal in mind.

Derrick shook his head. "Too late. Mom wants all of us to stop by her room after the reception."

Dylan closed his eyes. His thigh began to burn.

"Flip you for it?" Derrick said.

His eyes flew open. "No way. You cheat."

Derrick's fake offense was funny. "Hey."

"I saw the double-sided coin last time."

His brother sent him a sheepish smile. "You can't blame me."

"Deke does. He got stuck going with Mom."

"Guess that explains why he punches me in the arm every time he sees me."

"You deserve it." He leveled his brother with his meanest special-agent glare. "We'll check the coin before we toss it."

"Spoilsport," Derrick grumbled. "I don't want to lose."

"None of us do, bro."

CHAPTER TWO

KADY PARKED THE van in the alley behind the shop and hurried inside. A smile still remained on her lips. Meeting Dylan had been a pleasant surprise. His cologne lingered in her memory. And those eyes? Unforgettable. Her mind shifted to the image of his face... Stop. She had to focus on the business. Whenever her parents called a meeting it was important and she expected this time to be no different. She needed to be on her toes, not crushing over a handsome guy she'd just met.

Her smile faded as she entered the workroom. Booming from the speakers, Elvis sang about a hound dog. Ugh. She admired the singer, but wasn't a fan of fifties music. Her parents loved those songs, despite Kady's suggestion they play a variety of music to appeal to their customers. In Kady's vision of an elegant floral shop where brides-to-be came to discuss their arrangements, they'd be better served with soft jazz or classical music in the background. Not folks going on about rockin' around the clock or waking up Susie.

"Hi, guys," she called out over the music, heading straight to the radio to lower the volume.

"How did the delivery go?" her mother asked as she added hypericum berries to the arrangement she was assembling.

"Everything went smoothly." Kady leaned against the table. "That's beautiful, Mom."

Her mother stepped back to scrutinize her creation. "Mr. Andrews will be in soon to pick this up. Would you mind placing it in the cooler while I clean up?"

"Sure."

Mr. Andrews came by every Saturday at noon to purchase his preordered arrangement. His wife had recently moved into an assisted-living facility and the sweet man brought her flowers every week.

Moving to the front of the shop, Kady placed the order in the cooler. Another cooler in the workroom held spare arrangements for sale to walk-ins. Kady had been in The Lavish Lily earlier, before the wedding, to put together some of the simple arrangements. She was glad to see three of them were gone.

"Were we busy this morning?" she asked

her dad. He was hovering by the cash register and glanced up but didn't look directly at her. Pushing his glasses to the bridge of his nose, he stared down again. Kady got the distinct impression he'd intentionally avoided looking at her. "Where's Will?"

At her brother's name, her dad's head came up. "Ran down the street to buy lunch. Once Mr. Andrews collects his order, we're closing down for the day."

"What? But it's beautiful out and people are sure to stop in. We'll lose business."

"We have things to discuss."

"Things more important than waiting on customers?"

Her father frowned. "Depending on how this meeting goes, we may reopen later this afternoon."

"But—"

"Not now, Kady."

Reprimanded, she returned to the workroom. Her mother hadn't yet tidied up the table, so Kady did, returning the tools to their correct places. When Kady started here full-time, she'd organized the cluttered space. Her mother's tendency to leave tools around drove Kady crazy, so she'd purchased medium-sized storage bins. With a labeler, she'd marked each bin—one for tape, another for glue sticks, wires, foam and the list went on.

Her parents hadn't been thrilled by the extra expense, since they ran the shop on a shoestring budget. Mark and Ruthie Lawrence operated a tight ship, financially speaking. The Lavish Lily had been in the Lawrence family for three decades. Lately, when Kady suggested ideas to spruce up the shop, her folks hesitated, like when she requested the storage bins. She'd finally broken down and bought the items herself.

"Mom, what's up with this meeting?"

Her mother wiped her hands with a paper towel and tossed it in the garbage can in the corner. "You'll find out when Will gets back."

"Is it about hiring storefront help? We could really use someone to take orders."

"I'm sure the topic will come up."

It did quite frequently. Her parents were notorious for not being able to keep good employees, but with Kady courting the wedding market, they needed a reliable assistant.

"So what's the big secret I don't know about?"

When her mother wouldn't meet her eyes, Kady realized there was something huge going on. Something the three of them must have already discussed without her. Her stomach sank.

She knew she was always the odd man out, but not being included in whatever the family had decided hurt more than she expected.

"Kady, honey…"

She held up her hand. "It's fine, Mom. We'll wait until Will gets back."

The bell over the front door chimed and Kady's stomach twisted more. She heard her father speaking, then a softer male voice, and she knew it was Mr. Andrews. She swallowed. Will would return soon. She mentally prepared herself for the battle to come.

While she girded her emotional defenses, her mother scurried about the workroom, gathering paper plates and utensils for their upcoming lunch. The bell sounded again and Will's unmistakable voice boomed from the other room.

"I'm back. Let's all meet up front."

Her mother sent her a nervous glance and exited the room. Taking a deep breath, Kady followed, fisting her hands. She smoothed her facial expression to neutral and joined the others, determined to keep a level head no matter what happened.

Standing amid open folding chairs, her brother handed out wrapped sandwiches as she walked in. Three years older, he had blond hair like their mother, along with intelligent blue eyes.

"Hey, sis. How did the delivery go? The flowers were spectacular."

"Fine." Her suspicions doubled. Will being nice after he'd been dogging her this morning? "This bride was easy to work with. I didn't expect any problems."

"You remembered to set up a pick-up time to get the glass containers back, right?" her father asked. He handed out to-go cups of iced tea.

"Yes, Dad. I spoke to the manager myself."

Kady delivered flowers to many functions at the Grand Cypress Hotel. She and the staff had developed a real camaraderie.

"It's not like I've left anything behind on purpose."

"There was a time when we had to keep tabs on you with the inventory and the van."

Kady wanted to shout. Would her parents ever let go of the past?

"Everything is taken care of, Dad. No worries."

"Good. Then we can get started." He passed Kady her food, which she hadn't had a say in. Will probably got her a tuna fish sandwich when she would have preferred turkey. She pulled back the paper, and sure enough, the fishy smell made her wrinkle her nose. With her stomach already roiling, she set it aside. Tuna probably wasn't a wise choice right now.

Will bit into a pickle, chewed and took a sip of his tea. "Dad, would you like to start?"

Her father cleared his throat. Why was he so nervous?

"Kady, you know this shop has been in our family for generations."

She nodded. Her grandparents originally opened The Lavish Lily. Past history.

"As much as your mother and I have loved working here, proud that our efforts supported the family and we made a name in the community…" He stopped. Sent a pleading look to her mother.

This was not good.

Her father took a deep breath. "We've decided to retire and sell the business."

Silence descended upon the room. After a few seconds, Kady reminded herself to breathe. "What?" she finally spluttered.

Her mother reached over and covered Kady's hand with hers. "We're tired, Kady. It's time for a change."

She studied her parents, who were sitting side by side. They were in their late fifties, kind of young to retire, but they'd worked all her life with few vacations. She regarded them in that light now and noticed fine lines on her mother's face and circles under her father's eyes, his dark brown hair graying. Just as they'd admitted, they did indeed seem worn-out.

So many questions filled her head, Kady didn't know where to start. "How long have you felt like this?"

"Six months," her mother answered, as her father responded simultaneously, "A year."

She sank back in her chair. "Wow."

Will opened a notebook by his side. Probably filled with numbers to satisfy the logical part of his brain. "As the family financial adviser, I need to bring you up to speed." He rattled off figures that made Kady's eyes go wide. Over the years, her parents had invested and saved up a considerable amount of money. More than Kady'd ever imagined.

"If you have so much money, why sell the shop?"

Her parents exchanged glances.

"It's time," her mother answered.

"But you know about my goals. I've already started to make inroads into the wedding market. With that income, I can upgrade the shop. And the florist convention is next week. I'm entered in the wedding-bouquet design category and this year I can beat the competition."

"We appreciate your dedication," her father said. "But we don't have the energy to rebuild the business."

"I do," she protested. "I thought you were on board with my ideas."

"We are…were," her mother said. "But lately we've been talking about going away, and, well—"

"You don't trust me with the shop."

Another abrupt silence sucked the air out of the room. She knew her parents had questioned her commitment ever since she'd started full-time, but in the past year, Kady thought she'd worked hard to erase these doubts. Apparently not.

"Kady," her brother said quietly, "we've talked about this and decided to take a vote. It's the fair thing to do."

Years ago, the ownership of the shop had been divided four ways, each member of the family holding an equal share. Kady already knew which way her parents would vote and assumed Will was on their side.

"Why bother?"

"Now, Kady," her mother admonished. "Don't be like this."

"Be like what? Shocked that you've been talking about a major family decision and didn't think to include me? Heartbroken over the fact that I love this place and now you want to take it away? I thought you believed in my vision." She glared at her brother. "I brought you projections and a business plan. You agreed it was solid. And now you want to yank that out from under me, too?"

"I never said—"

She held up a hand to stop her brother and then faced her parents. "You still see me as the girl who makes mistakes, even though I've proven the opposite. No messing up orders. No losing keys to the delivery van. My mind is focused." She stopped for a breath. Her dreams were evaporating right before her eyes. "Let me buy the shop. I can apply for a loan, work extra hours—"

"Kady—"

"Please give me a chance." She hated begging but what other choice did she have? She could start her own business elsewhere, maybe, but she loved The Lavish Lily.

Tears pricked the backs of her eyelids. No. This couldn't be happening.

"Maybe we could sort something out," her

mother said, clearly troubled by her emotional reaction. "Mark?"

Her father was scrutinizing her. She could see the indecision in his eyes. For the first time since the meeting had started, Kady felt hope.

"You guys can go on a trip or travel in a motor home or whatever you want. I'll be right here, making money."

Her father's brow rose. He always brightened at the prospect of making money. "Our plans aren't carved in stone."

Buoyed by his positive reaction, Kady threw caution to the wind. "How about this—if I win first place in the bridal bouquet competition this year, you give me a real chance to build up a wedding clientele. I'll run the shop. You don't have to be involved at all."

She bit the inside of her cheek, waiting.

"Kady, you've come in second place for three years now," her mother responded. "What makes you think you'll win this time?"

"I've been practicing all year." And she had. She was tired of losing. She'd studied trends and questioned her friends about what kinds of flowers and styles they would choose for their own wedding bouquets. "After coming in runner-up for so long, I'm ready with a stand-out entry. I'll knock Queen Jasmine off her throne for sure."

Her parents didn't seem convinced.

"This year the convention committee's opened the event to the public," Kady continued. "Brides-to-be from all over the area have been invited to come view the bouquets and centerpieces and other contest entries before announcing the winners. We couldn't pay for that kind of exposure."

"That is true," her father agreed.

"And what are you going to do when Mom and Dad go on their vacation?" Will asked. "I can't do deliveries or run the shop. I have my own business to worry about."

Unease trickled down her spine. She hoped her next suggestion didn't blow her case. "I could hire someone. Part-time? Then you wouldn't have to worry about anything except enjoying your time together."

Her mother stood. "Mark, let's go in the back and talk about this."

Together they walked to the workroom.

"I doubt this'll happen, Kady," Will said. "They've made up their minds."

"Really? If that's so, they wouldn't have gone off to consider my proposal."

"Kady, what are you thinking?"

"That I want to run this business, Will. Do you really believe I can't do this?"

She thought about the success of her floral designs at today's wedding. She'd done it all, professionally, and with no errors, even though she'd nearly dropped one of the arrangements.

She suddenly thought about the man with the strange-colored eyes. Dylan had been impressed with her. And why was she even thinking about this? Because it was easier than the alternative—losing all she'd begun to build.

Her brother stood. Paced. Ran a hand through his normally styled hair. "I want what's best for Mom and Dad."

"Even if they decide to give me a shot?"

He met her gaze. "Yes. You've really stepped up, taking over most of the running of the shop. And I agree with your idea to corner the wedding market."

"Wait. What are you saying?"

"I'm on your side. I've seen your drive and dedication. I'm—" He was interrupted by their mother.

"We've talked it over." Ruthie came to a stop in the middle of the room, her eyes dancing as she met those of her husband's. "We're willing to reach a compromise for now. We are going to go away, on a cruise, I think. Kady, you take over daily operations. Hire help."

"Kady, this should give you time to implement your plans," her father added. "Win the competition. Prove to us you can handle taking over the business permanently. When we come back, we'll revisit the subject."

Kady jumped up, smiling. "Thank you," she said, hugging her mother. Then she grabbed her father. "You won't be sorry."

"No, we won't be because your brother will be checking in on you." Her father stopped her before she could protest. "Deal or no deal?"

Kady decided not to argue with the offer. "Deal."

"Good," he said, though he'd taken a little wind from her sail. "Get the job done, Kady, or we'll sell."

DYLAN STOOD BY the window, lost in the beach view. The sun, orange in the fading wash of the purple sky, dipped closer and closer to the horizon. The reception had officially ended around three, but the family had remained, happily catching up with each other. Dylan and his brothers fell into that category. They'd mingled long after the bride and groom had left for their honeymoon.

Hanging out wasn't as painful as Dylan imagined. His family had been very considerate of his request not to talk about the situation surrounding his injury. Instead they razzed him about not having a girlfriend, which he could handle much easier than reliving the shooting and the loss of Eddie. He reserved that pain alone for the dark hours of the night, when he wrestled with his guilt over the shooting. His brothers probed, but he shut them down. His mother hadn't put her two cents in yet, but he knew it was coming.

"Sit," his mother commanded. Tall and regal, her olive skin announced her Mediterranean heritage. Her dark hair held little gray and her brown eyes were sharp, not missing a thing where her sons were concerned. "I saw you limping down the hallway."

He didn't argue. He loved this woman, as did his brothers. That was why even though they griped about the convention every year, one of them would always be with her.

She was right, though. He'd limped all the way to her room. Time to rest.

"Now, my darling boys—"

Deke groaned. His mother sent him a stern look.

"It's time for the annual Sunshine State Florist Convention. Which of my loving sons is going to escort me this year?"

Dylan peered at his brothers, all of whom wore the same long-suffering expression. No one would question if they were related. Dark like their mother, only Dylan and Derrick had their father's lighter eyes. And like their parents, all four were tall and lean. All in law enforcement of some kind.

"Mom, we love you," Derrick began. "But this has to end. Can't you find a friend to go with you?"

"If your father were here he'd be shocked at you all. Trying to pawn your mother off on someone else."

"Oh, great. The dad card," Dante mumbled in Dylan's direction.

"I don't know why this is such a burden for you boys. It's not like I ask anything else of you."

"I take your car for an oil change every five thousand miles," Deke pointed out.

"I still cut the grass, even though I've offered to pay a lawn service to do it," Dante added.

"And I call you every week," Dylan said.

All heads turned to Derrick. "I got nothing."

"That's because you cheat," Deke told him.

"That's enough," their mother proclaimed. "I know you are all adults. And I can't tell you how much I appreciate every one of you." She eyed Derrick. "Even you."

Deke punched him in the arm.

"But this year is different. I was asked to give a workshop and I've accepted. It's my first public-speaking event and I need moral support."

Derrick brightened up, the first of the brothers to cross the room and hug their mother. "Awesome news, Mom."

"Congrats," Dylan said, his heart softening as he viewed his mother's teary eyes. He thought her wiping away a fake tear was a little much, but it was the way Jasmine Matthews worked.

"I promise after this year I won't ask any of you to tag along with me. Aunt Betty has expressed an interest, especially since Uncle Frank is going to retire. She can come with me next year."

Dylan was about to throw out an excuse for not attending this year when his cell rang. He slipped it from his pocket, frowning when the division office number appeared on the screen.

"Can't this wait?" his mother asked, a reprimand in her voice.

He held up the phone. "The office. I should see what they want."

She nodded and turned her attention back to the captive audience. He eased open the sliding door, stepping onto the balcony. The temperature had dipped with the impending night and a heady breeze kicked up. Dylan pulled the collar of his jacket closer to his neck. "Matthews."

"Dylan, it's Tom Bailey. I've got some news I think you should hear."

"I'm at a family wedding. Can't it wait?"

"It's about Esposa."

The man who'd disappeared after killing Eddie. Dylan had searched high and low, as had other law-enforcement agencies, but the dealer disappeared underground. No one had seen or heard from him since.

Anger burned in Dylan's chest. "What have you got?"

"A buddy of mine in Tampa is on a joint task force with local police departments. He heard about what went down with Esposa. One of his contacts made a positive sighting."

"Where?"

"Just outside of Tampa. I remembered you said you'd be near there, so I'm giving you a heads-up."

In his research, Dylan had learned that Esposa had family in the Tampa area, but after having the local district office keep a watch on them, the agents hadn't found any evidence to corroborate that Esposa had relocated there. Esposa was able to lie low in a place the DEA wouldn't know of because he'd built a loyal network of people who would hide him indefinitely. But maybe Dylan had caught a break.

Cypress Pointe was only forty-five minutes outside of Tampa. Dylan needed to act on the tip.

"Thanks, Tom. I owe you."

"Pizza and a round of pool should make us even."

"Deal."

Dylan ended the call and slipped the phone back in his pocket. He wrapped his fingers around the cold metal balcony railing. The breeze cooled his heated face. Finally. This was his chance to make Esposa pay. Time to get justice for Eddie.

Except he couldn't allow Esposa to have any inkling he was here. If the dealer caught wind that Dylan had received a credible tip, he'd take off. Dylan might not have an opportunity like this again. He had to play this smart or his chances of catching the guy would again drop to zero. He needed to hang around and come up with a strategy.

His brothers' laughter pulled him from his thoughts. He went back into the room. Being here with his family, seeing them safe and healthy, made his chest hurt. Since living in Miami, he'd been too far away from them. The wedding had been a worthwhile reason to reconnect. He'd missed sparring with his brothers, missed the creative ways their mother found to keep her sons active in her life.

It also reminded him this was why he did the work he did. To keep families, like his and so many others, safe from dealers who cared about only money and power.

"Excellent," his mother said. "You're back. I was just telling your brothers about my workshop. It's all about making the bride imagine what she needs for her special day, not necessarily what she wants. I've found…"

Dylan pulled Derrick to the corner of the room, his gaze glued to his mother while he asked, "You still have the fake two-headed coin?"

"I'm not saying anything without a lawyer."

"Chill. You want to get out of convention duty?"

Derrick eyed him suspiciously. "Of course."

"Then let me flip the coin. I need to stay in town."

"Are you crazy? Still on pain meds?"

"No. I have a lead on Esposa."

His brother stilled.

"He's close, Derrick. I have to stick around and see what I can dig up. The convention will be a great cover."

"I don't know, Dyl. Are you up to this?"

"I haven't thought of anything else since I woke up after surgery and found out Eddie was gone."

"I get it, but you're too close, man. And your bosses wouldn't go for it."

"Esposa's been in the wind too long. It's now or never."

Derrick went quiet. Mulling it over? No matter what his brother decided, Dylan was sticking around Cypress Pointe until he got some answers.

"I don't like it, but okay. You need backup?"

"Not yet."

"I'll only give you the coin if you promise to keep me in the loop. Call if you need anything."

Dylan hated to get anyone else involved. This entire mess was on him and he intended to keep it like that.

"I can do that," he assured his brother. "And another thing. Keep this between us. I don't want going after Esposa to turn into a family affair. He's mine."

Derrick nodded.

"We're good?" Dylan asked.

"We're good," his brother answered.

His mother turned her gaze toward him. "What are you two whispering about over there?"

"It's nothing, Mom," he replied. "Your workshop sounds exciting."

Dante coughed.

"It is." She stood, glancing at the gold-and-diamond wristwatch their father had given her on their last anniversary. "You boys have until tomorrow to decide who will attend the conference with me. Now, go back to your rooms and get changed. We're meeting your aunt and uncle down at the beach in twenty minutes. They tell me the bonfire is lots of fun." She took a long moment to glance at Dylan. "We don't get together much anymore, so let's enjoy ourselves."

Dylan and his brothers filed out of the room. In the hallway, with the door closed and their conversation out of their mother's earshot, Deke blurted, "When do we flip?"

Derrick pulled out a coin and flicked it in the air. "How about right now?"

"Not until we check the coin." Dante reached out to grab it.

"Wait. Let me." Dylan snatched the coin in midair and made a show of looking it over, first one side, then the other. "We're good. Dante, you and Derrick go first."

"Heads," Dante called.

Dylan flipped the coin, and when it landed back in his hand, he said, "Heads. You're out, Dante."

His brother let out a long, relieved breath.

"Okay, Derrick and Deke."

"Heads," Deke called before Dylan tossed the coin. Again he read the face when it landed in his hand.

"Sorry, man. Derrick is safe."

Derrick backed away. "Don't ever punch me again."

Dante snickered.

"Get it over with. Heads," Deke said, pain etched on his face.

Just for fun, Dylan stretched out the suspense. "One. Two. Hey, Deke, did Mom really make you follow her around with the flower bucket last year?"

Deke glared at him. "Do it."

Dylan chuckled. "Three."

He sent the coin in the air. Four sets of eyes watched it twirl, each brother holding his breath at the outcome. Dylan captured the coin in his fist and snatched it to his chest. Opening his hand, he looked down. Closed his eyes.

"Well?" Deke asked.

Dylan held the coin up between his thumb and forefinger. "Heads. I lose."

Deke slumped against the wall, clearly relieved. "You guys kill me."

"Guess I have convention duty this year. Wish me luck," Dylan told them.

Deke straightened. "It's not so bad."

Dylan lifted a brow.

"Okay, it is, but you're injured. I wanted to cut you some slack."

"I'm a big boy. I can handle anything Mom throws my way."

"Be careful what you say," Deke warned.

"At least this is the last coin toss," Derrick said. "After this convention, we're free men."

"Until Mom decides she wants daughters-in-law," Dante pointed out. "I saw her searching the crowd during the wedding. She's already making plans."

Deke shook his head. "Just shoot me now."

Normally Dylan would agree with his brothers, but an image of the pretty florist he'd met at the wedding flashed across his mind. He blinked, surprised at the pleasure it brought him. He just as quickly shook it off. He was a long way from wedding bells. Until he put Esposa behind bars, nothing else, including a woman, came first in his life.

CHAPTER THREE

IT DIDN'T TAKE Dylan long to get the ball rolling. Knowing Esposa might be near infused him with an energy he'd been lacking. He had to do something now, because waiting was no longer an option. Closing the book on Esposa meant moving on with his life.

The beach teemed with locals enjoying the wintery Saturday night. The bonfire burned bright, the wood crackling as the steady wind kept it stoked. His brothers had spread out among family and friends, sharing their brand of humor and chatting up the fine people of Cypress Pointe. Dylan stood alone, dwelling on his next move.

A hoot of laughter caught his attention. Derrick, holding court. He wished he could laugh as easily, but his mind was elsewhere and his thigh ached in the cold air. He chose to ignore it, focusing instead on the prospect of nailing Esposa.

When his mind started going around in circles, he finally entered the merry group, hands jammed deep in his pockets. After asking a couple of leading questions, his uncle pointed out the police chief, Bob Gardener. The older, stocky man lingered on the edge of the gathering, dressed in his official uniform, obviously on duty. Dylan made his way over, gritting his teeth as he tried not to limp, and introduced himself, mentioning his agency and title.

"Your office gave me a heads-up," the chief said.

"Already?"

"We're with the joint task force," he explained, directing a no-nonsense look at Dylan. "They made sure to let me know you aren't active in the field at this moment."

"I'm not. I came to town for my cousin's wedding, but I can't ignore it when a suspected big-time drug dealer might be in the area."

The chief nodded. "Figured as much."

"Do you have information you can share with me?"

"First, I have to establish whether this is this coming from you in an official capacity or personal interest. I know this guy shot you and your partner."

"Esposa. Yes."

News traveled fast in the law-enforcement

world, but he didn't blame the chief for asking. Finding Esposa was a personal matter, as well as a professional one, and the chief had a right to know. Dylan had already spoken to his superior since the call from Tom. He was on leave, but they could command him not to nose around, though how would they stop him? The unspoken code was that Dylan had better be discreet, and if he did indeed find Esposa, he better not play cowboy and go after him alone. Dylan had been a field agent long enough to know that the hero always died, except in the movies. He was part of a team for a reason and would call upon them if needed.

"It's both, personal and private, at this point. Is that a problem?"

"Not as long as we follow protocol. Until your supervisor says otherwise, you have limited authority in my jurisdiction, but if we find the guy you're looking for, I'd like to work together."

"I intend to."

The chief regarded him once again, sizing up the man who'd come into his town requesting information. Dylan didn't like it, but he understood. He didn't always play well with others, but in this case he'd liaise with local law enforcement to a T. Esposa wasn't going to get away because Dylan went rogue.

"We've had activity at the marina," the chief revealed, having made sure they were far enough away from the crowd so no one would overhear. "Usually we get an influx of weekend tourists who dock and head into town to shop or visit the restaurants. The locals keep their boats moored there. But lately there have been vessels coming in and out that are suspicious."

"How so?"

"Idling in during the early morning hours. Docking for short periods of time. Definitely not tourists."

"What can you tell me about the marina?"

"Run by a private company. Got a guy on duty during the day."

"Have you checked him out?"

"No red flags. Been working there for years. Company man, runs the place efficiently."

A gust of wind whipped up the flames of the bonfire. Bright sparks shot up in the air before burning out, ash drifting down to the sand. The scent of burning wood floated toward Dylan as he processed the information. The chief knew the locals, so he'd have to trust him on this.

"Who noticed the boats coming in and out at night?"

"Local fishermen. They're a tight group, watching out for each other. Notice when strangers show up snooping out their favorite spots."

"Are you looking at any possible suspects?"

"A few guys have come across our radar."

He reined in his impatience at the chief's vague answer. "Names?"

"A couple of young punks showed up here about three months ago. Been hanging around the marina. Had a couple run-ins with 'em. Ran their names through the system. Petty stuff mostly, but with the news of a drug dealer in the wind, we're taking it seriously. I got the names back at the station."

Good. Somewhere to start. "Anyone else you're looking at?"

The chief hesitated. Dylan had to hand it to the man. He'd shared a lot so far, but now wasn't the time to backpedal.

"Still think I'm going to interfere?" he asked.

The chief met his gaze head-on. "Look, I'm bein' careful. For both of us."

Dylan's hands fisted in his pockets. Patience, he reminded himself. He wasn't going to find

Esposa tonight and he needed the chief's assistance. No point blowing it by ticking off this man.

"Got it."

The chief chewed on Dylan's answer before replying. "Local guy. Will Lawrence. Also been hangin' at the marina, which is odd 'cause he doesn't own a boat."

"Does he have legitimate reasons for being there?"

"He's an accountant."

"So he could be there on business?"

"Yeah. The company that runs the marina is out of town, so Will does the bookkeeping. Known the guy since he was a kid, but I gotta say, something feels off."

A jolt of excitement charged Dylan's veins. He never ignored a fellow officer's gut when he claimed something was hinky. "I'll run his name. See if I can find anything more."

"Doubt it. He's a Cypress Pointe resident. Never been in trouble with the law or run with the wrong crowd. He was popular in school. Runs a stable business."

That the chief knew of. People involved with criminal activity didn't usually announce it to the world.

The chief's face remained tight, his gaze

daring Dylan to contradict him. "I pride myself on knowing the people around here. Just 'cause something might be off doesn't mean he's a criminal."

"Fair enough." Dylan scanned the crowd, still jazzed that there might be some leads in this town. "Is he here tonight?"

"Haven't seen him." The chief craned his neck, his gaze hunting over the people assembled. "His sister is by the fire. Over there, talking to two other women."

Dylan searched in the direction the chief pointed out, his chest tightening when he saw Kady, the woman from the wedding. Just to be sure, he asked, "Her name?"

"Kady Lawrence."

"You don't say."

The chief shot him a sharp look. "You know her?"

Dylan shook his head. "Only met her briefly at my cousin's wedding."

"She'd be the one delivering the flowers." The chief squinted, like he was searching his memory. "She got into some mischief as a kid, but nothing serious. She works at the family flower shop. Nothing to tie her to her brother's activities besides the family business."

But there was a connection and Dylan never

took opportunities like this for granted. Kady's brother might be innocent, but he was a solid lead Dylan planned on pursuing. Spending time with Kady to get to the truth was an added bonus.

The few minutes they'd spent talking at the reception had him thinking about her on and off all day. She'd managed to snag and hold his attention, something that rarely happened when he was deep in a case. Well, he wasn't technically on a case, but he had been focused on Esposa for the past few months. She might not have any tie to this investigation, but now he had an excuse to seek her out. Not that he'd reveal a thing. He still intended to keep his cover hidden until he learned anything useful.

Watching Kady laugh with her friends, Dylan resisted the urge to pull her from the group and question her. Because he wanted to be near her again? Smell her sweet perfume? *Slow down, Matthews. She's part of the puzzle.*

The chief's voice cut into his thoughts. "Got a local PI by the name of Max Sanders keeping an unofficial eye on things. He helps me out from time to time when I'm down on manpower. Good guy. You'll probably want to speak to him."

Dylan nodded, tucking the information away.

"Thanks, Chief. I really appreciate you filling me in."

Hands on his hips, legs spread in a military stance, the chief said, "Look, Matthews, I don't have anything substantial to book these guys on, let alone connect them to Esposa. I haven't searched the boats because I don't have cause to. On top of that, your guy hasn't been seen around here. This could be a complete misunderstanding."

"Even strange boats in the marina?"

"I don't know for sure if they're involved in illegal activities or transporting drugs. It could simply be some fishermen I haven't met before, looking for a place to drop their lines."

Dylan watched the chief, his gut churning. The older man said one thing, but his eyes said another. He suspected the events were connected; he just couldn't act on it. Yet.

"But you don't think so."

The chief went silent for a long moment. "No. I don't."

"Then we keep investigating. By the book."

The chief shook his head. "You aren't gonna give up on this, are you?"

"Not until I find the guy who killed my partner."

The chief puffed up his cheeks and blew out a breath. "I get it, but I gotta say, be careful."

"Always."

Loud voices carried over the crowd, catching their attention. The chief perked up, his gaze assessing the situation on the other side of the bonfire. A heated argument between two burly guys looked like the makings of a fight. "Gotta get to work. Stay in touch."

As the chief lumbered away, Dylan stared at the fire, lost in his thoughts. A group of women deep in conversation caught his eye, Kady among them. A strong protective streak swept over him, reminding the agent in him why his job was so important. But the urge to see her again reminded him that he was attracted to this woman. The brief encounter at the reception wasn't long enough. Another chance to talk to the pretty lady presented itself and he wasn't going to squander the opportunity.

WILL LAWRENCE STARED at the numbers, his eyes blurring. The dim lighting didn't help. He could look at them a million more times but nothing would change. He needed more work, or a miracle, to replace the money in his family's accounts.

He'd been an idiot. Knew better than to fall

for get-rich-quick schemes. He'd been lured in by the promise of easy cash, sure this onetime venture would secure retirement not only for his folks, who'd worked for years to support their children, but also for Kady and himself. Flat out, he'd been played. Now he found himself in serious trouble.

Never look a gift horse in the mouth.

His granddad's old saying. What would the old man say now if he knew what Will had done? Getting involved in an investment through the friend of a friend was a risky choice, but with his parents talking seriously about retiring, he'd hoped to add more funds to their portfolio.

From the partially open office window, Will heard a commotion from the beach, a mere block away. Rubbing his eyes, he stood and crossed the room. Stared outside. Normally he'd be part of the rowdy crowd, enjoying his friends. Joking around like he didn't have a care in the world.

All that changed three months ago. It felt like a lifetime.

He turned, going back to his desk. He'd reviewed his personal budget, but even drastically changing his lifestyle wouldn't be enough to make a difference. His only hope was the two appointments set up for next week. Through the grapevine he'd learned the country club needed a new bookkeeper. It was a big job, meaning lots of extra hours on top of his already established practice, but he would do it. If he was offered the job.

Then there was Jenna at Charming Delights Catering. Her business had grown quickly, so he scheduled an interview for next week. Every new account he could secure would help in the long run.

He'd already picked up additional work at the marina. Lined up some safe investments, which would bring in close to half of what he owed, except it took time. He was amazed at how quickly one could lose a bundle of money versus it slowly trickling back. But he had no one but himself to blame.

Slumping in his chair, he scanned the room. Anything else beat concentrating on the unchanging numbers. His gaze came to a screeching halt when he viewed the diplomas on his office wall. Top-ten college. Graduated summa cum laude. His CPA accreditation. First in his class.

What good was it all now? If word got out that he'd lost his own family's money, his reputation would be useless. Unless he fixed the situation. Fast.

This morning, when his sister balked at selling the shop, he'd been relieved. If his folks reconciled their true financial situation, they would learn money was missing. Demand explanations. Wanting his parents to be set when they retired was a lame excuse for his losing their money, even if it was true. They would be disappointed in him, with cause. He'd let them down. Thank goodness they didn't have a clue.

But instead, Kady's argument about running the shop saved him. Changing their parents' minds bought him more time. They could go on a much-needed vacation and enjoy themselves. He would make it up to them no matter how long it took.

Kady managing the shop and weddings would keep her in the dark as well. He actually agreed with her vision, was happy she finally settled down to make a wise career choice. They didn't usually see eye to eye, but her plan to build up their wedding market share made sound financial sense. Her business plan was good, as were her projections. She could actually make a name for The Lavish Lily since his parents wanted out. He was proud of her.

He only hoped he hadn't ruined her dreams.

Kᴀᴅʏ's ᴇʏᴇs ʙᴜʀɴᴇᴅ as the bonfire smoke blew in her direction. She blinked, which only caused tears to well. What was she? A smoke magnet? It seemed smoke had radar and blew in her direction, no matter where she sat. "Why do I let you guys talk me into coming out here?" she muttered, her throat drying up as the smoke engulfed her again.

"Because you need a night out with the girls," her friend Nealy answered.

"You're so busy conquering the world of wedding flowers, we don't see you," Lilli added.

"Except this isn't a girls' night out. It's the entire town of Cypress Pointe out. And you're both here with your significant others." Coughing, she grabbed the water bottle from Lilli's outstretched hand.

"You make that sound like a bad thing," Lilli said.

"Look, bonfires are special to both of you. I get it. You have wonderful memories associated here. All I do is end up going home with a scratchy throat and smelly clothes and hair."

Nealy laughed. "You are so not a romantic."

Lilli tapped a finger against her chin. "We need to find you a guy."

"Whoa. Put the brakes on." Kady held up her hand. "I'm not looking."

"That's your problem. You should be."

"Why bother? I know most of the single men in town. Dated some of them. It didn't happen."

"That's no reason to close yourself off," Nealy argued.

Sure it was. Most of the guys she'd dated were as busy as she, always canceling at the last minute with work obligations. She got it, but for once she'd love to be put first in a relationship. Take Brad, for instance.

She'd trusted him. Thought she'd fallen hard for the country-club general manager she'd met while attending a business meeting there. She'd been talking with the event coordinator about her floral services when Brad walked into the office. They'd clicked. One date led to another and soon they were an item. Kady couldn't believe how well they'd synced.

Until they didn't.

After three months of assurances that he wanted to settle down, Brad jumped at an opportunity to move to a big club in Texas and hadn't asked her to come with him. Worst of all, he'd bragged about acquiring only quality vendors, like Kady, to land the job.

While still in Florida, he'd promised she would be the exclusive florist for the club, which quickly fell through when the new general manager didn't agree. Not only had her heart been bruised, but Brad had also cost her business she'd been counting on, while using her to advance his own career. After that, her trust level in men plummeted.

Since then, having gone on too many bad dates to count, Kady decided she and dating were like oil and water. Didn't mix well. She accepted that. Why couldn't her friends? Running her business and building a brand were the most important relationships in her life right now.

"You two are disgustingly happy and I'm thrilled for you both—truly I am. But not everyone is looking for their soul mate."

Nealy leveled a glance at Lilli. "That is true. Things weren't smooth sailing for either of us when we started out with our guys."

"But they are now."

Lilli's smitten expression made Kady laugh. "Spoken like a bride-to-be."

"The bride-to-be who has venue choices to make," Nealy reminded her. As her event planner, she'd been after Lilli to make decisions so she could get the wedding ball rolling.

"And flowers to select," Kady added.

"I will." Lilli's eyes went all dreamy. "We're enjoying the moment."

Nealy sputtered, "You're making Max crazy. The PI is ready to drag you down the aisle."

"There is that, too."

Kady smiled at her childhood friend. She was delighted about the upcoming nuptials, especially since she'd be doing the flowers for the wedding and all the other related events. If Lilli ever set a date, that was.

"Hey, look. Dane's waving at me." Nealy stood, waving back to the man who owned the Grand Cypress Hotel, home to this year's florist convention. "I should see what he wants."

Lilli followed, brushing sand off the seat of her jeans. "And I should find Max."

"Nice," Kady mumbled, still seated. "You drag me down here then dump me."

"We'll be back," Nealy assured her as the two took off. Yeah, right. From past experience, she knew once those two got with their men, there was no separating them. She smiled.

The wind picked up again, blowing the acrid smoke in Kady's direction. Her nose burned and she blinked back fresh tears. Pushing up from the sand, she was ready to call it a night. The entire population of Cypress Pointe might enjoy the revelry of a bonfire on the beach, but Kady was not one of them.

Zipping up the jacket she'd layered over a sweatshirt and jeans, she coughed again as she weaved through the crowd, headed to the parking lot. She passed a group of laughing guys, swerving out of their way when she heard a deep male voice.

"Kady?"

She swung around, her foot sliding in the damp sand. Her pulse jumped as the hunk from the wedding headed in her direction.

"Hi. Dylan, right?"

"Yeah. Enjoying the bonfire?"

She brushed ash from her sleeves and answered, tongue in cheek. "Sure."

His metal-colored eyes sparkled with humor. "I'll take that as a no."

She laughed. "You'd be correct."

"Then why are you here?"

"Friends dragged me out. You?"

"Family dragged me out." His smile, somewhere between sad and amused, reminded her of just how attractive she found him.

"Part of the wedding festivities?"

"Apparently." He rubbed his leg and tried to hide a grimace.

She nodded toward his leg. "Are you okay?"

"Injury. Been standing out in the cold for too long."

"There's a bench over there." She pointed. "You can have a seat."

"If you'll join me."

Her stomach fluttered at his invitation. Trying to act nonchalant, she shrugged. "Why not? I was only planning to go home and take a nice warm shower to get the stench out of my hair."

"Bet you're loads of fun on a camping trip."

"Never been."

"Fun times."

Kady slowed her pace to match Dylan's gait. He'd changed into a jacket over a Henley shirt, with jeans and boots. Shedding his formal wear hadn't made him any less attractive.

When they reached the bench he eased down gingerly. Not sure how to act around him, she perched at the far end, leaving plenty of space between them. Not that she had to worry—it seemed like the entire town surrounded them. If he started anything sketchy, she'd yell at the top of her lungs.

"I promise you, I have no evil intentions."

Great. Obvious much? "A girl can't take chances."

"Very wise of you."

She sat back and relaxed a bit. "And kind of insulting to you?"

"Nah. I get it."

His easy acceptance made her loosen her tense shoulders. Here she sat, on a bench, curious about the good-looking guy who'd not only kept her from ruining a flower arrangement at the reception, but was also the man she'd been thinking about all day. Why not enjoy it?

"Do you have these public bonfires on the beach often?" he asked after a few moments.

"Yes. It's a tradition. They've been part of Cypress Pointe history for as long as I can remember." She drew up her leg and turned to angle herself in his direction. "Kids used to start the fires on their own, so instead of banning them, the town council decided to set up specific nights for the fires so the authorities could monitor the crowd."

"Smart. Although starting fires when you're not supposed to is more fun, it is more dangerous."

She tilted her head inquisitively. "Is that a guy thing?"

He chuckled. "Just an observation. Our family gatherings are usually barbecues, so we always say fire fixes everything. Well, except for the time my brother Dante accidentally set the field behind our house on fire. We all ran outside to contain it before the fire department arrived. On the way, he grabbed an heirloom quilt my great-grandmother had made and used it to try to smother the flames." He shook his head, a crooked grin lighting up his face. "My mother was not happy."

"I imagine." She bit her lip, then asked, "How many brothers do you have?"

"Three."

"Wow. Your mom must be wonderful to put up with your antics."

He glanced at the crowd. Looking for his mother?

"She is." He turned his attention back to her. "You have any siblings?"

"A brother. But he hasn't started fires or destroyed heirlooms."

"Why not?"

She silently chuckled at his serious face. Like fire and destruction were normal parts of life to him.

"My brother is too upstanding and too good at everything he does to engage in troublemaking."

"Oh. Sorry to hear that."

Her eyes went wide. "Seriously?"

"I'm just saying, my brothers and I have lots of great stories."

She shook her head, trying not to laugh.

"So you're saying your brother is a decent member of society?"

"He is." Her eyes narrowed. "What's with all the questions about my brother?"

"Nothing. Just making conversation. Family is usually a safe topic."

And why had she suddenly gotten so prickly? Because Will always ended up being part of the conversation, no matter where she was. With her folks. On the job. People always wanted to know how Mr. Wonderful was doing, even people who didn't know him well. She hadn't realized how defensive she'd gotten about her brother until just now.

"Okay," Dylan said, bracing his arm along the top of the bench. His fingers were mere inches from her shoulder, which she found very distracting. "We'll switch off the topic of family. So, the bonfire. Do folks from surrounding towns join in as well?"

"It's usually just Cypress Pointe."

"Seems like you have a nice town. Safe place?"

"Why, are you planning on moving here?"

Now, wouldn't that be interesting, running into this hunk around town.

He chuckled. "No. Since my cousin lives here I'm curious."

"Well, not much crime. A nice tourist spot. Not much traffic. Good restaurants. Awesome beach views."

He nodded, watching the people on the beach. Like he was looking for someone. She ignored the regret washing over her. Already tired of talking to her? It shouldn't matter, but it did.

The moment dragged on until he spoke again. "Did you grow up here?"

"What are you, a census taker?" she teased, afraid it came off more defensive than joking.

"You got a chip on your shoulder?" he responded.

Okay, he gave as good as she did. His aim directly hit its target. "Fine. I deserved that." She ran a shaky hand through her hair. "To be honest, it's been a while since I spent time talking to a nice guy."

His mouth thinned and his gunmetal eyes turned serious. "You sure I'm a nice guy?"

If his expression was supposed to make her nervous, it didn't. If anything, she wanted to know why he'd think differently. "I haven't seen otherwise."

"We don't really know each other." He paused, leaning in close. His fingers nearly skimmed over her jacket. In a quiet voice he said, "But I do know I like spending time with you."

His statement caught her off guard. Made her blood race.

"Um, thanks."

His chuckle sent chills over her skin. "You're welcome."

Nervous now, she tucked her hair behind her ear. "I'm sorry for coming off rude. I'm not usually hard to get along with."

"No worries." He glanced at his watch. "I need to get back to my family. They're probably heading over to the hotel soon."

He stood, a little shaky on his leg, but caught himself. She wondered what had caused his injury. How long ago he'd been hurt. Not that it was her business, but honestly, in the short time she'd known him he triggered the inquisitive side of her nature. She wanted to know more.

He held out his hand. "Nice to meet you. Again."

She rose and took his hand in hers. The zing

of pleasure she'd experienced earlier returned, stronger this time. "Likewise."

They remained there, gazing at each other. Kady held her breath, hoping he might say more. Maybe ask her out? When he didn't speak, she realized he wasn't going to do as she'd hoped. Disappointment wrapped around her. What did she expect? She'd only just met the guy. He was probably leaving town soon. No point in starting anything if he wasn't going to be around, even if he'd admitted he liked spending time with her.

"So I'll see you around?" she asked.

She couldn't quite interpret the expression in his eyes when he said, "Never say never," before walking away.

Was that a yes or a no?

Tugging the car keys from her jeans pocket, she trudged to her car. How had she managed to screw up a possible date? She really needed to try harder. Lilli was right. But this thing with Dylan? It was different. Made her want to get out there again. She would hate to admit this to her friends, but maybe she did need their help. If not with Dylan, maybe another guy.

Once she got to the car, she slid inside, curling her hands over the top of the steering wheel and resting her forehead against them. Had she really blown her chance with Dylan? Her parents always accused her of being difficult. Maybe they were right. It would explain why her relationships never lasted. Even though Brad had been ages ago, she realized now he'd never been the man for her. But Dylan? He wasn't like any man she'd ever met. He had her second-guessing herself, while at the same time he sent her pulse racing. It was out of the ordinary for her and she liked it.

Lifting her head, she stared at the beach. It looked like the party was winding down. Folks would return home and tomorrow things would go back to normal in this sleepy town. For her, it would be business as usual. Right. Once she convinced her folks to let her run the shop, lined up more wedding jobs and won the bouquet competition at the florist convention. By that time Dylan would probably be gone and she'd have missed her chance to learn more about the most interesting man she'd met…ever.

CHAPTER FOUR

BY THREE O'CLOCK Tuesday afternoon, Kady had interviewed four women for the front-counter position. After her parents agreed to let her hire help, Kady had called her friend at the local newspaper to place a want ad. She'd also posted the position on employment websites and been pleased by the quick responses.

Until now.

Of the four, one had sales experience, but very few hours she could work. Another was just out of college and wanted an administrative position. Kady scratched her head at that one. Her posting had clearly stated it was a sales position. The last two were local teens looking for part-time jobs. Not exactly what Kady was hoping for.

Thankfully, her parents opted out of the interview process. Kady's mother had managed to book a cruise that sailed out of the Port of Tampa on Friday. She was busy shopping and getting ready to hit the high seas. Her father decided to wean himself from coming to the shop so he didn't suffer withdrawal while they were gone. Only been a few days in, but so far, so good.

Leaving Kady alone to pick out their newest employee was a huge sign of confidence on her folks' part. They'd kept their word and let her assume control of the business. As long as Will didn't stop by too often and interfere, she was golden.

Glancing at the wall clock, she realized her final interview for the day was to arrive soon. She tidied up the worktable after finishing her last arrangement, just in time to hear the shop bell ring. Hurrying up front, she was met by a smiling woman close to her age.

"Hi. I'm Kady Lawrence," she said, holding out her hand.

"Christine Wallace."

As they shook, Kady observed her newest recruit. Shoulder-length curly blond hair, sparkling blue eyes and a megawatt smile. Average height. The girl-next-door look customers would respond to.

Kady got right down to business. "You know this is a sales position?"

"Yes. I've worked in retail, so I'm aware of how to engage customers. I'll work hard to represent your business and help increase productivity."

Okay, finally someone who understood. But by her word choices, Kady got the impression Christine had done far more than sales. Was she too good to be true? "What kind of other relevant experience do you have?"

Christine rattled off her management and office skills from time spent with respectable companies.

"I have to ask, why this job? You're overqualified."

"I just moved to the area. To be honest, I've done my time in the nine-to-five grind and I want a change. I love Cypress Pointe and plan on settling here. This job would be perfect for what I have in mind." She grinned. "And I like flowers."

"Perfect answer." On instinct, Kady made a quick but firm decision. "How soon can you start?"

Christine blinked. "That was fast. And I can start as soon as you want."

"I have a good feeling about you." She paused and bit her lower lip. "There is one thing."

"Okay."

"My parents are a bit…challenging to work

with. They're very picky about the shop. I feel it's only right I give you a heads-up."

Christine seemed to consider Kady's words. "I've worked with a variety of…shall we say, temperamental bosses in the past. I'll be fine."

Kady let out a breath. "Great. That said, my folks are leaving on a cruise and I'll be attending a florists' convention here locally, so I'll be in and out of the shop. Think you can handle it?"

"Absolutely."

"My older brother will be around, too. He doesn't work here, but pops by occasionally. I'll make sure you meet him and he can get the info he needs for his bookkeeping. During the convention, I'll be in early in the mornings to complete orders before attending the workshops.

"But for today, let's go over your duties and I'll give you a rundown of the shop." Kady smiled. "Welcome to The Lavish Lily."

ON WEDNESDAY AFTERNOON, Kady stepped away from the registration table at the Grand Cypress Hotel, her convention packet in hand. She looped her name tag, which was attached to a lanyard, around her neck. The buzz in the hotel lobby ramped up the energy level as people checked in and caught up with old friends. A poster, propped on an easel right inside the front door, announced the upcoming floral competitions in which Kady was already registered. After her parents' bombshell several days earlier, she had to make the most of this conference, which meant winning the wedding-bouquet category.

To her relief, Christine had taken to the job immediately, easing any concerns Kady had about leaving her new employee alone at the shop for a few hours without Kady there to guide her. Will promised to stop by and check up on things sometime during the day. While she was glad he was on her side for once, she could tell something was off. He was distracted and edgy. More so than usual. She thought about asking what was up, but then she doubted he'd confide in her anyway. They hadn't been close for a long time, not since he opened his own accounting office and she finally stopped wandering around trying to find aim in her life. Do-no-wrong Will could take care of himself, as he'd always done. Without her.

Groups of attendees mingled in the huge lobby, excited chatter echoing off the marble floors. For the next several days, anything and everything floral-related would be focused upon within these walls.

In the years Kady had been attending the conference, it had always been located in different cities in Florida. When it was announced that this year's event would be held right here in Cypress Pointe, Kady couldn't believe her luck. On her home turf, maybe she could beat the reigning queen of wedding bouquets and finally win first place.

She waved to a few women she knew as she moved to a quiet corner of the lobby to take a seat and go over the itinerary. Scanning the workshop schedule, she discovered the next few days were packed with all sorts of interesting topics. This year, organizers added actual hands-on workshops for newbies to experience floral designing. Interesting. The welcoming reception was tonight and the awards ceremony would cap off the convention on Sunday evening. At each previous convention, she'd held her breath at the ceremony, waiting to hear her place in the competition. And each year, she'd missed out on being number one.

She had three days to worry about her entry. This year, the competition held an extra perk, thanks to a new feature the convention committee developed. All day Sunday, the entrants in different wedding categories would display their floral designs to the public, specifically targeting brides-to-be. The open house had been publicized around town and all over the Tampa Bay area, in order to lure prospective brides to the showcase. That meant a day's worth of publicity for The Lavish Lily. Kady would be able to show off her bouquet entry, as well as connect with potential customers she needed to grow her wedding business.

Her drawings were hidden away in her apartment. The flowers she'd ordered would be delivered by her wholesaler early Sunday morning, ensuring her entry would be fresh for display. She'd established a contingency plan, just in case, and was totally prepared to beat her competition this year. Nothing was going to stop her.

There were only a few workshops scheduled for this afternoon. For the most part, it was a day to catch up with other florists. Kady checked off two topics she thought might be interesting. How to Improve Your Business was scheduled in ten minutes. Later, she'd stop by Floral Tips 101, then have time to run home, change into something dressy and return for the reception.

Pleased with her first decision, she stood,

smoothing the designer jeans she wore with a jade green top and high-heeled black boots, the picture of a successful businesswoman. Or so she hoped. She dropped the convention packet in her large tote bag, which held a notebook and several pens, then hitched it over her shoulder, ready to move on to the first meeting room. When she looked up, her gaze collided with the handsome guy she hadn't been able to get out of her mind since Saturday.

His low drawl sent a familiar awareness through her. "Surprise."

Her eyes went wide, but she quickly regained her composure. "Dylan? What are you doing here?"

"Attending the conference."

"I thought you were in town for the wedding."

"And the conference. Double duty."

She blinked. "I…"

His spicy cologne grabbed her attention and she forgot her next words. Today he'd dressed in a light blue, button-down dress shirt and black trousers. The loafers made his outfit casual, yet he carried it off with sophistication.

"Why didn't you mention you'd be here when we were together the other night?" she finally ventured.

He shrugged, his metal-colored eyes hooded. "I'm a man of mystery."

"That I believe, because you don't seem like a florist."

There was an edge about Dylan. She couldn't see him patiently creating a floral arrangement. No, more like he needed action in his life.

He chuckled. "I'm not, but it is a family business. Just like everyone else here, I'm ready to learn more about the floral industry."

She glanced down at his chest and back. "Where's your name tag?"

"You caught me. I haven't picked it up yet."

"You can't get into any of the workshops unless you have one." Did she come off as stuffy as she sounded?

"Which I'll rectify right now. See you around?"

"Sure. I hope so."

Shaking her head, Kady went to the designated meeting room. Why hadn't Dylan told her he'd be here? Not that he needed to announce his schedule to her. They'd only bumped into each other a few times. Of course, this was Cypress Pointe. If he was going to hang around town, she'd eventually run into him.

As her mind worked out the logistics of

Dylan's presence at the convention, Kady nearly missed the room. Clearing her mind, she entered, determined to concentrate on the speaker, not Dylan's motives. Glancing around, she noticed a few early birds scattered about in the empty seats. She chose a row in the middle, a few seats in from the aisle. A few minutes passed and someone took a seat beside her. Dylan.

"Are you stalking me?"

"No. You're the only person I know here. And I can always learn how to—" he glanced at the workshop schedule and read "—improve my business."

She slanted a look his way. "You own a floral shop?"

"My mom. I help her out occasionally by coming to these conventions."

"So you don't actually work in the floral industry?"

"Not in the traditional sense."

Kady wrinkled her brow. "What other sense is there?"

"More like I'm into the growing end of the business."

"You mean, like a wholesaler?" she asked.

"Plants are more my area."

"Interesting. Are you planning on broadening your expertise this week?"

His eyes grew warm. "Most definitely."

The speaker stepped up to the podium and started her speech. She droned on about buildings and taxes and finding good employees. Nothing new here, all things Kady had already discovered and implemented on her own. Fifteen minutes later, she stifled a yawn, wondering how the woman hadn't lost her business out of sheer boredom instead of improving it.

Dylan leaned over and spoke in a hushed voice. His breath tickled her ear, which, to Kady's chagrin, triggered a set of chills. What was wrong with her?

"Is this as excruciating as I think?"

She tried not to groan. "Yes."

"How about ditching the rest of the lecture and getting a coffee?"

"Lead the way."

They quietly left the room. Once outside, Dylan held up his program folder. "I hope that isn't a preview of things to come."

"No. Most of the speakers are interesting. I've never heard the businesswoman before."

He steered her through the lobby then to the poolside Sandbar Café.

"Want anything in particular?"

"Decaf," Kady told him. "A little cream."

"Got it," he said, removing his lanyard and stuffing it into his pants pocket.

While Dylan ordered two coffees, Kady found them a table. The sun shone brightly and reflected off the sparkling water of the hotel pool. Brisk and pleasant, the afternoon air held a slight hint of orange blossoms. Appropriate for a floral convention. Kady dug a sweater out of her tote. January in Florida could be fickle, so she always tried to be prepared. Despite the weather, it was a perfect month for a convention.

Dylan joined her with two tall cups.

"So, do you own your flower shop?" he asked conversationally.

Kady blew on her coffee before answering. "Technically my folks do, but I've recently taken over its day-to-day running."

"If the wedding arrangements you designed last weekend are any indication, you'll do well."

"Thanks." She took a sip of the richly brewed coffee then set down her cup. "If your family is in the business, why didn't you supply the flowers for your cousin's wedding?"

"We came from out of town. My cousin didn't want to add the burden of us getting here, finding a wholesaler and a place to prepare the flowers. She wanted this to be a mini family vacation without the logistical headache."

"Very considerate."

"My mom is always busy. It was a nice break for her."

"Will she be at the reception tonight?"

"Wouldn't miss it."

"Good. I'd like to meet her."

"So, what should I expect the next couple of days?"

"The usual convention stuff." She counted off on her fingers. "Workshops, networking, competitions. Oh, and this year? Hands-on workshops."

One of Dylan's dark eyebrows rose. "What does that mean?"

"Means you'll probably be up to your elbows in fresh flowers at some point. Problem with that?"

"No way."

"Even if your mom can't make it and asks you to fill in?"

"Maybe." His gaze pierced hers. "If you're in the workshop."

She swallowed. Those odd-shaded eyes got her every time. She imagined the deep secrets hidden there, secrets he'd never reveal to anyone. Especially not to her, anyway. And why would she even be thinking that way? He was here for the convention, just like her. Nothing more, or at least that was what she was telling herself.

"Are your brothers here?"

"No. Once they were off the hook, they left before Mom could change her mind and talk them into staying."

"And you aren't wishing you took off with them?"

He studied her intently until she felt her cheeks heat. "If I left with them I wouldn't be able to spend time with you. So, no. I'm glad I stayed."

She hoped her smile didn't make her seem as if she was easily impressed. Yes, she was intrigued, but he didn't have to be privy to that information. "You're a real sweet talker, aren't you?"

A cocky smile spread across his lips. "Given the right motivation."

"Save me from overconfident nonflorists."

"Is there such a thing?"

"Apparently."

He chuckled. "Really, I'm glad I met you. I'm hoping you might give me a tour of your town. If it's not too much to ask."

"Depends on the workshop schedule. This

convention is held once a year and I intend on making full use of the resources available."

"Spoken like a serious business owner. Bet you could give that last presenter a run for her money."

She tried not to be on the defensive, but after struggling with her parents over every detail at the shop to prove her worth, his words touched a sore spot in her. "Who knows—maybe next year I will be."

His eyes softened. "I don't doubt it for a minute."

Taking a bracing gulp of her drink to cover the pleasure from his words, Kady hoped to diffuse this…whatever, between them. She hadn't been reduced to klutzy conference conversation in ages. What was it about Dylan that had her blushing like a schoolgirl? And what if he was here with someone?

She didn't know, but she decided right then and there to find out. "So, um…are you alone—"

Just then a cell phone rang. She realized it was Dylan's when he patted his chest to find the device in his shirt pocket. He removed it, read the screen and said, "Hold that thought." Then he rose to take the call.

"And another one bites the dust," she muttered, watching his retreating back. With a sigh she gathered her belongings, intending to sit in on the next lecture.

"Leaving?" Dylan asked, catching her before she took off.

"Yes. Thanks for the coffee."

"Hope we can do it again."

At his easy smile, she decided to take a chance. "Going to the next workshop? We can sit together and critique the speaker."

His smile dimmed. "Sorry. Something's come up."

Of course it had.

"Then I'll catch you later." She waved and walked away, ignoring the twinge of disappointment in her chest and the regret reflected in Dylan's eyes.

DYLAN WATCHED KADY walk away. He liked her confident stride, liked the way her shoulder-length hair swung as she walked. Liked her smile and how she kept up her end of the conversation. He liked her, plain and simple. Yet he had no idea what, if anything, her connection might be to the drug dealer he'd come searching for.

He ran a hand through his hair. He wanted to tag along with Kady, sit through another workshop, but the police chief had just given him news he couldn't put on the back burner.

Since they'd talked at the beach last Saturday night, there had been a spike in activity at the marina. The chief wanted Dylan to meet Max Sanders, the PI in town whom the chief had pulled into the investigation. After reading the text containing the address to Max's office, Dylan pocketed the cell and headed to the nearest exit.

Fifteen minutes later, he sat in a cramped office overlooking Main Street, with the chief and Max.

"I don't know if this is related to your guy," the chief said to Dylan, "but I've busted two convenience-store owners for selling synthetic drugs."

Dylan nodded. "We've been trying to crack down on sales all over the state. Just before Esposa disappeared, he was a major player in synthetic-drug distribution. I can't imagine he's given up just because he's moved house."

"Then we better find him or whoever is in charge. A local girl ended up in the ER last night. Her folks are frantic."

Dylan sympathized. "So what's the plan?"

Max, who'd been sitting back in his desk chair, leaned forward. "I'm going to stake out the marina. Watch the activity. Take pictures. See if those involved match up to your database."

"I'll keep after those store owners," the chief added. "Bugging them isn't going to make them stop selling that junk, but I can make life difficult by threatening arrests."

"Good start," Dylan said. "I spoke to my supervisor this morning. Got permission to work with the Tampa DEA division."

The chief shot Dylan a steely-eyed glance. "I know this is personal for you, Matthews, but this is my town. The safety of the people here comes first."

"Always." He hated the reprimand, but knew the chief's words held merit. He rubbed his aching thigh, a constant reminder of what was at stake.

"Your cover at the convention should let you move around town and not raise questions," the older man continued. "We'll be in touch regularly with updates. Anything you need, let me know."

"I appreciate it. You've already given me a heads-up on some people of interest here in town." With the few names he'd gathered so far, he'd run background checks. No red flags as of yet, but he planned to dig deeper. "I'll be following up."

"Let's get busy," Max said, rising to his feet. He reached his hand over the desk toward Dylan. "Nice to work with you."

He took Max's hand. "Likewise."

Max grinned. "Florist convention?"

"Hey, you work with what you're given."

"Have fun with that."

Dylan pictured Kady's smiling face. "I intend to."

WILL STRODE DOWN Main Street. He didn't have time to babysit Kady's new employee. No, he had more pressing matters at hand. He'd discovered a lead on a solid investment opportunity.

He shook off his frustration. Kady didn't ask for much. The least he could do was pop into the shop, make sure things were running smoothly. His folks had already taken off on a road trip before the cruise, so with them gone and Kady at the convention, he had to step up.

A heavy afternoon crowd browsed along Main Street, encouraging for the town's shopkeepers. Tourist season in full swing. Add in the pristine sandy beaches and blue waters of the gulf, and Cypress Pointe had become a favorite destination spot. Brushing past tourists, he made tracks to The Lavish Lily. Once he checked in with the new girl, he could get back to his busy day. Besides this, he had three other stops to make. Tax season was looming and he had clients to prepare.

The distinct welcome bell pealed as he entered the shop. From behind the counter, a smiling woman greeted him. Definitely not a girl.

"Welcome to The Lavish Lily. How can I help you?"

He crossed to the counter. "My name is Will Lawrence. Kady's brother."

"Hi. She said you'd be coming by."

"Christine, correct?"

Blond curls bounced and blue eyes shone as she nodded. Will frowned. No one should look that happy.

"Any problems today?" he asked, more brusquely than he intended.

"Not one. Foot traffic has been heavy but I've only rung up a few sales." She pushed an open magazine aside and focused her attention on him.

"Orders?"

"I already let your sister know. And I took detailed notes from the callers."

"Did you set up a time for the wholesaler to make a delivery?"

"Tomorrow. All taken care of." She shot him an amused look. "Are you always so to-the-point?"

"Usually." Will knew he was being abrasive, yet her smile didn't slip. He sighed. He needed to stop being a pain to everyone around him. "So, you're new to town?"

"Yes. I'm really thankful your sister hired me." Her teeth worried her lower lip.

Interestingly enough, so was he. Christine came across as a professional and unflappable woman. A plus in his book. Until the small tell of biting her lip said otherwise. He realized he wanted to know more.

"Do you have family here?"

"The answer is complicated." Christine straightened her shoulders. "I'd really rather not talk about it."

Not what he expected. Or wanted to hear. There were enough problems attached to this shop. His family didn't need whatever drama Christine might be mixed up in.

But on the other hand, he was intrigued. Someone else with complications in their life. And by the look on her face, they were serious. Were her problems as big as his? Or was he projecting his own predicament on her?

"Does my sister know? About your...complications?"

"No. And I'd like to keep it that way."

He watched as Christine blinked, her gaze swiftly changing from troubled to unconcerned. So, she didn't want to talk about it, whatever it was. He could relate.

He drew closer to the counter, nodding in the direction of the open magazine. "What are you reading?"

Her cheeks flushed. "I found a floral designing magazine in the workroom. I figured since I'm working here, I could learn a thing or two. Possibly help your sister at some point."

A go-getter. Maybe hiring help wasn't such a bad idea after all. "She'd like that." Or at least Will thought she would. They'd drifted apart, and because of that, he and Kady hadn't engaged in any in-depth conversations.

His cell pinged and he checked the screen. Frowned. A text from his dad. Keep me up-to-date with the shop. Great. His dad depended on him, only he didn't know the truth. His folks thought Kady might be the one to somehow ruin The Lavish Lily, not knowing he'd already done just that. He was the one they should be looking out for.

"Are you okay?"

Will glanced up, meeting concerned blue eyes. "Yeah. My dad."

"Kady said they're booked on a cruise?"

He nodded, distracted. "He wants me to check in from time to time. See how the shop is doing."

"Um, I don't mean to overstep, but doesn't Kady run the shop?"

"She does. Day-to-day." He scrolled through his messages. "I take care of the big picture."

"Good to know."

When he heard a steady beat rapping on the counter, he looked up to find Christine tapping a pen.

"Are you always so…distracted when you talk to people?"

"I'm busy, got a lot on my plate at the moment."

Christine shrugged. "It's kinda rude."

His brows rose. "Excuse me?"

"I'm just saying, this is the first time we've met. Do you treat your clients like this?"

Did he? He'd been so stressed ever since the investment tanked. Had he been taking it out on his clients?

"I've been in business for years," Christine explained when he didn't answer. "There's nothing worse than working for someone who doesn't pay attention."

"You do realize I'm your boss."

She didn't look the least bit concerned. "I'm an employee of your sister's."

"We're family. Same thing."

"You might be, but she hired me to do the job. I answer to her."

Will blinked. This woman was actually arguing the finer points of his family business? Unbelievable.

"If you have a problem," she continued, "take it up with Kady."

Gone was the polite face that greeted him when he walked in. She meant what she said. So did he. The first whiff of trouble and she was gone, no matter what Kady wanted.

"I admire your stand."

"I assure you, Mr. Lawrence, I'm not a pushover."

So. She thought she had the upper hand. "No, I don't believe you are. But you do realize when you mentioned a complication, you gave me leverage. If I were the type to use that information at a later date…" As his words trailed off, he figured he'd made his point.

"Are you that kind of man?"

He couldn't deny the worry etched on her face, which made him a jerk for using her troubles against her. He certainly wouldn't win the prize for stellar boss, son or big brother. Deciding her secret was hers alone, he assured her, "Not today."

When she bit her lip again, he took pity. Glancing at the time displayed on his cellphone screen, he came up with an idea. "You'll be closing in a few hours. How about we go get something to eat then? Maybe we can share our complications."

"I don't think so."

"Fine. Instead you can list all the ways I'm not your boss."

It took a second for a hesitant grin to spread across her increasingly pretty face. "It would be my pleasure."

CHAPTER FIVE

KADY STOOD BEFORE the full-length mirror attached to her closet door, debating her dress choice. The shimmer of gold-threaded lace overlaying the bodice of a champagne-colored dress brought out the highlights in her hair and made her eyes sparkle. Of course, that could be attributed to excitement. Dylan may have had to take care of some kind of business, but he'd be at the welcome reception. They'd resume this…whatever was happening between them.

"I haven't seen you this flustered in a long time," Lilli, who had taken a break from her wedding preparations, observed from her position of lounging on the bed. "Gives me hope that you'll find your happily-ever-after."

"I'll be at a welcome reception at a floral convention. It's not like I'm going on a date." She smoothed the full skirt. "And I am not flustered."

"Really. Because the way you're going

through outfits, it sure seems like it." Lilli sat up and gathered the discarded dresses to place back on hangers.

"I'll be visiting people I only see once a year. What's wrong with looking my best?"

"Nothing, except you never worry about what to wear to these events. Every year I try to get you to go shopping before the convention and you always insist your old dresses are fine." She waved a hand over the pile on her lap. "Exhibit A."

Kady glanced over her shoulder. "I'm running The Lavish Lily now. I want to make new contacts, learn ways to attract new customers. I need to look my best."

"Uh-huh. And your change of attitude has nothing to do with a guy?"

"Why does everyone always assume that when a woman wants to look her best it's to impress a guy?"

"Because it's usually true," her friend said. "So, what's up?"

Kady turned away, hoping Lilli didn't notice her flushed face in the mirror. "Nothing."

Lilli laughed. "You are such a bad liar."

Twirling around, Kady jammed her hands on her hips. "What are you talking about?"

"Nealy called me earlier. Apparently Dane

saw you having a conversation with a certain handsome man at the Grand Cypress. Since he owns the hotel, he would know."

"I can't talk to a guy without it being front-page news? It is a conference, after all."

Lilli snorted.

"When did Dane turn into a spy?" Kady grumbled.

"Since he's involved with Nealy and she's your friend."

The bad part about the convention being held in her hometown? No anonymity. No "what happens at the convention stays at the convention."

"So I met a guy."

Lilli tucked her legs under her. "Spill," she said in an I-told-you-so tone.

Seeing her friend making herself comfortable, Kady knew she had to tell Lilli something or she'd never let up.

"First of all, don't look so smug. I could be dressing up for any reason."

"But you're not. Go on."

Kady held back a resigned sigh, but if she was honest, deep down she wanted to tell her friend. "His name is Dylan. I met him at Nellie's wedding reception."

"That was Saturday. Why haven't you mentioned him before now?"

"I thought he was leaving town after the wedding. Turns out he's here for the convention."

"A fellow florist?"

"Um… I don't know. He's infuriatingly closemouthed about himself."

"He's not competition, is he?"

"No. At least I don't think so. His mother is a florist and he's here with her."

Lilli frowned. "Mama's boy?"

Kady pictured Dylan's dark good looks, his take-charge attitude. "Far from it."

Lilli blew out a breath. "Good. Especially with your dismal track record with men."

"Hey!"

"C'mon. After Brad left, you just phoned in your dates. Even you have to agree the men you go out with are disasters."

"True. And sad."

"So tonight things are looking up. Maybe this guy is different."

Kady scooped up a pair of strappy nude heels and carried them to the bed. She sank onto the mattress. "I don't want to be disappointed again. My confidence really hit bottom after Brad dumped me, but yeah. Dylan is different. Not ever-after different—"

"Yes, because heaven forbid you find a nice guy and have a serious relationship."

"But I really like him."

The room went silent at Kady's admission.

"So there is hope?"

Kady grinned. "Yes, oh meddlesome one, there is hope."

"And you've decided on this dress?"

Yes, Kady realized. With her hair in an updo style and her makeup just right, she wanted to make a lasting impression on Dylan.

"Then strap on those dancing shoes and get this party started."

DYLAN CHECKED HIS PHONE. No text messages or calls. Good. Tonight his plans had less to do with the job and more to do with a woman. Kady, to be exact.

He'd actually taken time to dress nicely tonight. Found himself humming as he splashed on aftershave. It had been so long since he'd been happy, it took a few minutes for the reality of the emotion to kick in. Yeah, he still needed to confront the man who had changed his life, but not tonight. For the first time in ages, he was going to enjoy himself. Dial back on the guilt and see what a few hours in the presence of an interesting woman might do for his soul.

If she showed. He glanced at his watch. Eight fifteen. Where was she?

He stuffed his phone back in his jacket pocket as his mother approached him.

"Why are you alone?"

"I could ask you the same question."

"Unlike you, I've been mingling."

"Meet anyone special?"

She sent him the stink eye. "Watch yourself. You know your father was the only man for me."

He let out a long-suffering sigh. "I'm just saying, it's been a while since Dad's been gone. You deserve some fun. Take a chance on someone new."

"You're one to talk. It's been months since you were injured. Besides the wedding, this is the first time you've been in a social setting. I wouldn't mind you meeting a nice woman." She glanced at his leg. "You don't seem to be limping as much."

"I'm getting stronger."

She took his hand in hers and squeezed. "Dylan, you know I love you. I've been worried sick, but your brothers warned me about suffocating you."

He squeezed back. "I know it's been hard for you, but I appreciate the distance. I've needed time to think. Heal." *Find the guy who did this to me.* "I love you, too."

In the soft lighting of the banquet room, Dylan swore he saw tears glimmering in his mother's eyes. He hated that he'd made her worry, but he had to deal with the current state of his life without her help.

"Promise me you won't get hurt again," she said in a halting voice.

"You know I can't do that."

"Then promise to do everything in your power to stay safe."

Dylan leaned over and kissed his mother's temple. "I promise."

His mother let out a shaky breath and put some space between them. "Okay, then."

"So, don't you have friends to visit? You always go on about your convention friends."

"Yes. And next time I see you, you'd better be chatting up an available, single female."

He chuckled. "I'll see what I can do."

His mother moved on. Scanning the room again, he wrinkled his brow when he didn't see the only female he wanted to "chat up." He was about to make a circuit when a voice to his left said, "You don't have a drink."

He shifted and a smiling Kady came into view.

"I thought maybe you stood me up," he scolded, surprised at how much the idea bothered him.

"Well, that would have been difficult since this isn't a date. I'm here just like every other convention attendee, mingling at the welcome reception."

"Whatever. The point is, you're here."

"Yes. And I'm thirsty." She angled her head to look over his shoulder. He turned to see a beverage station set up on the far side of the room.

"After you."

As they crossed the room, he couldn't keep his eyes off her. *Lovely* didn't do her justice. Her dress shimmered in the lighting, and with her hair swept up in some kind of wispy style, she captured his complete attention. Let's just say he wouldn't be getting the image of Kady out of his mind anytime soon.

The soft music, chatter and laughter faded as he joined Kady to order a drink. He asked for his usual—club soda with lime. He never ordered anything with alcohol. Occupational hazard, he supposed.

Kady ordered white wine. As they stood, holding their glasses, he suddenly found himself at a loss for words. Proved the point that he'd been so wrapped up in finding Esposa, he'd let his personal life get stale, along with the ability to make small talk with an interesting woman. He'd been so much about the job, he'd forgotten there was a great big world to enjoy.

"So, is your mother here?" Kady asked.

"Somewhere. She's visiting with old friends."

"One of the advantages of a yearly convention." She scanned the room. "How about you? Any friends here?"

"No. I've been busy with my own job for a long time."

"Which is?"

"Time-consuming."

She laughed and shook her head. "How about friends at home?"

He sent her a sideways glance. "Is that your way of asking if I'm single?"

"I was trying to be discreet, but yes."

"No significant other."

She nodded. "It's always good to establish that up front."

A waiter interrupted, angling a tray of bacon-wrapped shrimp toward them. The spicy scent made Dylan's stomach rumble.

After tasting one of the tempting hors d'oeuvres, Dylan continued the more enticing conversation. "Then I gotta ask, are you dating anyone?"

"Not currently."

"Terrific. Awkward moment over."

She laughed. "Oh, I'm sure there will be more to come."

"Why?"

"Because getting to know people can be torture. What topics are off-limits? How much do we reveal about ourselves? Are we even compatible?"

"You've given this some thought."

"To be honest, I haven't struck gold in the dating department lately."

"Hard to believe."

A friend called out Kady's name in passing. Kady smiled and waved in return. "Believe it. Most of the guys I've gone out with are too busy to try and start a real relationship. Or they just aren't interested."

"Busy?"

She sent him an accusatory glance. "Like, on the phone all the time."

"Ah. Point taken. And sorry about earlier, but it was important."

"I've heard those words before. Right after I'd decided to give the guy a chance."

"Tell you what. No phone calls tonight."

To demonstrate he meant it, Dylan took his cell from his pocket and turned it off. He held it up for Kady to see. "I promise, no distractions."

She took a sip of her drink, eyeing him as though considering his actions. "Score one for you."

He grinned. "I'll be the first to admit I let the job get the best of me, but tonight I'd much rather focus on you."

"Make that two points."

He held up his glass. "To a night of getting to know each other."

"Sounds interesting." She clinked her glass with his. "I'm in."

They both sipped their drinks again, watching the crowd mill around them.

"So," Kady said, "will you be attending more workshops?"

"Probably. I'm here to support my mother."

"Please don't tell me you're signed up for one of the floral competitions."

Dylan nearly choked. "No. That would be all Mom."

"Let me guess." She tapped a finger against her chin. "Wedding-reception-table category?"

"To be honest, she hasn't filled me in. She's all hush-hush."

"I've been that way, too. I hope—"

"Kady? Is that you?"

With a squeal, the woman who approached didn't wait for an answer. She threw her arms around Kady.

"Sue," Kady said, barely able to reply. "How's it going?"

"Fantastic. I have *the* arrangement to win this year."

"Looking forward to seeing—"

"And I predict this is the year for you."

Kady blinked. "Thanks."

"Gotta run. Drama over in the corsage camp. Don't want to miss a thing."

While her friend hurried off, Dylan bit back a chuckle. "Drama over corsages?"

"The competitors take their categories very seriously."

Dylan didn't see it, but then again, he wasn't part of this world.

"Kady," a young man called as he passed by. "This year for sure."

Dylan raised a brow, enjoying Kady's flushed cheeks. "Care to explain?"

"Just some people who want to see me win this year."

"Is it really that important?"

"For bragging rights, sure. But it will also help my business."

Another woman walked by and gave Kady a thumbs-up.

"Do you mind if we get out of here for a bit?" Kady asked.

"Sure."

He followed as Kady exited through the doors leading to the pool patio. They rounded the empty pool to a pathway leading to the side of the hotel. A vast expanse of grass ran from the hotel to the beach. Small decorative lights lined the pathway on the side of the building. Kady headed in the direction of the surf.

Stars shone in the dark sky. The wind churned up the water as it rushed to the shore. Even in the crisp night air, Dylan discerned the scent of salt and sea.

Once they reached the beach, Kady let out a long breath.

"I wouldn't suggest wearing those shoes if you're going to walk on the sand," he advised.

"Here is fine. I just needed a minute."

"Mind my asking why?"

Kady sent him an amused grin. "See, this is when the uncomfortable questions start."

"We could stand here in silence if you like."

She laughed. "Three points for you."

"Okay, silence it is."

Brushing at a strand of hair escaping her hairstyle, Kady stared out over the undulating water shining in the moonlight. Her earrings sparkled as she moved. He could read the indecision on her face. Understood it as well.

"I always come in second in the competition. I hate for everyone to feel sorry for me."

"You think that's what it is?"

"Oh, yeah." She cut him a self-deprecating glance before looking back at the water. "It's frustrating enough to lose every year, and even though my friends want me to win, they doubt it. Shoot, even I doubt it from time to time."

"Maybe this year will be different."

"It has to be. I have a lot riding on winning."

"For your business reputation?"

"Partly. More because I don't want to lose my shop."

"Over a contest?"

"It's a big deal to my family."

"Because?"

He noticed her hesitation in answering. Was she thinking too much too soon?

"My folks are thinking of retiring," she finally said. "They want to sell the shop and I want to prove I can make it in the wedding industry."

"So, you think winning will solve all your problems?"

"Look, every business needs customers. I want to focus on brides and weddings. My folks aren't convinced, because they never ran the business that way. They've been happy to make arrangements for special occasions or funerals. I want to branch out."

"Sometimes family is the hardest to please."

"Exactly. Weddings are a multimillion-dollar industry. In time I know I could convince my parents that my ideas have merit, but I need the accolades and wedding customers to win them over. My brother is on my side, but he has his own career to focus on."

Dylan remembered Will's name coming up in his investigation. He had a clear opening to learn more about his person of interest, yet he found himself hesitating. Finally, he asked, "So your brother doesn't want to sell?"

"No. Usually my folks listen to him, since he's our financial guy, but they're pretty determined right now. I just hope he doesn't have a change of mind."

A change of mind that might affect Kady and her folks? In what way? Since her brother's name had come up in connection with the investigation, Dylan wondered if Will's decision could be of any interest to the case.

"I considered buying the shop from my parents since it's been in the family for generations, but I'd have to get a loan." She ran the sole of her shoe over the sand. "It's all so complicated."

"But it's what you want?"

"Yeah," she answered with quiet conviction. "More than anything."

While Dylan admired her conviction, he also knew that people could go down dark paths to accomplish their goals. Hadn't he done so by single-mindedly pursuing Esposa, sacrificing the safety of his partner because he'd been so obsessed? Yeah, he could admit it now. He was obsessed with nailing Esposa. He didn't want to see Kady get caught up in a sticky predicament that consumed her life just to achieve her plans.

When she shivered, he moved closer. Their shoulders brushed. He liked being here with Kady, standing in the outdoors, far away from the burden of his memories, the strangling ties of his job. Standing before this beautiful vista of sand and surf, beside an equally beautiful and fascinating woman, almost felt surreal.

Kady rubbed her hands up and down her bare arms.

"Are you cold?"

"Yes. I should have grabbed my wrap before we came outside."

Dylan shrugged out of his jacket and placed it over her shoulders. She took the lapels in her hands and drew the jacket around her.

"Better?"

She met his gaze. "Much."

They continued to stare at each other. Dylan didn't know what drew him to this woman, but he wasn't about to fight it. He slid his arm around her waist. When she didn't move away, he pulled her closer. Still, she continued to keep her eyes locked with his. Before he even realized what he was doing, he lowered his head and closed his lips over hers.

He kissed her slowly, gauging her response. When her hand landed on his chest, he placed his other hand on her hip. As she moved deeper into his embrace, Dylan's heart pounded. He'd hoped she'd kiss him back, but the reality? More potent than he'd let himself imagine. He'd never thought anything could beat the adrenaline kick right after a bust. Kissing Kady proved him wrong.

WHAT WAS WRONG with her? She barely knew Dylan, yet she'd melted into his kiss as if she'd been waiting for him her entire life.

She drew back, her eyes meeting his. Fire burned there. Oh, boy.

With a shaky breath she put some distance between them, at a loss as to what to do next. Dylan was the perfect distraction. When they were together she didn't worry about the competition. The shop. Her parents' decision to sell. No, with Dylan it was all long looks, fluttering in her belly and untimely chills. A girl could do worse.

Dylan spoke first. "The most important awkward moment. The first kiss."

She forced herself to better grip the lapels of his jacket, hoping he wouldn't notice the slight tremor. Awkward kiss? Far from it. Hiding her reaction, she turned her nose into the warm fabric, inhaling the masculine scent of tangy cologne and all man. All Dylan.

"I hope I didn't overstep."

"No. It's fine." And how lame did that sound?

"Blame it on the night."

Oh, she would later, when she went over the kiss in her head.

"Should we go back inside?"

"Probably a good idea."

As she moved by him, Dylan placed a hand on her arm to stop her. "Just so you know, I'm glad I kissed you."

She swallowed hard. The man got right to the point, didn't he? Well, if he could be honest, so would she. "Me, too."

She was rewarded with a roguish smile. Throw in nice guy and she was in big trouble.

Moments later they were in the banquet room, surrounded by opening-night revelry. The music ramped up and voices became louder. Dylan took his jacket, which she hated to give up, and this time they mingled. Before long, one of her florist friends corralled her.

"Melissa. I thought you weren't coming?"

"Last-minute change of plans. Hubby decided to stay home with the kids so I could make the convention." They hugged each other. As they stepped back, Melissa checked out Dylan. "I'm so glad I didn't miss it."

"How about I get us another drink?" Dylan asked.

"Thanks."

Dylan looked at Melissa. She held up her full glass.

"Be right back."

When he walked away, Melissa pulled Kady aside. "You're here with a hottie and I'm just now finding out?"

"I'm not *here* here with him. We met recently. We're just hanging out."

"The way he was looking at you? That wasn't a hanging-out look."

Kady felt her cheeks heat. "I don't know what to say."

"Take some advice from an old married lady. Enjoy the moment."

She glanced over to see Dylan headed their way. "I will."

He handed her a drink while Kady made introductions. Once that was done, Melissa got right to business.

"You'd better win the competition. I'll say it again—you were robbed last year. Your bouquets are always gorgeous This year, Queen Jasmine gets bumped off her throne."

At Melissa's comment, Dylan, who'd just taken a bite of an hors d'oeuvre, started coughing.

"Are you okay?" Kady asked as she pounded his back.

He nodded, tried to speak, but coughed again.

"I'll get some water," Melissa offered and disappeared in the crowd.

"Dylan. Can you breathe?"

He nodded, proving it by taking a deep breath.

"You had me worried. What happened?"

He tried to speak but still had no success.

"Don't worry. Melissa will be right back with the water."

She took the napkin from his hand to place on a nearby table, along with her drink. When she turned around, a woman was standing in front of Dylan, her hands on his arms.

"Breathe."

Kady could have sworn he rolled his eyes, but when his gaze met hers, they went wider. Concerned, she took a step closer to move the other woman aside. "Excuse me. I—"

The words died on her tongue. She was face-to-face with her archenemy, none other than Queen Jasmine herself.

CHAPTER SIX

JASMINE GLANCED AT HER, frowned, then returned to Dylan.

"Your last name is Matthews?" Kady barely got the words out.

"It is." A sheepish expression crossed his face. He finally found his voice. Though gravelly, it worked. "Kady, meet Jasmine Matthews. My mother."

Kady jumped back, as if electrocuted. "I know who she is. Here. I mean, at the convention." She shook off the confusion in her head. "Your mother?"

"We know each other," Jasmine confirmed, watching her son's face.

The shock started to give way, the thought of betrayal rapidly taking its place. She remembered his attention. The kiss on the beach. "Was this your plan all along? Distract the competition?"

Dylan frowned. "No. I didn't even know you two competed against each other."

And she'd hadn't bothered looking closely at Dylan's name tag earlier today before he stashed it in his pocket. How could she have known he was the son of her chief competitor? And if she had known, what would she have done anyway? Instead, she'd been caught up in his metal-gray eyes, acting like a teenager waiting for a first kiss from the good-looking boy. She'd let her guard down and ended up... with her chest so tight she could barely breathe.

She couldn't face Dylan, so she focused on his mother instead. "Despite our professional rivalry, he didn't learn any of my secrets. My entry is going to blow away the judges this year, Jasmine."

"Kady," Dylan said, "I was never after your secrets."

"Right." *And I suppose that kiss meant nothing.*

"You seem to be jumping to conclusions here," the Queen jumped in. "I assure you, Kady, I didn't send my son after your design. I didn't even know you two had met."

"Of course you'd say that, now that you're caught."

Jasmine's shoulders went stiff. "Are you insinuating I cheat?"

"What other reason could there be?"

"All these years in a row?" Melissa, having joined the group, launched headlong into the conversation. "We should have guessed something fishy was going on."

Dylan took Kady's arm and steered her away from the small group. Despite the pleasure of his touch, she yanked herself free, controlling the anger that was swiftly overtaking her. When she finally met Dylan's gaze, she was surprised by the genuine distress there.

"Kady, my mother and I were not plotting against you. It's been years since I came to a conference with her. I don't know the ins and outs or the important competitions."

"Even when I mentioned being in one of the categories?"

"C'mon. How many are there? I'm not that plugged in to what my own mother is doing."

"Then why bother being here?"

He ran a hand through his hair, his gaze moving to a spot over her shoulder. After a few seconds, he said, "I told you, she asked and I had some free time, so I stayed."

She glimpsed the guilt eclipsing his eyes. "Right."

Which made things worse when he didn't answer.

She hated to ask, but she had to know the

truth anyway since he'd thrown her off her game. "So the kiss? It wasn't meant to draw my attention from the prize?"

Dylan looked at her. His dark eyes grew darker. "Oh, no, that kiss was definitely *the* prize."

"I'd give you another point, but after learning the truth, you lost it and all three you earned earlier."

Dylan seemed to consider that statement for a moment. "Not a problem. Now I get to try all over again."

"You think it'll be that easy?"

"I love a challenge."

"Good for you, then, because you have your work cut out for you."

He sent her a confident grin.

"Be warned. I'm watching you and your mother."

She turned and walked away, her stomach in knots. That was what she got for hoping she'd finally met a man worth being attracted to. Worth getting to know.

Disappointed yet again.

What made it worse was that she'd have a hard time getting Dylan out of her mind. He'd managed to affect her so quickly, so thoroughly. And to make matters worse, she'd be running into him for the remainder of the convention.

Why couldn't life ever be easy?

EARLY THE NEXT MORNING, Kady rose with a headache. Sleep the night before had been hit-and-miss and she was up before dawn. She kept picturing Dylan's face when he introduced her to his mother. So while she lay awake in bed, questions tumbled one over the other, competing to make her crazy. Had he known all along that Jasmine was Kady's competition? He had seemed as surprised as Kady when she came face-to-face with his mother. And if so, was that why he kissed her? To sidetrack her?

Every time she thought about the kiss, about how her heart pounded and she enjoyed every tantalizing second, she felt the fool. Maybe it hadn't meant anything to him, but it had to her, and the events afterward burned.

She'd tossed, turned and punched her pillow so often she lost count. But the thing that bothered her the most was the underlying disappointment. Dylan had quickly drawn her attention. She found herself thinking about him frequently. Wondering if maybe this was the start of a new relationship. He might have said he didn't know anything about the competition, but how could she know for sure? She'd have to trust him, and frankly, she just wasn't sure. Look what happened with Brad.

So she'd pick up her chin, hold her head high and win the competition. Right after she went to the shop to sign off on the delivery from the local flower wholesaler. After a long shower and a bracing cup of coffee, she quickly dressed in a bright pink top, black pants and comfortable shoes. Tossing a denim jacket into her tote in case she needed it at some point during the day, she hurried to the shop for the early flower delivery.

"Hey, Tommy," she greeted the young man as she met him by the back door. After disarming the security system, he carried in her order, followed by a young man she'd never seen before.

"Ms. Lawrence."

"Who's your friend?"

He set the container on the worktable. "Oh, this is Scott. The new guy."

Scott chuckled. "I'm shadowing Tommy until I get a route of my own."

"Fun," Tommy muttered.

Kady nodded. Work drama. Everyone experienced it.

She inspected the colorful blooms, pleased

with the freshness of the flowers, as well as the brightness. While Tommy went out for another container, Scott stood by the door, shoving his hands in and out of his pockets. Clearly he didn't know what to do. Tough being the newbie, Kady decided as she separated the flowers into groups, keeping an eye on him as she readied to construct the two arrangements before going to the conference.

Tommy returned with the container of stephanotis, one part of the flower combination for her competition bouquet. The other blooms would come later. She ran her fingers over the white petals, visualizing the finished creation.

"You ordered more than usual. Something special coming up?"

"You could say so."

The young man grinned at her. "A secret?"

Kady smiled. This secret would remain hers alone. Tonight she'd bring these flowers back to her apartment for safekeeping. She turned her attention from the flowers to the driver. "Sorry you have to make two stops here this week. I hired a new employee, and with the convention going on, things are a little out of the ordinary."

"No big deal. The boss understands."

"Good. My special order will be here early Sunday?"

"Yes, ma'am." Tommy handed her a clip-board. "It's what we do."

Kady took the board and pen to sign off on the invoice. As she scribbled her name, Christine walked in.

"I'm glad you're here," Kady said. "I want you to meet Tommy. You'll be seeing him a lot since we're regulars on his route." She handed the board back. "And this is Scott, who's new."

Scott had wandered over to the organized shelving that took up a large percentage of the wall. He jumped when he heard his name, then turned and nodded to Christine. "Hey."

"Oh, Tommy, while I'm thinking about it. Do you have a reinforced box, about this size, in your truck?" She held out her hands to indicate a medium-sized space.

"Don't you have that size here?"

"No. I need to transport something home."

"I should." He turned to his helper, who was wandering the shop, not paying attention. "Scott, go out to the van. In the right back corner is a stack of medium-sized boxes. Bring them here."

"Got it." Scott jogged outside, returning a few minutes later with the boxes.

"Just place them on the counter," she instructed. "Are you sure you don't need them?"

Tommy shrugged. "Keep 'em. We've got plenty."

Kady grinned. "Thanks. You're the best."

Tommy smiled and dropped his head, but not before Kady noticed his face turning red. She took the copy of the invoice Tommy handed her when, to her surprise, Will walked in the room. She blinked. Deliberately held up her wrist to check her watch.

"Why are you here?"

"What? I can't stop by the shop?"

"At this hour?" She scowled at him. "Dad called you, didn't he?"

"He asked me to check in early, yes."

Kady threw up her hands.

"It's nothing personal, sis."

"It is to me."

Christine turned to Will. "You didn't have to come by at this hour. I told you I have the shop under control while Kady's at the convention."

"Look, I'm not out to throw anyone under the bus."

"Um, we're gonna take off," Tommy announced to the room. "C'mon, Scott."

Kady followed them to the door. "Thanks again. Tell Mr. Ness, too."

"Will do." Tommy jogged to the truck and jumped behind the wheel.

Kady closed the door to find Christine and her brother arguing. Arguing? And then she remembered Christine's comment about Will not needing to stop by this morning.

"So, you two know each other?"

Will eyed Christine. "You told me to come by and meet her. I did."

Hmm. Were Christine's cheeks red?

"And..." Kady prompted.

"We ate dinner together." Will shrugged. "I filled her in on what it's like to be a florist."

Right. And in her spare time, Kady masqueraded as the Easter Bunny.

"I hope that's not a problem?" Christine added, a frown wrinkling her brow.

Actually, it worked in Kady's favor. If Will focused on a woman, the attention would be off her.

"Not for me." She scowled at her brother. "Be nice."

"I'm always nice."

Kady decided to take the high road and not respond.

"Do you need any help?" Christine asked. "Since the shop doesn't open for an hour yet."

"When we were talking last night, Christine

expressed an interest in learning how to make arrangements," Will added.

Kady carried the container of stephanotis to the workroom cooler, enjoying the sweet scent of the blossoms. "I'd love it. With Mom gone, all the designing will fall on me." She glanced at a huge wall calendar. "I have the Smith-Thompson wedding in two weeks, plus the everyday arrangements. Another pair of hands would be appreciated."

"I'm a beginner," Christine reminded her.

"Which is great. I can teach you how we prefer things to be done."

Her employee smiled. Kady covertly glanced at her brother, who only had eyes for Christine. He must have noticed her because he shifted to meet Kady's gaze and frowned.

"I should get to my office."

"Go," Kady shooed. "We have work to do. You'll only distract us."

"Then I'll see you later. Both of you."

Christine waved in his direction. Kady sent him a knowing smile. Will hesitated, then exited via the back door.

Kady let out a mock sigh. "I thought he'd never leave."

"Really? Because I thought it was nice of

him to check and make sure I can handle the store."

With a laugh, Kady took the long-stem pink gladiolus from the container to add to the already cut greenery. The pungent aromas of eucalyptus and the sweeter flowers were like a symphony to her senses. "I was kidding. And it was nice of Will to stop by."

"Oh." Christine blinked. "Look, if I shouldn't see him…"

"You're seeing him?"

"No. I mean…we had dinner last night. Will filled me in on the town and the other merchants." Christine bit her lower lip. "Do you mind?"

"I can't stop you."

Christine blew out a breath. "It was nice to have someone to talk to. I haven't been here long enough to make any friends."

"Will is a great guy. I'm sure you'll be good friends." Or more, but for now Kady could only speculate. Still, the heat level in the room had risen at least ten degrees when the two exchanged glances. "So, back to work. How about flower arranging 101?"

"I'm ready."

While Kady gathered supplies, she went over the list of items Christine should be familiar with. Foam, stem tape, glass vases. First, they separated daisies for one group, a colorful array of yellow roses, orange and purple lilies for another.

"I always make at least two arrangements for the shop cooler. We have walk-in customers, so I like to have these ready. Next I make the preorders and store them back here. Since I'll be at the convention most of the day, do you mind making deliveries?"

"Not at all. If I can figure out how to get around Cypress Pointe."

"If you need help, call Will."

"I'll try on my own first. How else to learn about the town?"

"Good point."

As Kady moved through the steps, Christine watched and asked questions. By the second arrangement, Christine was working alone, slowly, but with good form.

"What are those white flowers you put in the cooler?" Christine asked.

"Stephanotis. I'm using them in a wedding bouquet."

"They're lovely."

"Aren't they? They represent marital happiness."

"Do you always use flowers with romantic meaning for brides?"

"I like to." Kady moved some of the blossoms around and stepped back to view her creation. "When I tell clients the meaning behind the flowers, it makes their selection personal. That's my hook with brides."

"I bet you have your wedding-bouquet flowers picked out."

Kady laughed. "Maybe. Someday."

Although when she thought about it, the bouquet she planned to display this weekend had taken hold of her. She supposed that when she finally did walk down the aisle, the design would be hers.

"Besides, there are no potential candidates for groom in my life at the moment." Dylan's face flashed in her mind's eye. She blinked him, and the residual hurt, away.

Christine placed the last stem in her mix. "I hear you."

In the time remaining until she went to the convention, Kady made up the orders. She answered any last-minute questions Christine voiced and made notes about any situations Christine might find herself facing during the day.

"I'm running a bit late," Kady said, removing the lid of the top box from the stack Tommy left behind for her. Into the box she deposited a pair of shears, tape and the wire she would need to work on her mock-up bouquet at home. She looked around to make sure she hadn't forgotten anything and asked Christine, "Would you mind carrying the boxes to my car? I'll pop the trunk."

"Sure."

Before Christine started to lift the stack of boxes, Kady stopped her. "Hold on a sec." Removing a heavy cut-crystal vase from the shelf, she added it to the items in the top box and replaced the lid.

Christine hefted the boxes. "Goodness. This is a heavy load."

"Do you want me to carry the vase? It's probably weighing you down."

"Nope. I got it. This is experience for when I make deliveries."

As they went outside, Kady pointed her key-less remote at her trunk. "I'll check in later, but please call me if you need anything."

"I'll be fine," Christine assured her, placing the cartons inside and closing the trunk.

Shouldering her tote, Kady gazed at the shop. Her heart pinched at the idea of losing this place. No way could she let that happen.

Dᴜᴜᴀɴ ʜᴜʀʀɪᴇᴅ ᴅᴏᴡɴ the stairs from the second-floor office of Sanders Security after an early meeting with Max to go over new information. He'd received more intel on the guys hanging around the marina, complete with pictures from Max and copies of arrest records the police chief shared. Kady's brother's name came up again, which bothered Dylan. There were multiple persons of interest in Cypress Pointe, but so far none were connected to Esposa.

In Dylan's mind, the only interesting person he'd met so far was Kady. And he'd pretty much blown it with her. Maybe if he'd paid more attention to what his mother was doing at the convention he wouldn't have landed in this mess. He'd been focused on Esposa when he should have gotten the lowdown from his mother. That would teach him. Beautiful, funny women didn't come his way often. He wanted to make things right with Kady.

He stepped on the sidewalk, taking his sunglasses from his shirt pocket to shield his eyes from the morning glare. Only nine, but the sun shone in full force. He dreaded sitting through workshops all day when he'd rather be outdoors, but if he wanted to keep his cover, he had to act interested in the scheduled events.

Only a few more days, but if it got him closer to Esposa, he could endure it.

He'd just turned in the direction of the Grand Cypress Hotel when he noticed Kady leave her floral shop. As she tossed her hair and hitched a bag over her shoulder, he admired her confidence. It was one of the first things that drew his attention when he'd first laid eyes on her.

He had some groveling to do. Might as well do it en route to the hotel. Picking up his pace, he jogged down the sidewalk to catch Kady. His thigh screamed at the exertion, but Dylan ignored the discomfort. At least he didn't fall on his face like he had in rehab after the shooting.

"Kady. Hold up."

When she didn't stop, he increased his pace. "Kady."

Finally she halted and glanced around, confusion on her lovely face. "I hear a buzzing noise but can't find the pest that goes with it." She met his gaze. "Must be you."

"Okay, I probably deserved that."

She continued walking.

"I told you I'm sorry for the misunderstanding."

"Fine. Doesn't mean I want to talk to you."

"Don't you think you're being a little juvenile?"

She swung around. "Coming from the guy who deliberately misled me?"

"Never. I didn't know about your history with my mother."

"And you expect me to believe you?"

"Yes."

He watched skepticism cross her features. She was struggling, which meant he might be able to salvage the entire mess. He waited, absently rubbing his thigh, allowing her the first chance to say something.

"Is your leg bothering you?"

"A little."

"What happened?"

"Work injury."

"I'm guessing it wasn't floral-related."

He shook his head, fighting a smile. "No."

"That's the first thing you've said that I actually believe. I never really bought your connection as a florist, or anything closely related."

She was quick; he'd give her that. He'd have to watch himself to keep from revealing his undercover status.

"My dad died about six years ago. Since then, one of my brothers or I accompany my mom to the convention. It's been five years since I've attended, so I tagged along. Decided to step up this year."

At his admission, he saw Kady soften. "So you really aren't snooping around to discover my secret?"

"Do I look like a guy who knows what kind of flower goes in a bouquet?"

He liked the grin that tentatively crossed her lips. "No. There's something about you. I can't put my finger on it, but flower guy? No."

"Then what do you say we start over?" He held out his hand. "Dylan Matthews. Son of Jasmine Matthews, who is apparently the queen of the bouquets. I am not trying now, nor have I ever tried, to coerce floral secrets from anyone, but most definitely, not from you."

After a few static moments, she took his hand. "Kady Lawrence. Florist, bouquet competition runner-up. I agree you aren't trying to pilfer secrets about my entry to give your mother an edge." She sighed. "Your mom is good. She doesn't need an edge."

"Thanks for the vote of confidence."

"While I was blindsided last night, I have to admit, you haven't asked any questions about my design."

"Then we can start over? Take up where we left off?"

He hoped she was thinking about their kiss as much as he was.

She pointed a finger at him. "I'm still keeping an eye on you. I don't want to inadvertently give you any information you can pass along to your mother."

"If keeping an eye on me means we hang out together, I'll deal with it."

After last night's debacle, when he expected Kady would have nothing to do with him, it bothered him to no end. He liked her, liked being around her. If she refused his company, well, it didn't sit right with him. And then there was the fact that she had connections to this town, so he really needed to find Esposa for her safety, as well as that of many others.

She glanced at her watch. "We need to get moving. The first workshop starts at ten and I want a good seat."

They picked up the pace and headed, along with a growing crowd, to the hotel.

"So where were you going when we met up?" Kady asked.

"I got up early. Took a walk along Main. Stopped at a few places."

"It's early. Most stores are just starting to open."

"The coffee place was hopping."

She grinned. "Cuppa Joe."

"They serve a good cup of coffee."

"And it's the place in Cypress Pointe to socialize."

Most coffee shops were. "I'm starting to like this town."

"As opposed to?"

He debated answering. "Miami."

"Cypress Pointe can't be anywhere near as exciting as Miami."

She had no idea.

"C'mon—South Beach? Shopping? The gorgeous beaches."

"The crowds, the crime," he countered, "and since I work, I don't get to the beaches."

"I guess it's the same for everyone. We never take advantage of the beautiful locales we live in."

"You've lived here all your life?"

"Yep. Left for a little while, but decided I wanted to work at my parents' shop…so here I am."

"Good for me."

She shot him an amused glance before they entered the hotel lobby. The noise level was high from people mingling before the morning sessions began. Freshly brewed coffee, and a sweet scent he hadn't noticed yesterday, filled the open area. Captured by the rays of sunlight streaming in from the large windows, Dylan noticed many arrangements scattered around the room. All he could think was *Thank goodness I'm not allergic to flowers.*

"Listen, I'm going to take off," Kady said in a distracted tone. "Maybe we'll see each other later."

Disappointment settled in his gut. "I could join you."

She hesitated, and then her eyes narrowed slightly. She looked ready to say something. Then the walls were back up again. Clearly she didn't trust him. "Thanks, but I'm good."

She turned on her heel and disappeared into the crowd, leaving him wondering what had just happened.

"I see you're making friends."

He heard his mother's voice before she stepped beside him.

"I was."

Jasmine waved her hand. "Kady will get over last night's mix-up."

"I thought she had."

"Until I materialized?"

He sent her a sideways look. "You do have a way of appearing at inopportune times."

"It comes from raising four boys. I seem to have trouble radar."

"I'm not in any trouble."

"Not yet. Just give it time." She raised a brow. "Do you think I don't know when you're up to something? This has to do with a case, doesn't it?"

"I'd rather not discuss it."

"I knew it."

"Mom. Please. Let it go."

"I worry. Especially since your injury."

"Which has healed." Okay, it was a little lie, but he couldn't have his mother babying him. If he needed any gentle, loving attention, he'd rather have it from Kady.

And where did that thought come from? What was up with him? He had a job to focus on, despite the fact that he wanted to walk the beach with Kady and kiss her again. Whoa, buddy. The case came first. Finding Esposa was his number one goal, not getting romantic with a woman he'd only recently met. A woman he'd leave when his job was done here. His pursuit of her had to be secondary. For everyone's sake, he needed to find Esposa.

Still, it bothered him that she dumped him when he wanted to be sitting beside her in a workshop, quietly critiquing the speaker.

"Look, I need you to run some errands for me. My workshop is this afternoon and I don't have a few things."

"Things you conveniently forget? Mom, you're always organized."

"Not when my topic gets changed."

"How did that happen?"

"I don't know," his usually calm mother cried. "This is my first time speaking."

Concern flooded him. His unflappable mother was headed for a meltdown. "Take a breath and tell me what happened."

His mother closed her eyes. Inhaled. Exhaled. After a few seconds, she looked at him.

"Way back when the committee asked me to speak, we decided on the romance of flowers. I thought they meant how picking the right flowers can make an arrangement romantic. When I read the workshop description last night, I discovered they misunderstood. I'm supposed to talk about what specific flowers mean, not the actual arranging." Her tote bag slipped from her shoulder. She rummaged inside until she pulled out a folded piece of paper. "I was up late last night gathering information for a new presentation. Here's a list of supplies. I've called around town and found the places that have what I need. I wrote them down as well."

He scanned the list she stuffed in his hand. "Oh, no. No way."

"You have to, Dylan. I'm counting on you."

He closed his eyes. Jeez. When he signed on to pretend to help his mom, he didn't think he'd have to actually do anything.

"You have three hours, son. I'm depending on you to be my assistant."

He flashed back to the horror on his brothers' faces when they tried to opt out of staying at the convention with their mother. He understood now just what they were feeling.

He glanced at the list, then his mother's panicked face. He had to do this for her.

As he walked out of the hotel, back into the morning glare, he decided that catching scumbag drug dealers was easier than being his mother's assistant at a florist convention.

CHAPTER SEVEN

STILL SEATED AT the table after enjoying a delicious meal and listening to a great luncheon speaker, Kady studied the workshop schedule, debating which class to attend next.

During the break before lunch, she'd run over to the shop. Christine had everything well in hand. Pleased, Kady decided to take the stephanotis home for her special bouquet in case she didn't have time later on. She arrived back at the hotel in time to grab a seat for the luncheon.

The only choices were a lecture on exotic flowers or the romance of flowers featuring Jasmine Matthews. Before everything happened with Dylan, she'd checked off Jasmine's workshop to attend. They may be rivals, but the topic played right into Kady's wheelhouse. The more she learned about the meaning of different flowers, the more ammunition in her arsenal when advising brides on their floral choices.

If she wanted to gain the reputation as the go-to florist for all things wedding, she needed to hone her edge. Learning everything there was to know about the romance of flowers, she could guide her brides to make choices that came from the heart, not the wallet, and therefore establish The Lavish Lily as the florist shop for weddings. She'd already received rave reviews from the brides she'd worked with. She needed to keep the momentum going in order to book so many weddings she didn't have time to breathe.

So going to the workshop might be awkward. She might have to see Dylan. Could she put aside her pride if it meant helping her business? She scanned the workshop description again and decided, yes, she could do this. Taking the class didn't mean she'd cower before Queen Jasmine. Instead, let the queen worry about her.

She gathered up her pen, notebook, conference binder and tote. Only a few minutes to spare. Maybe she'd be lucky and snag a seat in the back of the room.

Wishful thinking. When she arrived at the assigned location, almost every seat was taken, except for a few in the front row. *Figures.* She was just about to back out when Jasmine caught her eye. Kady read the silent dare there. Now she really couldn't leave.

Making her way down the center aisle, she took a seat at the end of the first row, next to the wall. After pulling out her notebook, she waited for the lecture to start. Jasmine seemed preoccupied. What was going on? She was just about to ask the woman sitting next to her when a commotion sounded from the back of the room. She turned, catching sight of Dylan dragging something down the aisle while balancing local store bags hanging from either arm.

He met his mother and she whispered in his ear. His head dropped and Kady got the distinct impression he didn't like what his mother said. She sat back, enjoying the show. Her afternoon was looking up.

He placed the bags on the long table behind the podium and wrestled with the big thing he'd dragged in. As he righted the object, Kady realized it was a life-size cutout of Cupid. Arrows and all. Just then Dylan looked up. His gaze scanned the room and finally collided with hers. He stopped, and she could have sworn his ears turned pink. She pressed her lips together to keep from laughing out loud as Dylan moved to help his mother empty the shopping bags.

Finally, Jasmine stepped to the podium and adjusted the microphone.

"Sorry for the delay. My assistant was late getting here."

Dylan shot his mother a wry look, which made Kady chuckle quietly. Assistant, huh? He must be loving the title.

"Today I will be discussing the romance of flowers. As you can see by our friend Cupid, romance is always the heart of the matter. Why, Valentine's Day is only a few weeks away. Perhaps Mr. Cupid has a thing or two to teach us."

Jasmine took a stack of papers from the podium and handed them to Dylan. "My assistant will distribute a handout I hope you find informational."

Dylan took the papers and handed them off to each person at the end of each row to pass along. He looked at her again, his metal-colored eyes warning her not to say a word. Oh, she would, but later, when she had him at her mercy.

"As you can see, I've used examples of the more commonly used flowers and their meanings."

When Dylan returned to the front, he removed single stems of flowers from one of the

"Then I suppose they'd like me to forward the pictures I snapped on my phone?"

His eyes grew wide.

"I'm kidding. Even I wouldn't sink that low."

"Thanks. I think."

"C'mon."

Instead of taking a seat at one of the bistro tables by the poolside café, they opted to stretch out in lounge chairs at the far end of the patio. From their vantage point they could see the beach and the blue water of the gulf beyond. A gentle breeze cooled the afternoon. A mixture of chlorine and salt water scented the air.

They sat quietly for a few minutes until Kady couldn't take it anymore and started laughing.

Dylan glanced at his watch. "Wow. I'm impressed. You held it in for a whole fifteen minutes."

"You should have seen your face. Classic."

"I guess I deserve it. Probably matched your face last night when I introduced my mother."

"So we're even."

"This coming from the woman who swore I was out to get her?"

"Karma is a beautiful thing."

This time he chuckled. A companionable silence fell between them.

Between not sleeping the night before and

going to the shop at the crack of dawn, Kady enjoyed this break in the action. Her lids began to droop when Dylan spoke up.

"Looks like a lot of boaters on the water. Is that because of tourist season or is it always busy here?"

Kady blinked and straightened. So much for a quick nap.

"The marina is busy year-round. We get plenty of tourists, but the locals use it as well."

"So you know most of the local people who anchor boats there?"

"Not all. It varies from season to season."

"Any trouble between the locals and tourists?"

She glanced at him. "I swear you sound like you're writing a travel brochure. If I were the suspicious sort, I'd assume you had an agenda behind all your questions."

"I'm curious by nature."

She narrowed her eyes at him, weighing his answer.

"What? Maybe I want to make a move in my life. Cypress Pointe seems like a nice place to live."

She considered his answer. "Would your sudden urge to relocate come from your work injury?"

"Why would you ask?"

"Call it a hunch."

Dylan gazed out over the water. Kady imagined he was deciding what to reveal. The man seemed to dole out only small tidbits of information about himself. She respected his privacy, but she was far too curious to back off now.

"I'm one of those people who really throws himself into a job. If I don't give one hundred and ten percent, why give anything at all? In my zeal to get the job done, I miscalculated. And the result ended in an injury."

He continued to look over the water. Not meeting her eyes meant one of two things. He'd revealed more than usual, or he'd only touched the tip of the iceberg. With him, Kady imagined the second. He hadn't told her what type of injury he'd received. And maybe it was too much to hope he'd confide in her. Honestly, if the tables were turned, would she spill all to him?

Dylan turned just then and their gazes met. In his eyes she saw a myriad of emotions. Hurt. Uncertainty. Before she could name the others he blinked and his gaze went blank. But still, she'd gotten a glimpse of the man she enjoyed spending time with.

So, yes. If the tables were turned, she just might tell all to Dylan. No matter how unwise the consequences might be.

He stirred and Kady realized it was time to get back to the real world. No more thinking that just because Dylan had let his guard down meant there was anything between them, last night's kiss notwithstanding.

"Are you going to the next workshop?" she asked, covering how much she'd let her attraction to the man get the better of her.

"Not hardly. I'm not sure I can show my face around here after Mom's lecture."

"Dylan, it's a florist convention. What happens here stays here."

"Isn't that the Las Vegas slogan?"

"Trust me when I say you aren't the first to be embarrassed at a conference. You won't be the last."

"Still, I'm heading up to my room. Have some calls I need to make."

She hid her disappointment. "Then I'll see you later."

They'd taken a few steps when he stopped her by laying his warm hand on her arm. She controlled the shiver skimming her skin.

"How about we grab dinner tonight?"

"Can't. I already have plans."

He jammed his hands in his pockets. "Well, maybe I'll run into you later."

"Maybe."

Hooking her tote over her shoulder, Kady forced a smile and walked away, regret squeezing her chest so tight she rubbed it once she was out of Dylan's view.

It was now official. Dylan Matthews had gotten under her skin and there was no way of letting him go.

DYLAN HADN'T BEEN in his room for five minutes when his cell rang. The caller ID showed the call was from Derrick.

"Cupid? Really?" He launched in without waiting for a proper greeting.

Great. His brother had a picture of his embarrassing moment.

"Don't start," Dylan snarled.

"Now you see why I cheat."

"Indeed, except this is the last year any of us has to worry about getting wrangled into helping Mom."

"At least we have the memories. You and Cupid. Stored in the cloud. Forever."

Derrick knew how much Dylan hated getting caught unawares. That made the brotherly joking so much worse. Until something nagged at Dylan. "Hey, where'd you get the picture?"

"Mom sent it."

When had she taken it? Clearly when he wasn't looking. Maybe if he'd kept his eyes on the environment around him, and not on Kady's reaction to him setting up a life-size Cupid, he would have noticed his mother's actions.

Dylan rubbed his forehead. "Which means Dante and Deke have a copy?"

"Yep." Derrick sounded way too cheerful for Dylan's liking.

"Fun time is over. What's up?"

"I did a little digging."

"I thought I told you I'd keep you in the loop."

"You know I was never one to wait to be asked to the party."

True. Derrick would rather jump in and ask questions later.

"And?"

"Esposa definitely has relatives living on the outskirts of Tampa. Whatever is going on in Cypress Pointe can't be a coincidence."

Dylan walked to the sliding doors and gazed out at the tropical vista. "I wonder if he realizes I'm here?"

"If he did, he probably would have come after you by now."

"I have been keeping a low profile."

Derrick snickered.

"What else?"

"My contact is getting the names of the families. Once we have them, we can check more thoroughly."

"What's this *we*? I told you I needed to do this on my own."

"Look, bro. I get that you want to bring Esposa down by yourself, but you're crazy if you think you're just gonna walk up and slap the cuffs on him. You need as much help as you can get. You owe Eddie that much."

If anyone but Derrick had said those words, he would have been all over them. But his brother was right. Eddie's memory deserved better, which meant Dylan needed to do this by the book. Make it count for Eddie's family.

"When you have the details get back to me."

"Will do."

Dylan paused, then asked, "You aren't going to catch trouble for helping me, are you?"

"Even if I was, I don't care. You're my brother. Eddie was a friend. I'm doing this."

There was no dissuading Derrick when he

was on the trail of a criminal. Dylan wouldn't bother trying.

"I'm working with a PI here in Cypress Pointe. When we get any new information I'll pass it on."

"Sounds good. And, Dylan?"

"Yeah."

"Watch your six, brother."

"Always."

He ended the call and tossed his phone on the bed. Out on the balcony, he clasped the wrought-iron banister and leaned forward, letting the breeze cool his face.

Except for the night Esposa surprised him, Dylan rarely let down his guard. It still stuck in his craw that he'd been so intent on getting Esposa that Eddie had been left vulnerable. The what-ifs had almost gotten to him after the shooting. The only way to make things right was to get Esposa off the streets and behind bars.

He ordered dinner to the room. Steak and a baked potato were definitely well earned tonight. Kady had plans, and his mother was with her friends, and honestly, he didn't want to be at the mercy of the florists who wanted to talk about the industry. He'd heard enough growing up, working during the summers delivering arrangements for his mother, or listening to shoptalk at the dinner table. He admired his mother's dedication to her craft, but if it wasn't for an ulterior motive, he'd have ratted out Derrick and his magic coin to escape conference duty.

While eating, he flipped through the sports channels. Usually, after a long day he'd come home and do just the same, but tonight he felt restless. He paced, watched the sun set, but couldn't settle down. He grabbed a jacket. Maybe a walk on the beach would blow the cobwebs away.

Attendees still mingled in the lobby. He couldn't blame them. This was a highlight in their year and most were taking full advantage of networking. He'd almost gotten to the front entrance when he noticed Kady coming from another direction. She was in conversation with her friends and didn't see him. He decided to wait and catch up with her as she left.

Leaning a shoulder against a decorative column, he was just out of Kady's sight line. She was very animated as she and her friends laughed. She must have gone to dinner after the last workshop because she still wore the same outfit from earlier. The only difference was that she'd pulled back her thick mass of hair into a soft style he'd come to like seeing on her. He imagined running his hands through the weight of it, and with any luck, he might lean in for a kiss…

His thoughts ended abruptly when the woman he'd been wishing to kiss stopped a few feet from him, chatting with her group. Although his intention was not to eavesdrop, he could overhear their conversation.

"Really, Kady. You need to get out there more," said the woman Dylan remembered meeting the other night. Melissa, was it?

"Look, you might all be old married women, but it doesn't happen for some of us. I'm happy at the shop."

Another woman barked out a laugh. "Right."

Kady's brow wrinkled. "No, I'm fine."

Melissa grinned at her. "Oh? I saw you sitting by the pool with Queen Jasmine's son."

Dylan winced at the description.

"You two were pretty cozy."

"We were just talking."

"Talking can lead to a relationship," another woman added. "My husband and I talked on the phone for two months before we met in person."

"Not everyone takes things that slowly," Melissa drawled.

The woman shrugged. "Worked for us."

Dylan wouldn't mind talking with Kady, but he wanted to walk along the beach with her. Alone. To see where things might go.

He hadn't missed the reluctant attraction in her eyes before she realized Jasmine was his mother. It was the same look she'd tried to disguise today out by the pool. He wanted to see the reluctant part removed and the attraction part increased.

"I'm happily single," Kady insisted.

Her friends exchanged knowing glances, but gave her a reprieve. They said their goodbyes and went in different directions.

Pushing from the column, he sidled up to Kady as she turned toward the entrance. "Headed home?"

She halted, her head jerking up. "Where did you come from?"

He nodded in the direction of the lobby. "Got stir-crazy and decided to take a walk."

"It's a nice night." Hesitating, she tugged at the tote strap over her shoulder. "So, um, I'll see you tomorrow?"

"I could walk you to your car."

"It's parked behind the flower shop. I have to go back and check on things anyway."

"Want company?"

She flashed a quick smile. "You must be really bored."

"No, but escorting a beautiful woman to her car just might make my night."

She chuckled. "You smooth talker, you." She visibly hesitated again, and when she met his gaze, he couldn't miss the longing there. It hit him smack in the middle of his solar plexus. But he could also see she was weighing her options. Deciding if she should spend more time with him. Smart girl.

"Cypress Pointe is a relatively safe town. Nothing much happens here. But a girl can't be too careful, so, okay. You can walk with me."

They stepped out into a clear, star-filled night. The temperature had dropped and the wind picked up again. Kady pulled the jacket from her bag. When she struggled to get it on, he helped. Their fingers brushed and he felt the adrenaline kick in his gut. The reaction he'd come to associate with Kady. The one that reminded him of how long it had been since he'd pursued a real relationship with a woman.

As they walked, he asked about the town. Kady kept up a running commentary, her nervousness evident. He smiled, amused and pleased.

Before long they reached the alley behind the shop. Kady dug for the keys.

"I should go inside and check on things. Christine is capable, but she's new and can't work with the flowers yet."

"Isn't there anyone else to do the job?"

"No. My parents are out of town, so the designing falls to me. Between the shop and the convention, I've been busy."

The lightbulb in the fixture over the back door flickered. "You should get that fixed."

"I will." Kady held the keys in her hand but didn't move. Loose papers blew across the asphalt. Did he detect the scent of rain in the air? When an especially strong gust whipped her hair free, he reached out to brush a strand from her cheek. Lost in the moment and the soft touch of her skin, Dylan stepped closer and lowered his head. Kady remained still and he touched his lips to hers, settling into a kiss that had the capability of rocking his world.

His tight chest eased when Kady leaned into him. He angled his head, settling his hands on her waist, sweeping them both into the intimacy of the kiss. He ignored the gravity of his feelings, instead giving himself over to the sensation of Kady in his arms. Reality would intrude later. For now, he wanted the magic of the moment, wanted the breathless kiss to last.

The wind gusted again, causing the bulb to flicker again, disturbing the electrifying bond between himself and Kady.

Kady pulled away, gazed directly into his eyes. "What's going on?"

"I'd say we're enjoying each other's company."

"But…what's the endgame, Dylan? You'll be leaving town soon."

He drew in a bracing breath. "Are you asking if this might turn into something permanent?"

"Maybe."

"I thought you liked being single?"

Her eyes went wide.

"Yeah, sorry. I overheard."

She punched his arm. "You were eavesdropping."

"Not intentionally."

"And that makes it okay?"

"No." He shifted uncomfortably. "I don't know how I keep ending up in these situations where I have to explain myself to you."

"So you're saying I bring out the worst in you?"

He ran a hand over his jaw. "This is getting

out of hand. Maybe you should just unlock the door."

Kady put the key in the lock, turned it and she pushed open the door. Before she or Dylan could move, he laid a hand on her shoulder. She looked at him, expectant.

"I can't explain what you do to me, Kady. And I can't make any promises. But I do want to see where this leads."

She nodded, then stepped inside, her hand running along the wall to locate the light switch. He waited while she flipped on the light, took another step and then abruptly plowed into the back of her.

"What the—"

His next word died in his throat as he took in the scene. Kady's shocked cry jolted him back to reality.

The room had been trashed. He'd been to enough crime scenes to know the act had been deliberate. And by the expression on Kady's pale face, she knew it, too.

CHAPTER EIGHT

"I DON'T UNDERSTAND what's happened," Kady gasped, her hands pressed over her aching stomach.

Dylan gently moved her aside. "Let me look around."

She grabbed a handful of his jacket. "Are you sure?"

He nodded. "Stay here."

Too shaky to do anything but follow his command, Kady processed her surroundings while Dylan made his way to the front of the store. A light came on in the distance.

"Clear," Dylan yelled in a calm, clear voice.

She shook her head. Now this?

Dylan returned, his cell phone in hand. "I'm calling the authorities."

Yes. Right. That made sense.

He jerked to a stop, his eyes fixed on her. "It'll be okay."

The concerned glimmer in his gaze made her straighten her shoulders and slowed her heart rate. Which worked, until she scanned the room more closely. "How can you say that?"

"Because you weren't here when the perps broke in."

Perps? Okay. But still...

Scattered on the floor were strips of floral tape, crushed foam molds, ruined baskets, a smashed glue gun and sticks. Dried lavender bunches were trampled among her supplies and emitted a sweet scent in the wake of all the destruction.

Running a shaky hand through her hair, she tried to wrap her mind around the fact that someone had torn her shop to pieces. Why? Cypress Pointe was a tourist destination, not a hotbed of criminal activity. And yet the scene before her said otherwise.

Dylan's strong voice broke through her fog. As he related the incident to someone on the other end of the phone, she finally drew in a few deep breaths. Setting her tote on the worktable, she tried to itemize the damage.

Only then did she notice she hadn't disengaged the alarm system. Yet the piercing sound had never blared through the room. Obviously someone else had beaten her to it. The unit was hanging from the wall by its wires.

She closed her eyes against hot tears. Why would someone violate the space she loved? What did they want or need so badly that they'd come into her business and trash it?

Taking another breath, she opened her eyes. It would help if she took inventory and saw if anything came up missing.

All the bins she'd lovingly organized and arranged on the shelves were dumped on the floor. The lower cabinet doors hung open, the contents also left on the floor. Broken glass littered the area, a rainbow of colors mixed together from the vases and decorative containers she used. The empty boxes she stored for delivery on the very top shelf were missing, probably mixed in among the mess she didn't have the heart to wander through.

The back door slammed as a gust of wind pushed it closed. Kady nearly jumped out of her skin, her hand moving over her rapidly beating heart.

Gingerly stepping over her materials, she noticed a crack in the glass door of the cooler. Hurrying over, she carefully felt inside. The air was cool. Relief swept over her.

"Broken?" Dylan asked as he joined her.

"Just the glass. The unit seems okay." She turned to him, drawing strength from his.

"The police will be here soon."

She wrung her hands. Where did she start cleaning this disaster?

"Everything has to remain where it is until the authorities survey the scene."

She nodded. She'd seen enough cop shows to know that much.

"How was it up front?"

"Barely touched."

Glad for a bit of good news, she suddenly thought of the cash register. "The money," she cried, sprinting down the hallway and skidding to a stop at the counter. The register was closed. She paused, confused.

Dylan came up behind her. "I noticed it, too."

"Why would someone trash the shop but not try to open the register to take the cash?" She hit a few buttons and the drawer slid open. She removed a few bills. "We only keep twenty dollars in the drawer overnight. It's all here."

Dylan took the bills, placed them back in the drawer and moved her away from the counter. "Try not to touch anything else."

As if her fingers had been zapped, she curled them together. This was so beyond her realm of experience. Now she didn't know what to do. Tears burned, and before she could blink them away, Dylan pulled her into a comforting embrace.

Stiff at first, the rhythmic rubbing of his hand up and down her back calmed her in slow degrees. Before long she relaxed against his chest, allowing the tears to fall. Just a few more minutes of this, she promised herself, and then she'd pull it together.

"It's okay to be upset," Dylan assured her in a steady voice. "This has been a shock."

"You think?" She choked on a half laugh, swiping at her eyes, trying for a little levity as she pulled from his warmth.

His hands braced her arms. "Once the police arrive, it'll be all business. Take this time to collect yourself."

Sage advice. "Voice of experience?"

His eyes were hooded. "Yeah."

"Police!"

Kady shuddered again.

Dylan rubbed her arms. "It'll be okay."

"If you say so."

Taking her by the elbow, Dylan led Kady to the back. An officer, making notes, looked up when they came in.

"One of you called this in?"

"I did," Dylan answered. "Ms. Lawrence is the owner."

"Are you okay, ma'am?"

"Yes," she replied, her voice still wobbly. "Whoever did this was gone when we arrived."

The officer focused on Dylan. "You are?"

"A friend," Kady quickly answered to reassure the young man.

He nodded. "I have questions, but I'm calling in the investigation team first." He spoke into the lapel mic hooked to his uniform collar. "B and E at Lavish Lily. Request additional assistance."

"Ten-four," came the crackly response.

The policeman stepped toward Kady. "I'm Officer Baylor. I need to ask you about a few things."

"Of course." Kady mentally prepared herself. She shot a quick glance at Dylan. After his brief nod, she joined the officer.

She answered whatever the officer asked her, but wasn't much help. She didn't know who would do this, nor did she have any reason to believe anyone had done it out of spite. Yes, her locks were up-to-date. Yes, she had an alarm system, but it was destroyed. This was all so bizarre. This was Cypress Pointe! After fifteen minutes of questioning, Bob Gardener entered the workroom. After a cursory glance, he approached her.

"You doing okay?"

How many more people were going to ask her that question? "Yes, Chief. More shaken up than anything else." This must be bad if the chief'd been called out. "Why are you here?"

"A few other locations called in suspicious activity tonight. Someone tried to jimmy the lock at Charming Delights Catering. Broken glass at Milly's Gifts and Things." He scrutinized the scene before him. "Your shop was the only one broken into."

"Any idea who's behind this?"

The chief shook his head, his eyes narrowed. "Not yet."

His answer did not inspire comfort.

"I'm sure your mama and daddy would want to know things are well in hand here."

Oh, no. She hadn't even thought about them. Great. They weren't going to be thrilled about this latest event.

"I haven't had a chance to call them. I've been—"

Before she could finish, Will stormed through the back door. His hair was a mess and his eyes, wild, roamed the room until he found her. He rushed over and tugged her into his arms, squeezing her tightly.

Surprised and touched by her brother's concern, she reveled in his hug until the lack of oxygen made her light-headed. "I can't breathe," she mumbled.

He loosened his hold but didn't release her. His eyes moved over her, as if to make sure she was in one piece.

"I'm okay. The shop was broken into before I got here."

Clearly unable to speak, he hugged her again. This time his hold was firm, not life-threatening. She stayed in his embrace until he calmed down, knowing he needed it more than she did. Finally, he let her go.

The chief slapped him on the back. "Will."

"Chief. What's going on?"

"B and E, by the looks of it. Don't know much more than you at this point. Kady gave my officer her version of events. The crime-scene guys will go over this place. Hopefully we'll get some answers."

Kady tried to relax. Answers. Yes, she needed them, too. By all indications, this was going to be a long night.

She glanced at her shell-shocked brother. "Earth to Will."

"Huh?" He faced her, scrutinizing her. "Sorry. A lot to process here." He frowned. "Why aren't you more upset?"

"Had my meltdown before you got here. Now I'm numb."

He squeezed her hand, and silently, they stood together for several minutes. "It could be worse, I suppose."

Will's brow rose. "Really? How?"

"No one was here when it happened, and nothing seems to have been taken. What kind of a robbery is that?"

The truth of her words made him grimace. "Robbery. What an awful word."

"I guess we got lucky," she told him, now that she'd had time to digest everything. "They didn't take the money in the cash drawer or the digital camera right there on the shelf. Who makes a mess and leaves empty-handed?"

She decided to ask the police chief, but didn't when she noticed him in heavy discussion with Dylan. Odd. It was almost as if they were thick as thieves. She cringed at the description.

As if reading her thoughts, Will asked, "Who's that guy with the chief?"

"Dylan. A friend from the floral convention."

He shot her a sidelong glance. "And he was with you late at night because…?"

"You're actually going to question the company I keep? After what happened here?"

"I'm your brother."

"And I'm glad Dylan was with me. He called the police and kept me from a major freak-out."

"In that case—"

"Thank you."

She caught Dylan's eye a moment later, waving him over to introduce her suddenly territorial older brother.

"Dylan, this is my brother, Will."

Holding out his hand, Dylan acknowledged him. "Good to meet you."

"Under these circumstances I don't agree necessarily, but I get it."

"Tough night all around."

An hour later, the police finished their initial investigation. Will called Christine, which Kady found interesting, and she arrived with coffee. With the final okay from the crime-scene unit, the four were left alone to clean up the mess.

Kady winced. "Where do we start?"

"I'll gather the bins," Christine volunteered. "Let's put the supplies on the worktable and sort from there."

Glad someone had devised a plan, Kady got busy. She found herself beside Dylan, who'd pushed up his sleeves and dived in with the rest of them.

"You don't have to stay," she told him.

"What kind of a guy do you think I am?"

"Generous?" she ventured.

"And concerned. Besides, you'll be here all night if everyone doesn't chip in. Honestly, I don't mind."

Her eyes welled up again. She turned away, not wanting Dylan to think she couldn't handle her emotions. But the fact that he'd volunteered to stay and clean up, well, it touched her.

Changing the subject, she said, "So. You and Chief Gardener?"

"I'm a stranger in town, so he needed to question me."

Sounded logical. Anyone out of place would be on the chief's radar.

"I'm not a suspect."

She grinned. "Mainly because you were with me?"

"There is that."

"I just can't get past the idea that whoever went to all this trouble didn't take the money. It's like this was deliberate, to get my attention away—" She sank back on her heels and sent Dylan a horrified look. "Please do not tell me this is your mother's plan to distract me."

Dylan rose, his face tight. "I can't believe you would even consider that."

Pushing herself up, she stood before him. "I didn't see you until late this evening. Where were you before then?"

"Excuse me?"

"Answer my question."

"It doesn't deserve a response."

She crossed her arms over her chest.

"Really? You think my mother and I would sink this low to win a stupid flower competition?"

"It's not stupid." Her burst of anger suddenly spent, her shoulders slumped. "What is wrong with me?"

He put a hand softly on her shoulder. "Delayed reaction to stress."

When her eyes grew wet again, she didn't try to hide it. "I'm so sorry, Dylan," she whispered.

Glancing at her brother, then back to her, he pulled her into his strong arms. "It's okay," he murmured against her hair.

The tears fell freely. She let them, wanting to get this emotional ordeal over with. Once she'd dried her eyes, she moved back. "I am so sorry I accused you."

"Apology accepted. We're even. Again. You laughed at me at the workshop earlier, then accused me of B and E. We're nothing if not wary of each other."

She choked out a laugh. "What a pair."

Will dropped a few bins on the table and walked over to them. "You okay, sis?"

"Yes. Once we get this place back to normal I'll be fine."

They continued cleaning. Dylan stayed near her, watching her as if afraid she'd fall apart again. Will darted around, doing one task, then another, while Christine worked silently, her face pinched with worry.

"Not a great way for you to start off with us," Kady said to her new employee as she refilled the bins.

"I'm just… It's a lot to take in."

"I won't be upset if you decide to quit."

"Quit?" Panic crossed Christine's face. "No. I can't do that."

"Are you sure?"

"Yes, especially after tonight."

On impulse, Kady hugged her. "Thanks."

Soon all the supplies were in bins and everything had been put back on the shelves. Will swept up the floor and Dylan found duct tape to cover the crack in the cooler door until a repairman could replace it.

Kady restocked the items dragged from the

cabinets. Something was missing. The package of white corsage boxes with the name of the shop printed in a lovely lavender script. Strange. She stood, examining each shelf. Empty. The small boxes from the wholesaler she kept for deliveries were missing.

"Christine?"

"Yes?" Christine said, joining her.

"Where are the corsage boxes?"

Christine frowned as she searched the room. "You know, I don't remember coming across them tonight."

"How about those empty delivery boxes?" She pointed to the shelf. "Did they get tossed in the garbage?"

"I have no idea."

"It's not a big deal, but it's odd we can't find them." She glanced around the room again. "I'll have to order new corsage boxes."

"Are you looking for these?" Will called out from the hallway, carrying in the larger, now flattened delivery boxes.

"Where'd you find them?"

"By the cooler up front." Will grabbed hold of a stepladder and climbed up. "Must have gotten moved in all the commotion," he said, placing the boxes on a shelf in their usual spot.

"What about a package of small, new white boxes?" Kady asked.

"Didn't see them."

Why would someone go to all this trouble to take the small boxes that were of little use outside the shop? The feeling that something was off continued to plague her.

"What?" Dylan asked as he watched her circle the room.

"I can't put my finger on it." She checked the entire room, still not sure what was bothering her. "Maybe I'll figure it out tomorrow when I've had some sleep and have a fresh perspective."

A frown wrinkled Dylan's brow as he searched Kady's face. She glanced at her watch. Going on 4:00 a.m. "We should call it a night—I mean, morning."

"We cleaned most of it up," Dylan agreed. He tossed the duct tape on the counter. "How about I get you home?"

Kady shook her head. "You've done enough. My car is out back. I can get home myself. Go to the hotel and get a few hours' sleep."

His dark eyes met hers. "Sure?"

"Positive." She collected her tote and purse. "Will, we're heading out."

"We're right behind you. I'll lock up."

"Thanks."

Kady stepped into the alley, pulling on her jacket. The early morning temperature had turned downright frosty in the hours they'd spent inside the shop. The sky, a murky black, held only a smattering of stars as clouds hung overhead. Humidity dampened the air.

"Dylan, thanks. You went above and beyond."

He shrugged. "I'd do it again."

A yawn sneaked up on her and she tried to stifle it.

"Get home. I'll see you later at the convention."

The convention. Right. It seemed worlds away.

Dylan turned, but Kady reached out to stop him. When he looked at her, she went on tiptoes and brushed her lips over his rough cheek. "I mean it. Thanks. I don't know what I would have done without you."

"You'd have handled the situation."

"I'd like to think so."

He ran his thumb over her lower lip. "You would have."

They stood still, Kady waiting to see if he'd kiss her again. Instead, he nodded and strode down the alley.

"My hero," she whispered under her breath. Not that she'd ever tell him that. After all the false starts between them, she'd never hear the end of it.

"WHAT'S WRONG?" WILL ASKED Christine as soon as Kady and her friend left. She'd been quiet, which he supposed was not uncalled for given the situation, but in the little time he'd spent with her so far, he could read her mood. And right now, she radiated more than concern for her bosses. No, that twinge of guilt he noticed in her eyes told him otherwise.

"What are you talking about?"

"You've been jumpy all night."

"I'm helping to clean up after a break-in, so, yeah, I'm jumpy."

"It's more than that." Will set the broom in the corner and ambled to the worktable. "I get being wary after the break-in, but it's something else. I can't put my finger on it."

"Then don't try," she said, her reply clipped. Christine held a spool of wire in her hand and was turning it over and over.

"Whatever is going on, maybe I can help."

When she looked up again, doubt troubled her features. "It's not that easy."

He leaned his hip against the table. Crossed his arms over his chest. Waited.

Finally, she put down the wire. "Fine. I'm afraid my brother might be behind this."

Words Will hadn't been expecting. "Come again?" he sputtered.

"My brother has a drug problem. And he's broken into businesses before looking for ready cash or items he can sell."

"But why would he be here? Did you move to Cypress Pointe with him?"

"No. I followed him." She waved her hand. "It's a long story, but I need to find him. Help him get out of whatever mess he's gotten himself into."

"The complication you mentioned the day you started working?"

She hesitated. "Yes."

"I'm assuming you haven't talked to him since you arrived."

"I was able to follow him here, but I've lost his trail. He hangs out with a group of guys who move around, selling that synthetic drug stuff. Bryce got caught up with them and, well, he's not the same sweet-natured kid I grew up with."

"So he's dealing?"

"I think so."

Will shook his head. "You realize you can't do this alone."

"What choice do I have? I can tell the police what little I know, but they'll search for him and probably arrest him. I can't let that happen."

"Maybe that's the best thing for him."

Her eyes went wide. "How can you say such an awful thing?"

"He has to own up to what he's done." Will winced at the irony in his advice. He hadn't told the truth about his family's financial situation. Who was he to tell Christine what her brother should or should not do? Yet deep down, he knew it was sound advice.

"He's my brother," she cried in an anguished voice.

"I know what I'm talking about, Christine. He has to come clean."

She tilted her head, her gaze questioning.

Okay, so she'd let him in on her secret. Not that he needed to reciprocate, but he did want to tell someone. Share his guilt before it weighed him down so heavily he couldn't hold up under the strain any longer.

"I've been keeping something from my family. A financial secret that affects their future."

She blinked. "I'm not sure what to say."

"Me, either. Otherwise I would have told the truth already."

A calm settled over them. Christine carried the wire over to the shelf and placed it in a bin.

Will spoke again. "So what's your plan?"

"Find him. Talk some sense into him."

"If he's taking drugs, what makes you think you'll have any influence over him?"

"I love him."

"Sure, but does he love you more than getting high?"

Tears welled in her eyes. "I hate the thought of him out there, in trouble, with no one beside him."

"It's his choice, Christine."

"Don't tell me you wouldn't help your sister, even if she was making choices you didn't agree with."

"Actually, I've never tried to help Kady. She always did her own thing and I never got involved."

Christine's eyes went stormy. "My family isn't that cold."

Point taken. And it wasn't that he was cold; he'd just always been into other things. Now that he looked at it from her point of view, he understood how bad it sounded.

"Listen," he said, shifting the focus away

from him. He had enough garbage to sort through, but he wasn't going to solve all their problems tonight. "We should tell the police."

"Will, it's a lot to ask, but can you hold off? Until I find Bryce. Find out if he was behind this? Or knows who is?"

He really had no proof to tie Christine's brother to the trashed shop. What could it hurt to keep Bryce's name under wraps for a while.

"On one condition."

"Anything."

"You let me help you find him. Hear his story. Then we'll decide."

Christine threw herself at him, wrapping her arms around his neck. Surprised, he held her tight.

"Thank you," she said. There was hope in her voice.

"Don't thank me until we've discovered what's going on."

CHAPTER NINE

DESPITE THE HOURS of shut-eye, Kady couldn't shake the morning fog. The day dawned dreary, overcast with a good chance of showers. Winter weather in Florida. Great. Just what she needed—rain to match her gloomy mood.

She dressed in a white sweater, gray slacks and black ballet flats. Honestly, she couldn't work up much energy for anything more fashionable. Running a brush through her hair, she decided to keep it down. This was as presentable as she was going to get.

Try as she might, a good sleep had eluded her. She couldn't get the disturbing images of her shop out of her head. Nor could she forget how wonderful it had been to have Dylan by her side, to feel his reassuring arms around her while she was at her weakest. Fairy-tale dreams, for sure. How Dylan played into her reality from here was anyone's guess.

With an unsteady hand, she unlocked the rear door to the shop. A neat and tidy work space should greet her, but what if something else had happened? What if the people who'd destroyed her shop had come back?

Heart pounding, she stepped inside and flipped on the light. Only quiet greeted her. Everything was in its place. Thankful, she closed the door behind her and dropped her tote on the worktable. Okay, so she might have a touch of delayed shock going on. Honestly, who would expect less? Still, she wished she wasn't alone.

Gathering the materials she needed to get started, she jumped at every little sound. Even a pin dropping seemed magnified after the events of last night. Before long, the silence grated on her nerves. She turned on the radio, selecting a country station. A raucous song boomed from the speakers. Exactly what she needed—a little attitude to start her day.

Tapping her foot, she got into the rhythm of placing awesome flower combinations together. She snipped stems and fluffed baby's breath. Angled the lovely blooms for maximum "wow" factor. Completed three orders in no time.

At a lull in the music, Kady tripped when her cell phone blared. Fishing through her purse, she fumbled before finding the device.

"This is Kady."

"Darling, please tell me you're all right?"

Kady smiled, immediately appreciating the voice on the other end. Aunt Cynthia had a way of knowing just the right moment when Kady needed her.

"Depends on what you're talking about."

"Don't get smart with me. I spoke to Will a short time ago."

"I'm fine, Auntie C. The police were here, wrote up a report and promised to find out who broke in." She switched off the radio. "Apparently The Lavish Lily wasn't the only target."

"What on earth is going on? Cypress Pointe is always so safe."

"It still is. Hopefully the police will catch the guilty creeps soon."

Her aunt paused before asking, "Have your parents been informed?"

Ah, the elephant in the room. Kady may wish otherwise, but the awkward conversation with her folks was inevitable. "I haven't spoken to them yet, but I assume Will made an early morning call."

"If he hasn't, you should be the one to tell them. It will show them you're serious about running the shop. Taking matters into your own hands."

"Instead of Will tattling?"

"Exactly."

She hated the idea of ruining their vacation, but her aunt had a point.

"I'll do it after I hang up."

"Good."

Enough of this depressing conversation, Kady thought. Time to change the subject. "Have you sold any new pieces?"

"A friend held a private party last week and I sold five. It's back to the drawing board to come up with new designs."

"That's great. Happy to hear you have repeat business because if my folks are really upset and I don't win the bouquet competition, I may have to come work for you."

"Please. You are more than capable and you know it. I don't want to hear any more negativity."

Aunt Cynthia believed in her. For that reason alone, Kady would prove to everyone she had the drive to make The Lavish Lily more successful than ever. Before long, her family wouldn't be able to deny she'd been on the right track all along.

"Kady, don't fret. You certainly didn't cause the break-in and I have faith you'll win the competition this year."

"Thanks. But Jasmine is back in full force."

"She has to lose sometime."

"You'd think."

"Speaking of Jasmine, I understand her son has made quite an impression."

At least they'd talked about other important topics before her aunt pulled out the you-should-be-dating card.

"Yes. Dylan was walking me back to the shop, so I wasn't alone when I discovered the break-in."

"Is he as handsome as I hear?"

"Yes, and who told you?"

"My friend Maria. She works at the Grand Cypress."

Of course she did. "I was grateful to have someone here. I was shocked. Dylan called the police and calmed me down."

"I like him already."

"He's a very decent guy who has a job in another city. I'm not getting involved."

Liar, liar, pants on fire.

"Whatever you say, Kady. Though, it wouldn't be the worst thing in the world to settle down."

No, it wouldn't, but first she had to find a man she genuinely clicked with. Like Dylan. They'd known each other only a short time, but the comfort level between them was off the charts. Or was that the attraction level? Both, if she was honest. Either way, she wasn't rushing.

"You know my relationships never work out."

"I keep saying you haven't found the right man. He's out there, darling."

The memory of Dylan's dark good looks and dreamy eyes swam before her. He was handsome, but he was also more than that. He'd stuck with her last night. Made sure she was safe. Helped her clean up. No other guy had gone out of his way for her. Ever.

"Keep me abreast of what happens," Aunt Cynthia commanded. "And call your parents."

"Yes, ma'am."

After hanging up, Kady tapped in her mother's cell number. While it rang, she separated daisies and lilies for the last two arrangements.

"Kady? Is everything all right?"

She rolled her eyes at her mother's greeting. What? No "Hi, honey. How are you? Good to hear your voice." Had the news reached the ship already?

"Hi, Mom. Yes, I'm fine, but the shop was broken into last night."

Silence filled the void between them.

"Did you say 'broken into'?"

"Yes. There was little damage and nothing much was taken."

"What is Will doing about it?"

She tried not to let the fact that her mother immediately defaulted to her brother bother her. Nonetheless, it rankled. She should be used to it. Until it dawned on her that Will, the child who always got to them first, hadn't called.

Why hadn't he called their parents?

"Will and I both spoke with the police. There's little we can do until they find whoever broke in, but The Lavish Lily wasn't the only business affected."

She heard a shuffling on the other end, then her father's voice. "Let me speak to Will."

Kady frowned. "He's not here."

"Where is he?"

Home sleeping, if he was smart. "I'd guess at his place."

"Why isn't he there handling the situation?"

"Because I handled it last night. We cleaned up the shop together. Everything is fine."

"You and your brother worked together?"

"Yes, Dad. I hated to even tell you guys about the break-in, but I thought you'd want to know."

"That's very…responsible of you."

Imagine that.

"Here's your mother. She can tell you about our vacation so far."

While she waited for the phone to change hands, Kady arranged the daisies and added a healthy amount of greenery. Four done, one more arrangement to go.

Her mother started by describing the food. Kady oohed and aahed in the appropriate places over her vacation tales while she whipped up the final floral creation. By the time her mother wore herself out with her stories, Kady had completed her task.

"Kady, you are okay after last night?"

Touched by her mother's rare concern, she blinked away the surprising moisture welling in her eyes. "I'm good, Mom."

"Okay, then. Stay safe and let Will take care of things. He's good in a crisis."

With those words, her tears dried up. She wanted to shout, "Yeah, if he's so dependable, where is he?" Instead, she said, "Have fun. See you when you get back."

What did she expect? Her parents to change their thinking instantaneously? They didn't see Kady as the reliable one, which only firmed her resolve to prove them wrong. As long as there were no more disasters, she might get them on her side before long.

Shaking off her brief pity party, she placed the completed orders, along with their tickets, in the cooler. Her steps echoed loudly. Even though she normally spent hours alone in the shop, she couldn't shake her uneasiness today. Anxious to leave, she cleaned up the last of her tools, placing everything in its proper spot. She kept looking over her shoulder, hating to admit it, but after last night? Being here by herself and not freaking out would take time.

After locking up, she shouldered her tote and hurried to Main Street. A light drizzle coated the concrete, making it slippery as she went. When one foot slid out from under her, she quickly corrected herself. Slowing down, she watched her step. Not a great start to the day.

"Calm down," she told herself. Once she got to the hotel she'd be surrounded by noise, laughing people, and her worries would dissipate. Attending workshops and focusing on flowers would ease her mind, she hoped.

Head down, she decided to cross Main, even though she hadn't reached the crosswalk. Light morning traffic crawled along, so she didn't pay much attention. How many times had she journeyed down this same street? Crossed wherever she wanted?

Three steps into the street, a blaring car horn

jerked Kady from her mental fog. She stopped. Turned. Set eyes on a sedan barreling directly at her. With a yelp, she took off running, only to slip on the slick road. Her balance thrown off, Kady tottered. Her tote slipped from her arm to land on the asphalt. Lunging for the sidewalk, she smacked into the curb, falling on her knees and palms just as the vehicle passed, the wind from its acceleration whipping over her.

Heart pounding, she plopped down on the sidewalk. The seat of her slacks grew uncomfortably damp and her palms stung from scraping the road to break her fall. She watched the car's route, incensed when the driver didn't slow down or even circle around to see if she was okay.

"Nice driving," she yelled, not that the driver would hear. The car took a turn and disappeared.

As she started to rise, powerful hands helped her up. She straightened, the object of Dylan's worried gaze.

"We have to stop meeting like this," he said, giving her the once-over.

She yanked herself from his hold. "This is embarrassing."

"What? Your swan dive to safety?"

"Yeah. That," she said, righting her overcoat. She brushed her pants, noticing a small tear in one knee. "What are you doing here?"

"Going back to the hotel from Cuppa Joe." Dylan jogged into the street, retrieved the tote and rejoined her. "What happened?"

"I wasn't paying attention. The driver warned me with his horn, the street was wet and…" She took a bracing breath. "Disaster averted."

"Barely."

Her eyes went wide. "That close?"

He nodded.

She pushed her hair from her eyes. "What a day this is starting out to be. I was hoping my luck had changed."

Dylan inspected one of her wrists, turning her hand to see the injury. "Looks nasty."

"I'll survive."

She had to admit, her palms looked bad. They were red and scratched badly. Once the adrenaline wore off, she suspected the pain would intensify.

"You need to clean those scrapes." He took hold of her other wrist. "Sooner rather than later."

"I will." She looked down at her ruined pants. "I need to go home and change anyway."

"Let me take you. We're closer to my car

now than yours. Plus, whether you want to ac-knowledge it or not, you're shaky. Please. Let me drive."

She fumed for a good minute before relent-ing. "Fine."

Glancing over her shoulder, she glimpsed Christine headed toward them.

"Kady," she called out, her voice breathy.

"Here comes the cavalry," Kady muttered.

"You sure don't like anyone's help, do you?"

Did she? It wasn't anything she'd ever dwelled upon before. She'd always depended on herself.

"Kady, are you okay? I saw what happened."

"Yes. My mind was elsewhere and I crossed the road without looking."

Christine put a hand on her arm, asking, "Are you hurt? I saw you fall."

"I'm fine. My pride hurts more than my hands."

As Christine quizzed her, a small crowd formed. Local businesspeople Kady had known forever were checking on her welfare. After re-assuring her friends multiple times, she caught a glimpse of Dylan on his phone. Whom was he talking to so intensely? Too strung out to speculate, she kept her weak smile in place. It was only 10:00 a.m. and she wanted nothing more than to return to her apartment and tend to her injuries.

Dylan broke through the crowd. "Kady needs some space."

"I'm fine," she repeated, grateful for Dylan's presence.

"Let's get you somewhere quiet."

He led her to his black SUV, his gait slightly steadier than on the first night Kady met him. She wondered if his thigh still bothered him. Without any fuss, he helped her climb inside the roomy cab before getting behind the wheel. Once settled, she gave him directions to her apartment building.

"You know, for a guy who is only visiting my town, you sure get around."

"Like I said, I went to Cuppa Joe."

"You don't like hotel coffee?"

"It's fine. Honestly, I didn't feel like mingling. I sat at the coffee shop and read the paper, uninterrupted."

"Sounds nice."

"I was going to return to the hotel when I saw you." He shot her an amused glance. "And before you suggest it, no, my mother did not send someone to run you down."

She went to cover her face with her hands,

wincing when her stinging palms made themselves known.

"It never even crossed my mind."

He grinned. "I appreciate that."

She puffed out a breath. "You haven't seen me at my best. I promise, I don't usually attract so much drama."

"Usually?"

She chuckled. "There was a time, but not anymore."

"Care to share?"

"I was...less than reliable when I was younger. Never put the shop first, so my parents were wary of giving me responsibilities. I was always looking for... I'm not sure really. New adventures, I guess. Because of that I messed up from time to time and my parents haven't forgotten." Her smile wobbled. "Let's just say it took me a while to decide what I wanted to do with my life."

"Not so unusual."

"Turn here."

When she told him the building number, he found a parking space and turned off the engine.

"Want me to wait?"

Kady debated and decided Dylan had already seen her at her absolute worst. Besides, she didn't want to be alone. "C'mon."

He followed her to the ground-floor apartment, taking the keys to unlock the door when her fingers were clumsy.

"These scrapes better heal quickly. I can't afford butterfingers if I'm going to make arrangements for customers."

"And your competition bouquet," he pointed out.

She groaned out loud.

They walked into her cool, dim apartment. The cloud cover remained, causing shadows inside and out. She went to the kitchen, fumbling in a cabinet to find ointment and bandages.

Dylan watched her from the half counter that separated the living room and kitchen. "I know you're independent, but do you mind if I help?"

She stared at the angry red scrapes on her palms. "I'm gonna have to take you up on the offer."

He strode into the kitchen, started assessing her palms. "I need to clean the skin first." He looked around. "Washcloth?"

She nodded to a drawer. He opened it and removed a fresh cloth, then ran it under the tap.

Adding a little soap, he gently dabbed around the red skin. Kady hissed once, then ground her teeth so she didn't sound like a baby.

He lightly applied ointment and pulled the backing off a large bandage. Before long, he'd finished the job without too much fuss.

"Let me guess. You're a doctor in your spare time?"

"No. But I have three brothers. Been down this road before."

She wiggled her fingers to make sure they were working properly, then smiled at him. "Thanks. I could have cleaned myself up, but it was nice to have help."

He grabbed a bottle of pain reliever and shook out two tablets. "You're going to need these."

She swallowed them with a tall glass of water. "Let me get changed. Then we can head back to the convention."

Dylan stopped her, his gaze piercing hers. "You're sure?"

She tried not to blink, astounded by the gentleness in Dylan's eyes. She'd never been with a man who took the time to care. Whose presence made her heart beat a little faster. Who had actually been there when she needed him, unlike her ex, who took off on her to further his own interests. Dylan fit the bill, and she'd known him for only a few days. Did that matter? She needed to be sure.

She'd always felt a disconnect with her parents and brother. Tried way too hard to please them, only to mess up. She'd wanted their love but received disapproval. Yet she'd had more calamities around Dylan than she cared to remember and he never once made her cringe under his censure, never said a negative word about her. Never once made her question herself. Hadn't even asked what was wrong with her for stepping into the street without looking first. No, he was only kind to her, protective, attentive. So was she falling for him because he'd been there when she needed him? Or was there something more?

Wait. Falling for him? She must have hit the ground harder than she thought to come up with that conclusion.

When Dylan's eyes grew dark, heat rushed over her. Fighting the attraction between them suddenly seemed foolish. Without worrying about the consequences, she told herself, *Might as well go all in.* Recognizing what she wanted, Dylan didn't hesitate to brush his lips over hers.

The kiss started softly, just a gentle touch,

much like the way Dylan had handled her scrapes. Before long, the tentative sweetness turned passionate as she tightened her arms around him and his hands spanned her waist. In the silent room, their breathing sounded loud in her ears. The scent of the freshly cut flowers she always kept on hand flitted around them as the kiss grew deeper and more meaningful.

Taking a hasty step back, she breathed in his scent, met his steady gaze. Oh, yeah, she was falling. More than she'd ever admit.

Why couldn't this attraction be delayed stress? Leftover shock? Right now she was too overwhelmed to scrutinize her feelings.

"I, um, need to get changed," she told him. "I'll be right back."

Not waiting for his response, she hurried to her room, her emotions a jumbled mess. She traded her slacks for a pair of dark jeans that went well with her white sweater. She took a moment to run a brush through her unruly hair. She ignored her pink cheeks. Yes, she'd have to come to terms with her growing feelings for Dylan. But that conversation had to be back burnered for now.

Coming out of her bedroom, she found him at her bookshelf. He turned and smiled.

"Better?"

"Much. Thanks again, Dylan."

He nodded. "We should go."

As they drove downtown, Kady stared out the window. The clouds were thinning and faint sunshine lightened the sky.

"You know," she said, wanting to address some of the questions circling her mind, "it occurred to me that you're a handy man to have in a crisis. What gives?"

His fingers tightened on the steering wheel. When he didn't answer right away, Kady wondered if she'd asked an upsetting question. Still, she was curious. How would he explain his innate authority, especially on the night of the break-in?

"Growing up with a bunch of guys, you learn to either take care of matters or get into trouble."

"Let me guess. You fall into the first category."

"Yes. Seems I've always handled the messy situations." He paused. "When my dad died, I helped my mother navigate all the necessary steps—you know, visiting the funeral home, planning the service, looking after everything that follows. She's tough, but losing my dad nearly took the spirit out of her."

Kady held back a shiver. She couldn't imagine loving someone so much and dealing with the reality after losing them. Another check for Dylan in the keeper box. "You're a good son."

He grinned. "Who else would let their mother talk them into carrying a life-size Cupid in public?"

"You know you'll never live it down."

"That's okay. I'd do anything my mom asked." He turned to her briefly, then focused on the road. "You, too."

Her heart stilled in her chest. Why would he say that? Was this attraction more than that?

"Not that I expect you to ask for help. You seem to take everything in stride."

And her expectations went back to zero. She was definitely reading too much into their relationship.

He pulled into the hotel parking lot in the nick of time. She needed distance. A few minutes away from Dylan and her tumultuous emotions. When they entered the lobby, she immediately went toward the lecture rooms.

"I'll see you later," she said, ignoring his puzzled look. She scurried away, hoping to get her mind off Dylan and onto other matters. Like flowers. Beautiful designs. Weddings. No, not weddings. Future brides-to-be.

"Coward," she muttered under her breath, knowing at some point she'd have to fess up to seriously enjoying the way Dylan made her feel.

CHAPTER TEN

DYLAN DUCKED OUT of the banquet room as the luncheon speaker started. From what he could tell, the president of the floral association enjoyed doling out accolades to certain members. Not his cup of tea. Especially when Max texted him, informing him he had new intel. Now, that piqued his interest.

After making sure Kady was surrounded by friends, he strode down over to Main Street. The sun had finally broken free from the cloud cover, but a heavy humidity still hung in the air. If only the day had cleared earlier, instead of the drizzle that had made the ground slippery enough for someone to fall.

His heart had twisted when he'd witnessed Kady barely escaping the speeding car. He'd been in plenty of dicey situations over the years, but he wouldn't forget this one very soon. When he'd finally had Kady in his arms, safe and in one piece, his worry eased. Her face, so pale and anxious, and her hands, so cold to the touch, had him barely restraining his anger. What was wrong with that driver? Hadn't he been paying attention? At least she was okay. A little scraped up, but alive.

He didn't want to leave her side, but after last night and the misadventure this morning, he suspected these were not coincidences. Better he find out what was going on now, while Kady was busy, than to leave her alone later.

On the way to meet Max, he called the Tampa DEA office to check in on the Esposa case. Special Agent Turner told him they were still looking into family members around the bay and hoped to find someone or something linking Esposa to the area soon. After the break-in at The Lavish Lily and other establishments in town, soon couldn't come fast enough for Dylan.

There may be no concrete proof of Esposa hiding out here, but Dylan's gut said otherwise. He'd been after the guy for too long, spent too many hours combing over details of his life, not to know there was a link here. He just had to connect the dots.

He climbed the stairs to Sanders Security, opening the door to find Max standing before a large computer screen.

Max greeted him. "Hey, glad you could take a break from the convention."

"I'm happy for a few hours away. I can only handle so many conversations about flowers."

Max clicked on an icon and closed a file. "Heard about what happened at The Lavish Lily. The chief said you were there?"

"I was escorting Kady. The convention had closed for the night. Her car was at the shop. We walked in to find the place tossed."

"The chief mentioned other stores were affected." He waved his hand. "Let's sit down."

They moved into Max's office, both taking a seat.

"Think this has anything to do with Esposa?" Max asked, getting right to the heart of the matter.

"I thought about it, but why target a floral shop? Besides, I don't have confirmation that he's been seen in or around Cypress Pointe."

Max opened a folder on his desk. "I'm still researching that angle, but here's what I have so far." He handed him a sheet of paper.

As Dylan read the report, his stomach dropped. Apparently Will Lawrence and The Lavish Lily were on the verge of bankruptcy.

He looked up. "How accurate is this?"

The leather chair squeaked as Max leaned

back. "Very. My computer whiz managed to follow Will's money trail. Large amounts have been removed from the Lawrence business and funneled elsewhere. As the accountant for The Lavish Lily, Will knows where every cent goes."

"Into his pocket?"

"That's what I thought at first. But the investments he made don't have any sort of pattern. Also, if you check the bottom of the report, he's slowly putting money back into the business account."

"So what's he up to?"

"Can't answer that question. Bad investments? Owes someone we don't know about? Embezzling? Take your pick."

Dylan didn't want to. He could already visualize Kady's devastated face if she learned her brother had stolen from the family business.

"Any connection to the guys you're watching? The ones we suspect are distributing the synthetic drugs?"

"No. So far it looks like the only reason Will goes to the marina is for legitimate business. Unless the marina management is involved, which so far hasn't been proven, Will is strictly doing tax prep for a client."

"So we aren't sure what's going on with Will

and haven't gotten any further on the drug distribution."

"That about sums it up." Max's steely gaze pierced his. "Will may not be mixed up with the drug situation, but he's definitely up to no good."

Dylan's thoughts exactly. He tossed the report back on the desk. "And Esposa isn't flashy or dumb. He wouldn't risk involving an established businessman who would stand out in surveillance."

"Agreed. Your agents find anything new?" Max folded his arms across his chest.

"Nothing. It's like Esposa's gone with the wind."

"The chief and I are still investigating the kids who hang around the marina. Maybe something will pan out."

"Hope so." Dylan took a few minutes to digest the facts. He didn't like the scenarios he came up with. "I should get back. I don't want to leave Kady alone for long."

"And why would that be?"

Dylan explained the almost hit-and-run from earlier.

"You were there?"

"Nearly had to scoop her up from the ground after it happened."

Max regarded him with a serious expression. "Something going on with you two I should know about?"

"I happened to be there and saw the entire incident." Dylan pushed back his annoyance at the curious look in Max's eyes. "I know Kady and your fiancée are friends, so enough with the big-brother concern."

Max raised a brow.

"Heard talk of it at Cuppa Joe."

"What can I say? Lilli, my fiancée, wouldn't be happy with me if I didn't at least ask."

"With the investigation going on, hanging out with Kady gives my cover credence. That's it."

"Is it?"

Dylan stood. "This meeting is over."

"Hey," Max said, as he walked Dylan out of the office. "It's nothing personal. Just looking out for a friend."

"I appreciate the gesture."

Max chuckled. "Somehow I don't think so."

Dylan smiled reluctantly. "Let me do my job."

"Got it. I'll be in touch."

Dylan nodded and hurried down the stairs, glad to be leaving. His feelings for Kady were... unsure right now. She made him laugh, and he admired her backbone when things got dicey. She was intelligent and focused on her goal to grow the business. Most of all, he liked her. He couldn't say that about most people. Sure, the drug trade made him cynical, but Kady seemed to have slipped past his stony outer wall to breathe life into the guy he used to be.

And aside from wanting to kiss her pretty much every time they were together, his intentions were still a bit hazy. Until the Esposa case got resolved, he expected his relationship with Kady would remain the same—exciting and nerve-racking, with no indication of how it would end between them.

"Get a grip," he warned, as he got to the sidewalk. If they could see him now, his brothers would love this. Thankfully, they were far, far away and he had to deal with only his mother. Still, given her eagle eyes, he'd better keep things casual with Kady or she'd be on him to settle down and give her grandkids. Like he could even think that far ahead at the moment.

Before returning to the hotel, he detoured to the beach. Walking always helped him sort out his problems.

Normally when he thought about marriage and a family, he broke into a cold sweat. How could he promise to love a woman then put himself in danger every day? True, not all cases were life-threatening, but the night Eddie was killed had marked his memory forever. His wife had lost the man she loved. Would that painful hole in her heart ever heal?

And his son? He'd grow up without a father. All because of some jerk afraid to stand up and pay for his crimes.

As Dylan worked on this case, he found the guilt from his part in Eddie's death wavered. Most times he could take one step in front of the other without the remorse swallowing him whole. It was like the cop part of him had resurfaced and he could deal with his emotions. Other times? He thought about Eddie's family and he could barely breathe. Would he carry this heavy burden around his entire life?

A young guy jogged by, feet pounding on the surf. Dylan jerked. So entrenched in reflecting on his life, he'd lost track of his surroundings. Disconcerting, especially after the outcome of his last meeting with Esposa.

He hoped with time he could manage the jumble of emotions overwhelming him. In the short while he'd spent with Kady, some of the weight had lifted. She didn't even know his situation, yet her sweet disposition helped put him on a path of accepting his role in Eddie's death. His future would get better, but what if she wasn't there to remind him?

He thought again of what it would cost a woman to love a man who went after bad guys for a living. Being an agent was his entire life. He couldn't imagine doing anything else. But since meeting Kady, he didn't get all tied up in knots at the idea of his career not being his future. And that scared him more than anything.

So he'd do what he always did with a topic he wanted to ignore. He'd bury it. Deep. Besides, Kady didn't know his true intentions about his being at the convention. What would she think when she found out? She was no dummy. She'd be hurt and angry. But he couldn't stop until this case was settled once and for all.

He stopped and he trudged all the way back to the hotel, readying himself for more fun with the floral crowd.

As soon as he reached the main entrance to the hotel, hot and tired from the exertion of pushing his still healing leg, he realized the tension in the lobby was high. A group of women hurried by, their voices high-pitched as they spoke over each other. The clerk behind the counter spoke rapidly into the phone while pointing the women in the direction to the right. Shouts carried from the banquet room just down the hall.

Out of habit, he reached for his firearm, then muttered a curse when he came up empty. Since he was only meeting with Max this morning, he'd left his weapon in his room. Feeling naked without protection, he decided he should check out the commotion and ascertain the situation.

Before he had a chance to move, Kady came from the opposite hallway to join him, thrusting one of the two large flower arrangements she carried into his arms.

"Good. You're back. We can use your help."

"With what, exactly?"

"Impromptu wedding."

"Excuse me?"

She seized his arm and dragged him along. "Sissy Thompson's longtime, I mean, super-longtime boyfriend proposed to her on the beach. She isn't taking any chances, so we're throwing together a wedding ceremony."

"That's what all the commotion is about?"

She stared at him. "Yes. What else would it be?"

He could come up with a list of options. "A wedding at a convention? Doesn't she want a church ceremony and all the usual stuff?"

"No. She wants Ned to be her husband."

After realizing he hadn't walked into a hostile situation, his pulse rate lowered. Then quickly rose again when he entered the large room teeming with all kinds of activity. People setting up rows of chairs. Others creating a makeshift altar. The Cupid from his mother's lecture stood on the sidelines. A sense of anticipation fueled the already frenetic energy in the air. "This is crazy."

"I know. Last year we had a similar situation and pulled off a spectacular wedding. Who knew it would become a thing?"

A thing he didn't want any part of. "Kady, it would probably be best if I stayed out of it. I'm not—"

"There you are," his mother called out as she barreled toward him. "We need some heavy lifting done."

Seeing the resolute expression on his mother's face, he knew there was no place he could hide that she wouldn't find him. He bit back a sigh, wishing he'd taken Derrick's advice and not used the trick coin. But he needed to be here to find Esposa, so heavy lifting it was.

He joined in the chaos and every once in a while caught sight of Kady, right in the middle of the action. He actually did a double take when he noticed Kady alongside his mother as they arranged the flowers. Was this a dream? Or possibly a nightmare?

Before long the banquet room had transformed into a chapel and reception venue. The convention attendees took their seats and soon a jumpy Ned stood at the front of the room, tugging at his shirt collar. Dylan silently commiserated with the man.

Music suddenly filled the room via speakers and the wedding guests rose. A small woman in a pretty lace dress, a smile as wide as her face, power walked up the aisle to meet her groom.

Dylan chanced a covert glance at Kady. Her expression was endearing. She'd had a part in this ceremony. Despite the break-in at her shop and her near miss from a hit-and-run driver, he could tell she was enjoying every minute. When she caught his eye, her gentle smile made his heart shift in his chest.

He was in more trouble than he thought.

They sat as a justice of the peace—one of the florists, Kady told him—read from a prayer book. Despite Ned's green complexion and Sissy keeping a manacled hold of his wrists, Dylan had to admit the ceremony wasn't terrible. When the couple said their *I do*s, Kady sighed. He slipped his hand in hers, taking pleasure in the rightness of her cheek pressed against his shoulder. Once this convention was over he owed her a big explanation.

The vows ended. The justice of the peace announced the couple husband and wife. Sissy yelped in victory, grabbing poor Ned by the lapels and pulling him in for a big kiss. It wasn't until after they surfaced for air that Dylan noticed a goofy smile on the groom's face. With all the hoopla over, the guy could finally relax.

As the guests mingled afterward, his mother, dabbing at her eyes with a tissue, found him.

"Wasn't the ceremony lovely?"

He noticed her meaningful gaze that belied her supposed tears. "Peachy, Mom."

"I'm sure Kady has dreamed of her own wedding."

Kady's eyes grew round. "No, um, just other people's who need my florist services."

"How could that be? No cutout pictures of gowns? Color schemes? Bridesmaids?"

"Mom—" Dylan warned.

"It's okay," Kady assured him. "Your mother is caught up in the moment."

"A moment I may never see if my sons have their way."

At Kady's giggle, Dylan coughed. "Laying it on a bit thick?"

"Keeping a mother from her one true wish to see her sons happily married? I don't think so."

"Wow," Kady whispered near his ear.

"I know," he agreed, thankful she picked up on the guilt trip.

Their conversation was interrupted when upbeat music started to flow. Kady nudged Dylan with her elbow. "Ask your mom to dance."

He leaned close. "I'd rather dance with you."

"You will, but you should take her for a spin first."

He gazed at her for a drawn-out moment. "You really are a nice person."

She beamed. "Aw, shucks."

He chuckled before turning to his mother. "Shall we?"

"I thought you'd never ask."

He took her hand and they glided into the crowd.

KADY BIT BACK a sigh as she watched Dylan lead his mother around the dance floor. No one seeing them could miss the pleasure on his mother's face. Kady couldn't believe she'd ever convinced herself the Matthewses were plotting to steal her design for the bouquet competition, especially as she watched them interact. Just a mother and son enjoying their time together. Clearly they liked each other.

Did her parents like her? Would she ever have that kind of relationship with her father? The more she'd wandered through the years, finding her way to the path that led back to The Lavish Lily, the higher the walls became on both their sides. Her parents had rallied around Will and she'd been left out. Even when she started working at the shop, there was always an odd tension between her and her folks. She didn't know how to breach it. Or if she should try.

Her smile faded as she watched Dylan laughing at something his mother said. Until now, she'd ignored how much it hurt to have such a strained relationship with her parents. She wanted what Dylan and his mom shared. Maybe when her folks came back from the cruise, refreshed and willing to give her the benefit of the doubt, they could make a change. Reconnect as a family.

Right after she won the competition and proved they had a good reason to trust her with the shop.

The music slowed to a sultry tempo. She

swayed to the beat. Dylan approached, his silver-gray eyes hooded as he held out his hand. Her stomach pitched from the heat she saw reflected in his gaze, the tug at one corner of his lips. How could she resist him? She couldn't, so she gingerly placed her hand in his and let him tug her to the makeshift dance floor.

His arm circled her waist and he gently held her hand as they rocked to the music. She recognized the song, a ballad about lost love and finding a treasure of the heart. She tried hard not to get sucked into the romantic notion.

"How are your palms?" Dylan asked, his lips so close to her ear she felt his warm breath.

She held back a shiver, but feared she'd failed, especially when he brought her closer. "Stinging, but I can handle it."

"Tough girl, huh?"

"Not sure about that. Resilient maybe?"

"You've had a few jam-packed days."

She smiled, dropped her head back to view his face. "Which you shared with me." A slight frown wrinkled her brow. "I'm not always such a calamity magnet."

"I didn't think you were."

Leaning her head on his shoulder, she closed her eyes. Drank in his masculine cologne. Reveled in firm arms surrounding her, keeping her safe, if only for this short time. She could get used to this, she mused, but once the convention ended, Dylan would be gone. Home to a life that didn't include her. They hadn't talked about the future. Did she want to? No, for now, dancing with an attractive man was enough. Because there was a very real possibility that he might break her heart and she didn't want to go there.

The song came to an end and they stepped apart. Suddenly feeling self-conscious, Kady's gaze darted around the room. Anywhere but Dylan's eyes.

"How about we get something to eat?" he suggested. "Looks like they've put out quite a spread."

Food. Yes. Her stomach growled at the suggestion and she welcomed the respite from her muddled emotions.

"I could eat," she said with a breezy tone. Best not to let Dylan know he'd been the subject of all her uncertainty.

They filled plates and sat among a group of Kady's friends. She tried to relax and enjoy the sumptuous food, but Dylan, seated next to her, made her jumpy. Maybe it was due to recent events. She'd never been like this before.

An hour later, the party broke up. Plenty of

food remained, so the staff brought boxes and encouraged the crowd to take the leftovers. There were still many activities and workshops scheduled for tomorrow, so the attendees called it a night and drifted back to their rooms.

"I should be getting home," Kady said as she and Dylan strolled to the lobby.

"My car is in the lot. I'll take you back to your apartment."

"No need. I parked behind The Lavish Lily."

"Then let me drive you there."

"I can walk."

He lifted a brow. "Yeah. That's not gonna happen."

Too tired to argue, she followed him out into the star-filled night. She shivered against the chill in the air.

As he opened her door and assisted her into the SUV, Dylan blew out a breath. "I love Florida in the winter."

She slid across the seat and tugged her tote onto her lap. "Yes. It's beautiful."

Dylan brushed a wisp of her hair away from her cheek, his fingers lingering. "Like you."

Kady smiled. "I bet you say that to all the girls."

"Trust me, I never do."

Her heart squeezed at his words. Oh, boy. This thing between them was getting intense, yet she didn't want to burst the bubble and let reality intrude.

Dylan closed her door and climbed in the driver side, then turned the key in the ignition. The ride to the shop passed quietly, making Kady more on edge. What was he thinking about? Did she dare ask?

Once she got into her own car, Dylan followed her home. After the events of the past few days, she appreciated it.

Before long she was unlocking the door to her place. As soon as she entered the living room, with Dylan close behind her, she dropped on the couch, rested her head against the cushion and closed her eyes.

"I'm beat."

Dylan carried her small box of wedding food to the kitchen.

While he was busy putting the leftovers away, Kady snuggled in a little deeper. After such a long day, she was quickly losing steam.

Dylan came back into the room. "All you have in your fridge are bagels, butter and carrots."

"I need to go shopping."

"Oh, and a bunch of really beautiful flowers."

One of her eyelids drifted up. "Stay away from my flowers."

"Right."

Her eyelid closed and she was vaguely aware of Dylan's presence. Really, he had to leave. Her bed called to her.

With a yawn, she rose, freezing when she saw Dylan standing beside her kitchen table, holding up a notepad with the renderings of her bouquet design. Spools of ribbon, seed pearls and a hot glue gun littered her table. She rushed over and snatched the notepad out of his hands.

"What are you doing?"

"Admiring your work."

"Dylan, these sketches are private."

Humor flashed in his dark eyes. "You're not still on that spying-for-my-mother kick, are you?"

She hugged the notepad close to her chest.

His humor quickly fled when she didn't disagree.

"I told you I'm not after your design."

Deep down she knew it, but couldn't take a chance. Couldn't trust he wouldn't somehow use her like Brad had. Yes, Dylan was different, so why was she still uncertain?

"And I've come in second place too many years behind your mother to take the risk."

He ran a hand through his hair. "I don't know how I can assure you otherwise."

"I may sound unreasonable, but look at it from my point of view. When we met, I didn't know who your mother was. Or why you were here."

"So you're saying if I'd told you who my mother was up front, you'd trust me?"

She bit her lower lip.

"Uh-huh. I didn't think so," he scoffed.

"Dylan, I like you. Probably more than I should. But this—" She held out the pad. "This is important to me. Important to me operating The Lavish Lily in the future."

"I get that, Kady. I do. But every time I turn around you're accusing me of conspiring against you and it's just not true."

Hot pressure built behind her eyes. She was blowing this.

"I'm sorry, Dylan. I have to protect my idea."

A shadow moved over his face. "I can't convince you, so I'm going to leave before one of us says something we might regret." He walked to the door, his gait unsteady. "I'll see you to-morrow."

He left her without looking back. Pressing her lips together to keep from crying, she followed his steps and locked the door. After turning off the lights, she deposited the notepad on the table and shuffled into her room to get ready for bed.

As she stood before the mirror in the bathroom to remove her makeup, she couldn't ignore the sadness in her eyes. Why did she turn on Dylan? It wasn't like he was being sneaky. He'd been looking at her drawings right out in the open. Yet she'd pulled the competition card again. As if accusing him would keep them at a distance because she wasn't sure about her feelings for him. Was that what she wanted?

What she wanted was a lifetime of his kisses, but she'd spent too many years floundering in her decisions, jumping into one crazy scheme or job after another, without a plan. Now she had a goal. Running the shop with her parents' blessing was within her grasp. Grabbing as much of the wedding market as possible was doable, as long as she remained focused. She wouldn't blow the opportunity, no matter how deeply she was attracted to Dylan. No matter how he made her heart accelerate or put a smile on her face. No matter how many times he played rescuer. She had to stay true to her commitment.

Even if it meant losing a chance with Dylan in the long run.

CHAPTER ELEVEN

DRUMMING HIS THUMB against the steering wheel, Dylan kept a steady beat. Frustration coursed through him like a swiftly moving river, threatening to overflow the surrounding banks.

Kady's refusal to believe he didn't want her bouquet designs irked him. After they'd talked about her wanting to prove to her parents she could handle the shop, he understood her reasoning. But how many times did he have to prove himself? And why did the lasting disappointment bother him so much?

Because she didn't trust him. Okay, she had every right not to, even if she didn't know the real reason why. When he'd decided to track down Esposa, he hadn't bargained on meeting Kady and becoming way too involved, way too quickly.

One more mess of his own making to clean up.

Deciding sleep would not come easily, he drove to the marina. It couldn't hurt to put in a little surveillance time on the project. Maybe he'd learn something tonight that would make him feel less guilty about keeping the truth from Kady and more positive about discovering where he could find Esposa.

He drove into the empty parking lot, easing into a space far enough away from the main entrance to the pier, but close enough to watch any activity. Cutting the engine, he lowered the window, letting the welcome chill invade the vehicle. He needed to cool down, both from his last encounter with Kady and his own over-thinking.

Palms swayed in the steady breeze, which kicked up the water, sending the scents of salt and diesel his way. He rested his head back against the seat, eyes steady on the marina. Boats bobbed in the waves, straining against the moorings. An occasional clink of the chain fencing surrounding the property sounded in the wind. A buoy light flashed in the ink-black night.

Dylan lost track of time. Another unproductive night. What was he missing? Obviously a big piece of the puzzle. Tomorrow he'd talk to Max, rehash everything they knew and look for a new angle.

He was just about to start the engine when

two figures emerged from the shadows of the marina office. He narrowed his eyes, watching as the huddled couple moved toward the parking lot.

Upon closer inspection he thought they might be out for a romantic stroll. They held hands and talked as they hurried along. It wasn't until they passed beneath a streetlamp that his adrenaline spiked. None other than Will Lawrence and the shop's new employee, Christine, were headed toward the sidewalk that weaved through the park to Main Street.

Easing his door open, he slipped out of the SUV. Took up a slight jog, ignoring the ache in his thigh, to fall in behind them. He heard their voices, pitched and animated, although he didn't catch the words. Will stopped and whirled around while pushing Christine to protection behind him, his body in a combative pose.

"Whoa, there," Dylan said, his hands up in surrender.

Will straightened. "Dylan?"

Christine peeked over Will's shoulder. "Are you following us?"

"You could say so."

She moved beside Will, stuffing something into her jacket pocket before tucking her hand into his elbow. "What are you doing out so late?"

"I could ask you the same question."

The couple exchanged a quick glance.

"We were taking a walk," Will answered.

"You usually come to the marina this late at night for a walk?"

Will lifted his chin. "Yeah. We do."

"And hide in the shadows? What, you don't want anyone to see you together?"

Her voice rising, Christine said, "What does it matter to you?"

"As much as I enjoy all the questions, I'm afraid I'm going to have to insist on some answers."

"We don't have to answer to you. You're not a cop."

"The federal government would beg to differ."

Christine's mouth gaped at the same time Will's eyes went wide.

Dylan pulled out the badge he'd tucked into his pocket before exiting the SUV. "DEA."

Shaking his head, Will eyed the badge, then met Dylan's gaze. "I'm confused. I thought you were a florist."

"I'm using the convention as cover."

"So no one knows who you really are?" Christine asked in a tone bordering on awe.

"Except the chief of police."

"Who are you looking for?"

He caught Will's gaze. "You tell me."

When Will sent a meaningful glance to Christine, Dylan knew something was up.

"I've got all night."

Will puffed out his cheeks. "Christine, we should tell him."

Christine took a fortifying breath. "All right." She stepped toward Dylan. The wind whipped her bouncy curls around her face. "We were looking for my brother."

"Why?"

"He's… He got caught up with some nasty guys. He might be dealing drugs. I came to Cypress Pointe, hoping I could talk some sense into him."

"You know for sure he's here?"

"Pretty sure. I haven't seen him in person yet. That's why Will and I were out here, hoping he might come to the marina and I'd be able to confront him."

"Why the marina?"

"Before he left, he'd been hanging out with guys who owned boats."

Could this be a break in the case? "How do you know he's dealing?"

She let out a heavy breath. "He's been using drugs on and off for a few years. About eight months ago he started hanging with a different crowd. He got all secretive and sneaky. Stole from people and businesses back home. When he disappeared, I knew he'd gotten involved in something bad, so I decided to look for him."

Dylan sliced his glance to Will. "Your part here?"

"Christine confided in me and I wanted to help."

He'd seen the two of them interact after the break-in at the shop, noticing the long looks and ways they would touch each other, thinking no one else noticed. It explained Will's part in tonight's outing.

"Do you know what your brother might be selling?"

"No."

"Did he ever mention any names of the guys he was running around with, like Esposa?"

She squinted, as if trying to remember. "Doesn't sound familiar. When I questioned him, he always clammed up. Not so much because he was standing up for his friends, but more like he was afraid."

"If he's working for one of the bigger distributors, he should be afraid."

Christine touched his arm. "He's not a bad kid, Dylan. Just always doing things without thinking and getting himself in trouble."

He knew those kids. Had arrested plenty of them. He'd always hoped for the best, never knowing which kids got the message and which ones didn't.

"What's his name?"

Christine went mute.

"Look, I know your name. I can easily find his."

She shuffled from foot to foot while she made her decision. Dylan could imagine the inner turmoil. If put in a similar situation and he had to give up one of his brothers, he didn't know if he could do it.

"Bryce. Bryce Wallace."

He'd have to check the report the police chief had given him to see if Bryce was one of the kids on the list.

"I appreciate you wanting to help your brother, but if he's working for the guy I'm after, he's in big trouble. I don't want to see you getting caught in the cross fire."

She nodded, and in the overhead light, he noticed the shine in her eyes.

"He's my little brother. What do I do?"

"Let us take care of the situation."

Using the sleeve of her jacket, she wiped at her eyes. Will put his arm around her, comforting her, which was what Dylan should have done with Kady earlier, instead of getting peeved and walking away. After the past two days, he really needed to cut her some slack.

Will spoke in a lowered voice to Christine, and at her nod, he leveled his gaze at Dylan.

"The reason Christine said anything in the first place is because of the break-in at the shop. She thinks her brother might be involved."

"I've been wondering about that," Dylan said. "What is it about the shop that's of interest?"

"Nothing that I know of," Will answered. "I couldn't make a connection, either. Until tonight."

Dylan went on red alert. "Why?"

Christine pulled away from Will and stuck her hand in her jacket pocket, extracting something white and square. She handed it to him.

"We found this on the pier," Will explained.

Dylan's heart nearly lurched to his throat when he examined the object. A flat, white box, with The Lavish Lily printed on top. Worn and dirty, as if handled, folded and reused multiple times.

"I'm guessing this is one of the corsage boxes your sister was looking for."

"Bingo."

Once his mind grasped the significance of finding the box, Dylan couldn't shake off the impending danger. Someone had gone to all the trouble to steal the small boxes. He had an idea why.

"You could easily transport a stash in this box. Who's going to question it with the name of a florist stamped on the outside?"

"But we don't deal drugs, obviously. So how would anyone even know to take them?" Will asked.

"That's an excellent question. One I mean to answer." He pocketed the box. "I'll fill in the chief. In the meantime, don't say a word to anyone."

"We should let Kady know about the boxes."

"No."

Will's eyes narrowed. "Why not?"

"Because your sister doesn't know I'm undercover."

"You haven't told her?" Christine squeaked.

"I need her to believe my cover, just like everyone else at the convention and in town."

"I don't like keeping this from her," Will argued. "She deserves to know."

"But she won't find out from you."

Will raised a challenging brow, stepping forward as if to change Dylan's mind.

"Do you want me to tell her about The Lavish Lily finances?"

At the mention of his secret, Will's bravado deflated. He angled away from Christine. "Would you stoop that low?"

"To preserve my cover, yeah, in a New York minute."

"Fine," he grumbled. "Just for the record, I don't like keeping the truth from Kady."

"Neither do I. After the convention, I'll explain it all." He pulled out his wallet and extracted a business card. "Here's my number. Program it into your phone. If you find anything, I mean anything that leads to your brother, call me. Don't handle it on your own."

Christine took the card and slipped it in her pocket. "Thanks."

Dylan thumbed over his shoulder. "I'm gonna take off. You two should head home."

Without any parting words, Will took Christine's arm and led her in the direction of town. Dylan turned on his heel and marched back to the SUV.

Finally, a concrete lead. While one part of Dylan was stoked at the prospect, the other side, the guilt-prodding side, poked at him about keeping the truth from Kady. He reasoned it was for her own safety, but knew deep down he didn't have a prayer when it came to her forgiveness if she learned the truth before he had a chance to come clean.

ON SATURDAY MORNING Kady obsessed over her bouquet design again. Her master plan hinged on the creation of blush-and-cream peonies, ivory garden roses with the tiniest blush of pink, which she'd special-ordered from the wholesaler, stephanotis and greens. She loved the double meaning, the peonies symbolizing a happy marriage, the roses embodying innocence and purity. The bouquet would have a classic look, unlike the more over-the-top submissions she'd created in years past to make a statement. Obviously that hadn't worked, so she'd gone back to the drawing board and opted for classic, all the way.

These flowers, delicate and lovely, would enhance any style wedding gown. Simplicity would draw attention. And while the flower choice was important, Kady had spent a great deal of time coming up with the perfect stem wrap to finish the bouquet.

She'd chosen ivory silk ribbon, which would tie in to the color scheme. Delicate seed pearls would be glued around the edges. And in the center, she'd affix a beautifully designed crystal brooch Aunt Cynthia had made for her. In truth, any piece of jewelry could be used as the focal point of the wrap. Kady's idea was to encourage a bride to find a very personal keepsake and incorporate it in decorating the wrap. Now the bride not only carried a beautiful bouquet, but it also had an artful design showcasing sentimental memories.

The central piece could be anything—a special gift from her fiancé, a family heirloom handed down from bride to bride, a keepsake from her parents. The inspirations were endless. In the case of her competition bouquet, Kady had chosen her aunt's brooch for good luck.

She hoped this would be a hit with the brides, but as trends went, one never knew what would be popular. She had to go with her gut on this one.

As much as she'd love to linger over her design ideas, she had to get to the convention. She'd already ditched the early morning workshops, not ready to face Dylan after last night's terse parting. But her friend Melissa was giving a hands-on workshop for newbie florists and Kady had promised to attend.

"No more procrastinating."

After a quick shower, she dressed in a gauzy mint-green top, flowing multicolor skirt, suede boots and a wide leather belt to finish off the look. Her palms didn't sting as much this morning, but she covered them with clean bandages just to be on the safe side. She stuffed a sweater in her tote and took off, running ten minutes late.

Once at the hotel, she navigated the crowded lobby, not bumping into Dylan, thank goodness, and hurried to the room designated for Melissa's class—How to Make the Perfect Boutonniere. She waved at Melissa, who pointed her to the far side of the crowded room.

"I've got you a partner," her friend mouthed.

Kady made her way to the table, stopping short when she found Dylan sorting through a selection of red and white carnations.

Handsome as always, today he'd dressed casually in a charcoal-colored, long-sleeved T-shirt, jeans and boots. He was probably angry with her, rightfully so. Yes, she could have handled last night better, but she'd been tired, achy and still didn't understand her emotions when it came to him. Today she needed space, not a partner.

"This can't happen," she said under her breath, taking a step backward. Melissa came up behind her.

"Going somewhere?"

"For water?"

"Wrong answer." Melissa nudged her toward the table. Dylan looked up, regarding her now with a put-upon glare. "I bumped into Jasmine and she suggested I wrangle Dylan into helping. He did such a good job assisting his mother, how could I pass up the opportunity?" Melissa explained.

He didn't look any happier than she did. He obviously hadn't shaved this morning, evidenced by the dark bristle on his cheeks. Dark circles shadowed his eyes. Because of her? The edgy, dangerous attitude he carried with ease was stronger than ever. In her uncertain mood, Kady was afraid she wouldn't be able to fight her ever-increasing attraction to him.

"Why us?" she asked.

"Do you see all the newbies in here? Someone has to look competent to encourage them."

As reasoning went, Kady thought it was a

little lame, but when she scanned the room again, she realized Melissa needed her.

"Fine. But you owe me."

Melissa took off and Kady reluctantly approached the table, meeting Dylan's gaze. "Good morning."

"Is it?"

Oh, yay. This was going to be fun, getting stuck with Mr. Grouchy.

Melissa began the class, pointing out the different supplies needed to complete their task. Scissors and clippers, along with ribbon, tape, stem wire and pearl-headed pins. With his big hands, Kady knew Dylan wouldn't find this exercise to his liking, which would most likely increase the crabby factor.

"Is there a prom later that no one told me about?" Dylan grumbled.

Kady bit back a smile. "No, but if you show your mom how well you did, maybe she'll give you a gold star."

"Funny."

"Not as funny as watching you pass the wire through the bottom of that flower without destroying it."

He narrowed his eyes as if accepting a challenge. "You think I can't do this?"

"I think I'm going to enjoy watching you try."

As per Melissa's instructions, the teams got to work. Kady rested her hip against the table, waiting for Dylan to take the lead.

"You aren't helping?"

"This class is for newbies, and since you don't work in your mother's shop, I'm guessing you haven't got a clue."

He braced his palms on the table, staring at the flowers.

"Mental telepathy doesn't work," she quipped.

His lips twitched. Okay, so maybe he wasn't totally ticked at her.

"How can you do this all day?" he asked as he picked up the delicate flower like it was a priceless artifact.

"I love it." She pointed to the wire. "Cut a piece about six inches."

He rolled out some wire and cut. "That's what my mom says."

She picked up a carnation and drew it to her nose, inhaling the clove-like scent. Ran her finger over the ruffled edge. "Next cut the stem about one inch from the bud."

"I guess I can see why this profession is a good match for you both," he continued. "You get to be creative and you love working with bright, colorful objects that make people happy." He snipped the stem. "Believe it or not, you and my mom are a lot alike in that way."

Kady had already discovered that fact when she worked with Jasmine at the impromptu wedding the day before, but she wasn't about to let Dylan in on her change of heart. Besides, Jasmine was technically her competition until after the conference.

"Now cross the wire through the base of the bud and bend the wire down between your thumb and forefinger," she instructed.

"I always remember her saying if she made people cry with her creations, she'd done her job well."

Kady lifted a brow.

"You know, because they loved the flowers. Although sometimes…"

"Sometimes?"

He glanced at her. "Never mind."

She shrugged, not revealing her never-ending curiosity. "Now, cut off about six or seven inches of tape. Then, starting at the top of the wire, wrap the tape around the stem."

Just as she thought, his big fingers were clumsy as he made a mess of the tape. He held up one hand, tape stuck to his fingers, carnation dangling in the air.

"Have pity on me."

She moved next to him, trying not to get drawn into his body heat or how his eyes held that gleam she'd seen only when they were alone. She took the wounded flower and untangled the tape, her fingers brushing his. She froze. Even after the way they'd left things last night, an awareness blazed between them. No amount of apologizing, secretly grinning at his clumsiness or helping him was going to change the fact that he was a very strong, very capable male who had his sights set on her. And hers on him. The question was, how were they going to deal with it?

Once his fingers were free, he cut a new length of tape. Learning from his mistake, he wrapped the stem more successfully this time.

"Now, finish with the ribbon."

He took the precut piece and wound it over the tape.

"At the top of the stem, make a loose loop and tie it off."

"With a butterfly, figure eight or running bowline knot?"

"Just tie it off, smarty-pants."

He did, a full-fledged smile greeting her as he handed her the finished product. Once again, his face relaxed. His smile floored Kady.

She wanted nothing more than to see that expression all the time, instead of the shadows in his eyes and the rare grins.

Taking the flower, she picked up the pin and attached his handiwork to his shirt. She smoothed the fabric around it, her fingers tingling at the defined muscle beneath the soft cotton.

"So, how did I do?" he asked, his voice husky.

Controlling the shivers his rough tone sent over her skin, she studied his creation. "Not bad."

"Just one of my many talents."

"Like?"

"Walks on the beach. Kisses in the moonlight."

She swallowed. "My favorites."

His unblinking gaze held hers until she finally looked away. Just in time for Melissa to come by and inspect Dylan's work.

"Hey, I'm impressed." She frowned at Kady. "Did you help him?"

"Nope. He's got talent."

She glanced at Dylan and they grinned at each other.

"I don't even want to know," Melissa said and moved on to the next table.

"Listen, after all this flower stuff, I'm gonna have to make you run with me or do push-ups. Just to get a little more guy activity happening."

"Well, I like to run, so you might have some serious competition."

"Bring it on."

Kady sneaked a peek at Dylan as he cleaned up. Right now, a run on the beach or going anywhere with Dylan sounded great, except neither of them were dressed for exercise. Plus, she had something to say whether she liked it or not.

"Instead of running, how about a stroll later on?" She paused. "And for the record, I should have apologized sooner. About last night. I was out of line."

When he didn't meet her eyes, her stomach twisted. Should she not have mentioned it? Just let it go since things seemed okay between them? She couldn't. That wasn't how she behaved, so she'd have to live with his answer.

"Yeah" was his one-word response.

Just like when she'd first met him, he reverted back to being a man of few words.

"Kady, I understand that your shop is important to you. Why you have big dreams. But not everyone is out to stifle those ambitions."

She thought about her ex. Her parents. Even Jasmine. "It sure seems like it."

"I get how it feels to be so focused on a goal that you lose sight of everything else in your life. How your extreme fixation causes problems for those around you. Don't go there, Kady."

Wow. What had happened to him? Maybe if they did take that stroll later, away from big ears and prying eyes, he'd confide in her. But his warning sure gave her a picture into his own life, reminding her she didn't really know this man.

"So you accept my apology?" she asked.

"I do. How about we move on?"

"To the beach?"

This time, when his trouble-free gaze met hers, she almost believed things would be better between them. "It's a date."

CHAPTER TWELVE

WHILE KADY SPENT the afternoon in workshops, Dylan spent his time on the phone. They'd agreed to meet later, but until then, he had work to do.

He spoke to Agent Turner, who relayed good news. He'd questioned an uncle of Esposa's and convinced the older man that it was only a matter of time before the authorities apprehended his nephew. The man decided to keep his immediate family out of trouble with the police by admitting Esposa was in the area. The agent promised to keep Dylan informed as the investigation progressed.

So close now. Taking down Esposa would be the highlight of his career, as well as close a painful chapter in his life. Going after Esposa had become the be-all and end-all of his life. He needed to move on.

Where do you go from there?

Dylan had no idea.

A child's cry rose from the beach. Dylan

stepped onto the balcony to view the scene below. A little boy ran to his father, who picked up the child and swung him in a circle. Legs out in the air, the boy's high-pitched laughter sliced at Dylan's heart.

He'd lost the laughter in his life. Lost enjoyment in the little things. Until he'd met Kady. She brought a smile to his face and unexpected joy to his life. He'd miss her when he left. Miss the possibilities of what could be.

As he watched, the father, with his son's small hand securely tucked in his larger one, moved to the water's edge. The boy jumped and played, splashing his father until the older man swooped up his son in his arms.

Would he ever have moments like that? Have a lasting relationship that didn't end when a case closed? Living in the shadows in order to smoke out dealers who broke the law had extracted a toll on Dylan. If he kept this pace, how could he ever connect to a woman, to someone like Kady, who could restore much-needed hope in his life?

But Esposa was still out there, and until Dylan found him, he would never be able to settle down. Kady deserved better than what he could give her, assuming she felt the same way. He thought she might, but knew the walls he'd purposely erected around his life since Eddie's death left little room for a relationship.

Shaking off the sad notion, Dylan went back into his room. He called Bob Gardener to tell him about his conversation with Christine and Will. The chief promised to run her brother's name through the system and get back to Dylan later with the results. Dylan also let the chief know about Will's part in the big picture. The police chief didn't like two amateurs searching for the kid on their own, but for now, would let them continue.

Next he checked in with Max and called a few other agents.

Calls made, Dylan sought the afternoon sunshine, reaching for his sunglasses. The temperature, while chilly, was still comfortable to be outdoors. The constant breeze ruffled his hair. He sat, captivated by the tropical wonderland. He liked it here in Cypress Point. The excitement of big-city life in Miami had faded. He'd tired of the traffic, the crowds and the crime. Even before the horrible night when Eddie was murdered, he'd been thinking about transferring. Only his dogged pursuit of Esposa kept pushing those thoughts aside.

Leg stretched out, the heat from the sun warmed his aching thigh muscle. Almost back to normal. Dylan hoped his leg would be as good as new in the near future. Maybe in time to race Kady down the beach.

He grinned at the notion, but quickly sobered. Just because he'd received confirmation of Esposa in the area did not mean the case was close to concluding. If Esposa caught wind of Dylan's investigation, who knew where Esposa would be off to next, with Dylan in hot pursuit. And when he left, there was no guarantee he and Kady would remain in touch.

His mood sour now, he almost didn't answer his cell when it rang. Derrick's name came up on the screen. Dylan pressed the talk button.

"Any more surprises from Mom?" his brother asked.

"She's busy. To be honest, I've kinda lost track of her."

"That's okay. She'll make you pay later."

"I've gotten further on the case, so I'm not worried."

"Fill me in."

Dylan took the next ten minutes bringing his brother up to speed.

"So what are your plans?" Derrick asked.

"Hang around town and try to find the guys transporting the product. Hope it leads to Esposa."

"And what about the flower shop? How does it fit in?"

"Not sure yet."

"Think the owner, what's her name—"

"Kady."

"Think she's involved somehow?"

Dylan pictured Kady. Her smile, her wit. Her determination to run the shop with her parents' approval. No way she could be involved. "No. I've spent time with her and it doesn't jibe."

"Spent time with her as in…?"

Dylan heard the humor in his brother's voice. "Convention stuff."

"Right. Because you're so into flowers. Wait—unless you are so long as Kady's around?"

"Don't make a big deal."

"Dyl, I live to make a big deal."

"Look, she's a nice woman. I helped her out when her shop was broken into. Nothing more."

"Sure. You keep telling yourself that."

Dylan held back a few choice words.

"I'm not one to give dating advice—" Derrick continued.

"Please don't."

"But I gotta say, maybe a distraction would be good for you. You've been so solitary since Eddie died. You don't have to get serious, but you deserve some fun. Go for it."

"So I should adopt the Derrick Matthews attitude and become a serial dater?"

"Works for me."

Except Dylan wasn't like his older brother.

"Even if I decided to go for it, Kady has no idea I'm undercover."

"That is a problem."

"I can't say anything."

"But you want to?"

He did. Found himself almost confiding in her this morning while they made boutonnieres. But this case relied on him keeping quiet until he found Esposa. He'd already confided in too many people. In his mind, the only way to keep Kady safe was for her to think Dylan was here for the convention only. Yes, the break-in at the floral shop was problematic, but he had no proof Esposa was behind it. Why worry her unnecessarily?

"So you said she's nice. Maybe she won't be mad at you when she learns the truth."

Deep down, Dylan doubted that was a possibility. Not after the kisses they'd shared. Or the fact that he hadn't confided his suspicions about the break-in at her shop. Besides, he wasn't much of a sweet talker, unlike silver-tongued Derrick.

"I never intended to feel like this."

"We all gotta fall sometime, bro."

"Well, the timing stinks."

"Usually does."

"You don't have to sound chipper about this, Derrick."

"Yes, I do. It isn't often you don't know which way to turn, Dyl."

"Just promise me you'll keep this between us. I don't need Dante and Deke calling me with advice."

"You know how to kill the fun."

"Promise?"

"Yeah, yeah. Any other requests?"

"When I do tell Kady the truth, and she gets mad at me, what next?"

"You learn how to grovel."

"That's what I was afraid of."

Dylan signed off. Glancing at his watch, he noted he still had a few hours before meeting Kady. He slouched down in the chair and closed his eyes. After being out late last night, catching a few z's held some appeal. Maybe after a short nap, he'd wake up and all his problems would be solved.

And maybe Derrick would find a woman and settle down for good. Nope. No chance of that happening, either.

By 5:00 P.M., THE WORKSHOPS were finished. Saturday night meant dinner on your own. The hotel restaurant, The Rendezvous, was already fully booked. Kady had checked. The lobby was practically empty. Everyone was off to find a place to hang out, eat and visit.

She sat by the main entrance, waiting for Dylan. Fifteen minutes crawled by. Had he changed his mind? She tried to relax, but the prospect of being alone with Dylan kept her antsy. Her palms were healing, but an occasional twinge reminded her of the fall. Maybe she'd be better off going back to her place after stopping for takeout. A quiet night at home while she caught up on her recorded shows.

Ready to give up on Dylan, she rose. She'd just exited the building when she heard her name.

"Kady. I'm here."

Relief flooded her. He hadn't stood her up. She swung around and spotted him. No lonely television watching with cold takeout.

"Sorry," he said, short on breath as he joined her. "Lost track of time."

"You made it. That's all that matters."

A cold breeze zipped over her and she buttoned her sweater. "So, where to?"

Dylan turned up his jacket collar. "You pick."

"Most of the restaurants are going to be serving the convention crowd. Let's walk down Main and see what's available."

They easily fell into step. Cheery streetlights pushed away the winter gloom. The temperature dipped some more, but walking beside Dylan, Kady couldn't deny her hot cheeks. Her warm heart. All because of the enigmatic man next to her.

"I should have asked earlier. How are your palms doing?" Dylan pointed at her hands.

She held them up. "Much better. Tomorrow I should be able to leave the bandages off."

"Good. Good."

Where did the awkward vibe come from?

"I have Dr. Dylan to thank for my speedy recovery."

He doffed an invisible hat. "Just doin' my part, ma'am."

"Really, thanks."

"Not a problem."

They continued on in silence. As they strolled down Main, a myriad of scents drifted in the night air. Seafood, burgers. Even the heavenly aroma of baking bread.

"I'm getting hungry," Dylan stated.

They passed Pointe Café. Busy. Master's Surf and Turf. A lineup.

Up ahead, a light shone from Charming Delights Catering. "Jenna must be sampling new recipes. She holds an open house once a month to get public consensus on her food."

Stopping by the window, Kady saw a large crowd mingling and holding filled plates. "What do you think?"

"Looks like fun, but not exactly what I had in mind."

"Me neither."

They passed the catering place, almost reaching the far end of Main, when inspiration struck. "I've got it." Tucking her arm through Dylan's, she guided him across the street to the public park. At the curb sat a big, brightly lit taco truck.

Dylan squeezed her arm. "Now you're speaking my language."

A decent-sized crowd was hanging out, enjoying their food. The spicy smells of onions and tomatoes and grilled meat, along with oil in a deep fryer, filled the air. Salsa music blared from speakers atop the truck. As they drew closer, Kady greeted the owner.

"Hey, Greta. Busy night?"

"Been at it for hours. You came at a lull."

Dylan leaned close to her ear. "Greta?"

"What can I say? Cypress Pointe is culturally diverse."

Kady continued the conversation with the truck owner and before long she and Dylan had placed their orders. Two beef tacos for Dylan, chicken for Kady, a side order of tortillas with a bowl of warm white queso cheese and a small dish of salsa. Dylan carried the bag to an empty picnic table nearby, while Kady followed with their drinks.

"Who says a picnic in winter isn't fun?" Kady asked as she chased after a wrapper picked up by the wind blowing off the gulf waters. "If we were closer to the beach, we could take cover in the pavilion."

"But where's the adventure? Not inside some warm restaurant surrounded by polite chitchat. We have the entire park practically to ourselves."

She shivered again. "Gee, I can't imagine why."

Dylan laughed. "C'mon. Sit down and enjoy your dinner."

She sat and they both dug into the food.

"You come here often?" Dylan asked after swallowing a bite.

"Lots. When I'm working late. I'll take a few minutes and run down here for dinner."

"Do you work late often?"

"When I have rush orders. Or a wedding. I've booked quite a few lately. It's been demanding, but I don't mind."

"Weddings. What's the draw?"

Kady dipped her tortilla in the gooey cheese. "It's a multimillion-dollar industry. I want a piece of it." She chomped the chip.

"I still don't get it."

She chuckled. "Such a guy." She took another bite and after chewing said, "It's not just the wedding itself. I create flower arrangements for the engagement party, bridal shower, rehearsal dinner, the ceremony, the reception, morning-after breakfast and, in the future, anniversary parties."

"That's a lot of flowers."

"Exactly. It's also good income." She dipped another tortilla. "Haven't you ever had this conversation with your mother?"

"My interests lie elsewhere."

"You mean you aren't still her delivery boy?"

He grinned and balled up the empty wax paper that had held his food.

"Really, what are your interests?" she persisted.

A long moment passed before he answered her. "I'm in the people business."

It took everything in her not to roll her eyes. "Which basically tells me nothing."

"I look out for what's important to people. Like safety."

"Insurance?"

"More in the field."

Could he be any vaguer? "If you don't want to tell me, just say so."

"I do. It's just…complicated."

In other words, *I don't want to confide in you.* She'd heard that a time or two over the years when dating guys who were unwilling to get involved. She'd hoped Dylan would be different.

"I don't mean to be a pest, but you've learned quite a bit about me over the last few days. Why can't you share some of yourself?"

Dylan gazed off into the distance and Kady thought she'd lost him, until she noticed his jaw working. There was a lot more to this man than he let on. Still, given how he'd acted around her, taking care of her, twice, and stealing a few kisses, she'd hoped he might see something developing between them. Who bothered with all the attention if they weren't interested?

"Forget I asked."

"Kady—"

When he tried to protest she held up her hand. "How about this? Instead of ruining what I've imagined by telling me you're a…plumber, let me keep my secret fantasy of you being a man of mystery."

"You think that about me?"

She shrugged. "Why not. I don't have anything else to base an opinion on."

A smile curved his lips. "Okay. Let's go with that description."

So much for hoping he'd reveal something about himself. Clearly that wasn't going to happen. The hurt from his holding back slowly moved into miffed territory.

She collected her empty wrappers. "But, Dylan?"

"Yes?"

"One day you'll tell me?"

Again he paused. Met her gaze boldly. "One day I'll tell you."

Satisfied, she stuffed the papers, and her temper, into the bag and carried the trash to the large can beside the truck.

She rubbed her hands together and blew warm air on them. "Thanks for dinner. I'm going to head home now."

"No walk on the beach?"

"Too cold."

"No kisses?"

No way. "Too little information."

A wrinkle furrowed his brow. He took her hand.

"Kady, something special *is* happening between us. I didn't expect this when I agreed to accompany my mom to the convention. But I'm not at a place in my life to make a commitment."

Kady tamped down the annoying disappointment. What had she thought would happen? A whirlwind romance that led to happily-everafter? "I get it. This is nothing more than a convenience of sorts."

"I can't make plans."

"And I'm not asking you to." He couldn't even tell her his profession, for Pete's sake. Why would he make plans with her?

The walk back to the hotel was cold and uncomfortable. Another stellar ending to another pointless date.

"I'll see you tomorrow?" Dylan said as she unlocked her car.

"Can't be sure. I'll be busy getting ready for the competition and displaying my bouquet. And don't forget the awards banquet."

He nodded. "I'll look for you."

"I'll be around."

Holding the door as she got settled, Dylan bent over to gaze at her in the dim interior.

"You are special to me, Kady."

But not enough to include her in his life. "Thanks, Dylan."

He closed the door and she drove away, chastising herself for letting herself get close to a man who wouldn't share one tiny fact about his life. His loss.

But the longer she drove, she had to ask, why? Was he a con man? A Casanova? Worse, a serial killer? Okay, maybe her imagination had gone overboard, but leaving her in the dark with so many unanswered questions brought out the skeptic in her.

Tomorrow was the last day of the convention. She'd keep her distance. By his actions tonight, Dylan proved he was yet another guy not terribly interested in her. It would take her a lot longer to get over him than she'd like to admit, but once he left town…? Out of sight, out of mind.

Or so she hoped.

With an aching chest, she unlocked her apartment door and ventured inside. A chill permeated the air, so she turned on the heat. Shrugging out of her jacket, she tossed it on the couch and wandered to the table.

Fingering the fake flowers she'd bought to experiment with her bouquet design, she wondered what she'd do if she couldn't work at the shop. If she lost the competition and her parents decided to sell. She'd hoped their ultimatum was just that, only words, but they could very well come home from the cruise, rested and more determined than ever to put their words into action. Maybe all her work to earn their trust would amount to nothing.

Sure, Kady could get a job with another florist, but it wouldn't be the same. The Lavish Lily belonged to her family. She had to get her parents to see that she could carry on the legacy.

As she headed to her bedroom, she realized the light was on in her bathroom. She'd turned it off this morning, hadn't she? Reliving the incident at the shop, fear trickled over her. She backed up, noticing for the first time that the scissors she'd left on the table this morning were now resting on one of the chairs.

Alert now, she took a serious pass over the room. Little things were moved. Nothing blatant, but enough. And with that knowledge came a frightening realization that someone had been here while she was out.

Grabbing her cell phone from her tote, she hurried from the apartment and dialed the direct number the police chief had given her after the break-in.

"Stay where you are," the chief told her. "I'll be right there."

Shivering, she ended the call, rubbing her hands up and down her arms to spark some warmth. Keeping a wary eye on her apartment door, she wished she wasn't alone.

Get used to it. Dylan won't always be around to play your knight in shining armor. You're on your own.

Lovely. Even her inner voice was against her.

The wind kicked up and Kady wished she'd snatched her jacket on the way out. She took shelter under the stairway a few doors down until the chief rolled up.

"Let me go in first and check it out," he told her as she joined him.

For the first time she became aware of her teeth chattering.

Soon the chief appeared at her doorway. "Clear. C'mon back in."

"With pleasure."

Jogging to the door, more than ready to get out of the cold, a weird thought hit her. *Clear.* Hadn't Dylan used the same wording the night of the break-in?

The chief stepped back to let her enter.

"There's no one here."

Relief flooded her.

"So what spooked you?"

Kady explained the nuances that had sent up her guard.

"After the break-in at The Lavish Lily, I'm gonna take your word on this." He nodded to the room. "Now that you know it's safe, take a look around and see if anything is missing."

The first place she checked was her refrigerator. Thankfully, the stephanotis she'd been storing there were still safely packaged. She let out a breath she hadn't realized she'd been holding. A flash of guilt, thinking that Dylan might be after her bouquet design, struck her. He wouldn't enter her apartment without permission, so why was she so quick to think he, or his mother, might be out for her design? In her weariness, she realized she wasn't thinking clearly.

Kady searched, but found nothing missing. The chief walked out of the bedroom. "Looks like the culprit came in through the bathroom. Window was wide open. Screen knocked out."

"I always leave it open a crack during the cooler weather." Kady gathered her hair into a ponytail, rolled her shoulders, then let her hair fall back into place. "Guess I won't be doing that any longer."

The chief nodded. "Being on the ground floor makes it easy for someone to crawl through."

She shuddered. "First The Lavish Lily, now this. Think the person will come back?"

"Hard to say. Without anything missing, I'd wager you didn't have what they were looking for. Still," he said, hooking his thumb in the direction of the bathroom, "follow precautions."

"You don't have to tell me twice."

"I'll write up a report. Have the squad car make a few more rotations around the complex tonight."

"Thanks, Chief."

"You gonna be okay by yourself?"

Kady fought down another full-body shiver. "I'll be fine."

"Should I call Will?"

"No. Please, don't call anyone. This could be nothing, but I don't want the word to get out and my folks to worry."

The chief lumbered to the door. "Call me. Anytime."

"I will."

Kady locked the door behind him, resting her forehead against the hard surface. When she finally worked up the nerve, she turned, her eyes scanning the living space. Suddenly her cozy apartment wasn't so inviting. Her two favorite places, the shop and her home, had been violated. What was going on?

She fought the urge to call Dylan. As much as she considered his warm arms a safe haven, he clearly wasn't as emotionally invested as she was. No. Tonight she'd tough it out, no matter how unsettling the circumstances.

Deciding she might as well get some sleep, Kady headed toward her bedroom. She stopped by the table, her assortment of tools scattered there. Wanting everything in its rightful place before she turned in, as if it would negate the fact that someone had trespassed here, she scooped them up, ready to deposit them in the empty box she'd carried in from her trunk.

Only the box, which she'd dropped on the floor when she'd carried it into her apartment earlier, was gone. She checked, thinking it might have been moved by the creep who'd broken into her apartment, but nope, it was nowhere to be found.

Of all the things to go missing. The other boxes Tommy had given her were still in her trunk.

Dumping everything back on the table, she went to her room and closed the door. Sleep would not come easily tonight, if it came at all.

CHAPTER THIRTEEN

"WE'VE RUN OUT of places to look," Will told Christine as they cruised down Main Street. Every night since she'd told the truth about searching for her brother, they'd traveled around town after dark, hoping to find him.

She shrugged and zippered her jacket. "I have to agree."

"Want to stop by my place for a bite to eat?"

"Why not…" Her voice trailed off as she stared out the window.

Will wanted to do more, but he couldn't make her brother materialize out of thin air. They'd just have to keep at it.

Suddenly, she straightened in her seat. "Will, the car we just passed? I swear I saw Bryce."

"Are you sure?"

"Yes. Yes, it was him. Turn around."

Pulling onto a side street, Will made a hasty three-point turn and swerved back onto Main. "Do you see the car?"

"No, but keep heading in this direction."

Before long they reached the marina. Will braked at the entrance to the parking lot. "We lost them."

Christine peered out the window, then pointed. "No. The car is parked right there."

Sure enough, a lone car sat in the farthest corner of the lot.

"Stay here," Will commanded after he shut off the engine. He hurried to the other vehicle, placing a hand on the hood. Heat radiated off the surface. Recently driven, he concluded.

He waved for Christine to join him. With caution, Will led the way to the pier. No sign of activity. They backtracked to the marina office and waited in the shadows.

"Where could he be?" Christine asked, frustrated at being so close, yet at a dead end again.

"Maybe he boarded one of the boats."

The longer they waited for Bryce to appear and the more the wind picked up off the turbulent water, the less Will assumed they were right. He stared at the docks, blowing warm breath on his hands.

"What do you say we call it a night?" he suggested after they'd been there for over an hour.

"A little longer, please?"

He couldn't resist her pleading eyes. Helping Christine had been a diversion from his own problems, but he'd quickly gotten caught up in her mission. He admired her firm commitment to finding her brother. She was convinced she'd locate him and everything would work out. Maybe his doubts of a happy ending were fading, because the more time he spent with this woman, the more he thought he could find a way out for himself. He didn't have to carry the weight solo.

After their run-in with Dylan, he'd confessed to her about how he'd used money from the flower shop to make questionable investments. How in his surety, he'd ended up losing it all— the secret he'd kept from his parents and sister. Instead of judging him with condemning eyes, Christine had laid her hand on his arm and assured him everything would be okay. Who did that?

Christine.

The relief of sharing his mistakes had lifted the pressure from his chest, replacing it with a different ache. An ache to hold this woman close and never let her go. Taking a chance, he'd leaned close, watching as her eyes went round, then soft as she realized his intention. Not giving him the opportunity to change his mind, Christine had planted a mind-blowing kiss on him. Once he got over the surprise, he wholeheartedly returned the gesture, keeping her locked in his arms until they pulled away, gasping for air.

They'd spent hours talking after that, hands clasped, shoulders touching. He'd never been this open and honest with a woman. The right woman. With Christine's support, he planned on coming clean once his folks returned from their trip. And then he planned on never letting Christine go.

But first, he had to convince his shivering partner they should call off tonight's surveillance. "You're freezing. We can at least sit in my car."

"I guess it wouldn't hurt," she agreed.

He reached out to take her hand when she grabbed hold of him and tugged him farther into the shadows.

"Someone's coming," she whispered.

They waited as someone moved quickly along the pier in their direction. Head down, the person didn't notice them. But as the figure drew closer, Christine let out a cry. "It's Bryce."

She rushed to her brother, who came to a complete stop when he heard his name.

"Chris? What are you doing here?"

She threw her arms around him. "Looking

for you. I've been so worried since you disappeared."

Bryce shoved her away, casting a quick glance over his shoulder. "You have to leave."

"No, silly. I just found you."

"It's not safe," he hissed, then dragged a hand through his shaggy hair. "No one can find you here."

Will stepped closer, understanding the urgency in Bryce's voice that Christine, in her joy at locating her brother, had missed. "What do you say we go back to my place? Talk things out."

Bryce glared at him. "Who's he?"

"Bryce, this is Will. A friend," she explained. "He's been helping me track you down."

"Chris, you should have stayed home."

"And let you deal with whatever you've gotten yourself into alone? No way."

The younger man frowned. "There's no helping me now. Not with this crowd."

"Of course there is."

Out came her innate optimism. A little misguided, Will thought, but true to her heart.

"Let's at least get out of the light," Will advised. If there were others around, guys Bryce was clearly afraid of, they made one huge target standing under the lamp standard.

They huddled on the far side of the building, protected from prying eyes and the steady wind.

Christine didn't waste any time. "What are you into, Bryce?"

Her brother looked at his feet, over the moored boats, anywhere but into his sister's eyes.

"It's okay," Will added in a gentle voice.

Finally, Bryce puffed out his cheeks and said, "I started dealing pot with some guys I met. I thought that's what they were doing at first, I swear. But before long, I discovered they were into different stuff and I couldn't get out. I know you're disappointed, Chris. I promised to get away from this life, and look, I've only made it worse."

"There's always a way out. A solution," Christine said, her tone firm. Confident. Sure.

"You don't know these guys. The boss would just as soon shoot me as wait for an explanation," Bryce responded, just as confidently.

"Can't you trust me to help you?" Christine grabbed her brother's arm. "Will you let me call someone who can actually do something about this situation?"

"A cop?"

"Sort of, yes."

Bryce scoffed. "Do you know what'll happen if I say a word?"

Will stepped forward. "What happens if you say nothing? It'll mean a life of looking over your shoulder, afraid of being arrested or worse…killed." Will paused, letting the scary reality of his words penetrate Bryce's stubbornness. "It won't be easy. You might even have to disappear for a while. But the alternative is a lot worse, not to mention your family will always be wondering if you're safe."

Though there wasn't much light, Will saw Bryce's eyes shimmer. Clearly he was terrified.

Christine moved beside her brother, placing her palm on his cheek. "We love you, Bryce. We'll do whatever we have to do to save you."

Bryce hugged his sister, shaking as he silently cried against her shoulder. Christine whispered soothing words. After a few minutes, Bryce stepped back, wiping his eyes and straightening his shoulders.

"I'm sorry, Chris. Mom and Dad, too."

She smiled. "When I get you home, you can tell them yourself."

"Let's go." Will left the shadows and walked straight into the path of two men. He stopped short, but it was too late. He'd been seen.

"Hey, who're you?" a burly guy asked.

"Nobody. I'm just leaving," Will replied, motioning for Christine and Bryce to stay hidden.

"I don't buy it," the other guy said. "Who are you waving at?"

"No one. I—"

Before he could finish, the burly guy grabbed him by his coat while his partner sprinted for the shadows.

"Bryce? That you?" the man called.

Bryce slowly came forward. "Yeah, Scott. I was just asking this guy why he was hanging around."

"You the cops?" Will's captor asked.

"No. An accountant."

A befuddled expression crossed the burly guy's face.

"A what?"

"Never mind," Scott spit, his voice trembling. "The boss is already on our backs. Shut him up and let's get outta here."

Will, a second shy of comprehending the command, doubled over when the man punched him in the stomach. Air heaved from his gut, leaving him breathless until an uppercut to his face replaced the first explosion of pain.

"You didn't have to do that," Bryce cried as he tried to pull from Scott's grasp.

"You want to be next?" Scott threatened Bryce.

Before he could catalog all his aches, another punch to his chest sent Will flying backward into the marina office. He shook off the effect, fighting the nausea swirling in his stomach.

"Stop it," Christine screamed as she went after Will's attacker.

He had to protect her. He launched himself at the big guy, catching him off guard, and they both went down hard.

"Run," Will yelled. "Call Dylan!"

Wild-eyed, Christine paused, recognition flaring in her eyes when she came face-to-face with Scott. "I know you. From the flower shop."

Scott lunged for her, but Bryce knocked him aside and shouted, "Do it, Chris!"

She took off running for the parking lot. Neither of the assailants could risk going after her and letting Will or Bryce go free.

"You know she's calling the cops," Will taunted. "You're going to get arrested."

The big guy staggered to his feet. His eyes darted to and fro. "We gotta run, Scott. The boss is already furious with us. If he gets wind of us talkin' to the cops, he'll kill us."

Scott, trying to take one last shot at Bryce, decided to heed his buddy's warning. With a shaking finger, he pointed at Bryce. "You're dead."

With those parting words, the two ran to the parking lot. Tires squealing, the vehicle fishtailed before peeling out of the lot to speed down the empty street.

Will slowly rose, rubbing his hand along his jaw.

"You okay?" he asked Bryce.

"Better than you."

Will tried to laugh, but groaned instead.

In the distance, Will heard the scream of a siren. Christine came running back from wherever she'd hidden, throwing herself at him. When her body hit his, Will let out an *oomph*. Thankful she was okay, he held her in his arms.

Taking his face gently in her hands, she said, "Oh, Will. Thank you." She kissed him softly. "Thank you," she whispered.

"All in a day's work for an accountant," he joked as his head started to throb with a vengeance.

"How can I ever repay you?" she asked.

"Promise to nurse my wounds."

A watery giggle escaped her. "I will." She kissed him again. "I love you."

"Medicine to my ears."

"And?" she prompted.

"I love you, too," he announced and followed it with a kiss.

Bryce hovered nearby. "The police are here."

Will looked over Christine's shoulder. Red and blue swirling lights illuminated the darkness, making him dizzy. A few seconds later another car barreled into the lot. Dylan.

Expelling a relieved breath, Will put his arm around Christine's shoulder to hold himself up.

"You ready for this?" he asked Bryce.

"After what you just did, yeah."

Dylan hustled toward Will, concern in his eyes. He took in Will's disheveled state. "I told you to call me."

"You'll learn that the Lawrences usually don't do what they're told."

"Already figured that out from your sister." Dylan glanced at Christine. "You okay?"

"Yes." She pointed. "This is my brother, Bryce."

Dylan sized up the younger man. "We need to talk."

Bryce glanced at his sister, then said, "I'll tell you everything I know."

The chief and a pair of policemen joined them. "Before we get any confessions, I'm guessing there's a boat we need to board?"

Bryce answered. "Slip number ten. The boat is being used as a meeting place."

"Drugs?"

Bryce nodded.

The chief pointed to another officer. "Watch him." Before following the chief, Dylan came to stand next to Will. "Keep your sister out of this."

"After what happened here tonight, you'll understand why I can't."

A CUP OF strong black coffee did little to blow away the cobwebs in Dylan's brain. He sipped the freshly poured second cup, buoyed by the bustling atmosphere in Cuppa Joe. For some reason the coffee shop had more than enough background noise to help him put together all the facts he'd garnered from Will and company just a few hours ago.

After boarding the boat and finding a stash of synthetic drugs, along with the real product, Bryce willingly spilled details about the operation. He also mentioned that Scott was nervous because he'd intentionally tried to run down a woman crossing the road in his frustration to find the box of drugs he'd misplaced. Dylan's blood had chilled when he realized the woman was none other than Kady. He really hoped they found the two missing clowns. He had more than a few words to share with the driver.

He'd been waiting on the doorstep when the owner of Cuppa Joe opened up. Dorinda Hobart was an institution in Cypress Pointe, with her spot-on coffee, ready ear to listen and, most important, willingness to let a person talk long enough to figure out their own problems. She would have made a fortune as a therapist.

After topping off his cup, Dorinda sat in the chair opposite him. "How is the convention going?"

He blinked, momentarily forgetting his cover. "It's been…busy. I've met a lot of new people."

"Kady Lawrence."

"You get right to the point."

"I'm old. I don't have time to beat around the bush."

He grinned. Chronologically she appeared to be in her seventies, but her clear eyes and snappy comeback proved the woman was young at heart.

"Yes, I know Kady."

"You were with her when she found the flower shop broken into?"

Dylan took a sip and nodded. "I was."

"Thank you. From everyone in Cypress Pointe. She's one of our own and if anything had happened to her..." The older woman stumbled over her thick words, tearing up.

"Nothing did. It was my pleasure to assist her." He placed his hand over her wrinkled, spotted hand and squeezed. "It all worked out."

"Except I heard there was some kind of trouble at the marina last night."

Dylan shrugged.

"You wouldn't tell me, even if you knew."

He sent her a bland look. "I'm just a tourist."

"Uh-huh. And I'm really a supermodel in disguise."

He smiled. "Um, I gotta be honest. I have no comeback for that remark."

Dorinda chuckled. "Nor any answers about the events of last night?"

"Sorry."

As she stood, Dorinda wagged a finger at him. "You're up to something."

"You're right. I'm looking forward to the last day of the florist convention."

"Hmm. Okay. Give Kady my regards when you see her."

If he saw her. They hadn't exactly left on good terms the night before. "Will do."

He settled back with his drink, wondering how to approach Kady today. He knew she'd be distracted by the competition. There was a lot riding on the outcome. And while he wanted her to win, he was still rather loyal to his mother. Running a hand over his jaw, he sighed. Could things get any more complex?

Last night—strike that, early this morning—they'd decided not to tell Kady about the assault on Will. Her brother agreed to keep silent for now, wanting Kady to have her special day without him grabbing the attention away from her. He seemed to recognize that was a bone of contention between them. From the remarks Kady let escape, Dylan agreed with him. Meanwhile, Christine promised to take Will back to his place and get him settled before she went to work at The Lavish Lily. Once the truth was revealed, Dylan would deal with the fallout.

Because truth time was growing ever closer.

He finally had solid intel on Esposa. Agent Turner had called an hour ago to tell Dylan they'd apprehended an informant. Esposa was close by. It was only a matter of hours before Dylan confronted him.

Glancing at his watch, he stood. The hotel

beckoned—he needed to shower and get ready for the day. Pausing at the counter, he dropped a twenty in the tip jar and waved at Dorinda.

"Promise you'll stop back after the convention," she said.

"I'll see what I can do."

After the convention, who knew where he'd be, what case he'd work on. Yet he was already a little homesick for the coffee joint that had become his go-to place first thing every morning.

He'd only just stepped outside when he heard someone call his name. He spotted Max jogging toward him.

"Chief called. I'm headed over to find out what went down last night."

"I'll go part of the way with you."

They walked briskly. "Can you fill me in?" Max asked.

"I'm sure the chief won't mind." He explained what happened to Will and Christine and the wealth of information they'd received from her brother.

"One of the guys who confronted Will last night works for the floral wholesaler."

"Let me guess. They deliver to The Lavish Lily."

"Bingo. Christine recognized him. Apparently he was shadowing the regular delivery guy."

"Casing the shop?"

"Hard to say since only corsage boxes were taken during the break-in. My guess is they were used to deliver product around town."

"Clever."

"Bryce, Christine's brother, agreed to give us everything he knew. So yeah, the boats were used to store the synthetic drugs, which explained the increase in activity the chief was concerned about. Bryce never met the boss, but he heard a name. Ness."

"Doesn't ring a bell."

"Nestor Esposa."

Max stopped. "Seriously?"

"Yep. I called one of the agents in our office in Tampa. He looked into the records for the wholesale business. Relatives of Esposa are listed as the owners."

"But he's really running things?"

"Knowing him, yes."

"Now what?"

"Something is keeping Esposa in the area. Bryce said part of a shipment went missing a few days ago. Unfortunately, the guys who work for Esposa took off before the chief and I got to the marina last night. Bryce is a small player, so he doesn't have enough particulars, but he did say the guys he was with last night were nervous. Jumpy at the least little sound. Like they were waiting for the boss to arrive and ream them out about something."

"So we find the missing shipment, covertly offer it to Esposa and it leads him to us?"

"That's the plan. It all boils down to the drugs he's supplying. Cypress Pointe doesn't have a lot of this kind of activity, but with the proximity to the gulf for delivery and Tampa for distribution, this is an important drop-off spot. If he has to move his operation again, it'll cost time and money. Not to mention he's looking for a missing shipment. His guard is down. Now is the time to get him."

"Not an easy task."

"No. The chief has his officers out looking for the two who fled last night. Hopefully they show up again and we grab them. Find out the rest of Esposa's strategy."

Max slapped him on the back. "Got your work cut out for you, buddy."

"And I'm running late." He held out his hand. "Can't thank you enough for your help."

Max took the outstretched hand and shook. "Anything to keep Cypress Pointe safe. I plan on raising my kids here."

"If you get your girl to take a walk down the aisle."

"Oh, she will. I'm making sure we set a date today."

"Good luck with that. I'm off."

The men parted company and Dylan made tracks to the hotel. It was still early enough that not much activity in town slowed his pace. The open house for brides to view the competition bouquets was still a few hours away. For Kady's sake, he hoped for a packed turnout.

He entered the lobby, which was still quiet for the morning. He'd just pressed the elevator button when his mother's voice echoed in his ears. She was barking out instructions to a concierge, his face stricken as he scribbled notes. Okay, Dylan hadn't gotten any sleep last night, but he had to save the poor guy.

"Mom, stop badgering the help."

"Dylan. Thank goodness." She turned to the man beside her. "This is my son. He'll assist me from here."

"If you're sure?"

"Yes." She patted the man on his shoulder. "You've been very helpful—" she glanced at his gold name tag "—Kevin."

"Yes, ma'am. If you need me I'll be at my desk," he said in a relieved tone.

"Wonderful." She twirled to face Dylan. "My bouquet is a failure."

"Aren't you a little overdramatic?"

"Do you see it in my hands?"

"No."

"Then I'm not being dramatic. A wholesaler was supposed to deliver the flowers I ordered this morning. So far they're a no-show."

He thought about Kady mentioning her own special order arriving this morning. "Maybe they're behind schedule."

"I knew this would happen. Derrick insisted I not bother bringing my selections with me. He wanted me to relax and insisted I work with a new company. This is a disaster."

"Call them and find out what's going on."

"I did. Multiple times. Starting at six o'clock this morning. No answer."

"Did you honestly expect someone to answer that early? On a Sunday?"

Her dismayed gaze met his. "Of course."

Checking his watch, he said, "It's going on eight. I bet they'll be here anytime now."

"And if they aren't? How can I win with only ribbon and tape?"

"You'll figure something out. You always do."

Her elegant shoulders sagged. "This was

easier when I was younger. When your father was here to help me."

He couldn't miss his mom's discouraged face. She lived for this stuff, especially since Dad had passed away. He and his brothers were out living their dreams, leaving her to continue a life she'd always imagined would include her husband.

"I can make some calls. There's got to be another source for you to get fresh flowers."

"Kevin was going to check on it."

"Then don't panic."

She glanced up at him, a wry twist to her lips. "I haven't lost this competition in years. Maybe this is the cosmos telling me it's time to hand my crown over to another florist."

"One, when do you ever question the cosmos? And two, I have faith in you."

"My only real competition is Kady. If everything falls apart for me, she just might win."

"Love the confidence, Mom."

"It's the truth."

"Is that a bad thing? To let someone else have a chance?"

"It depends." His mother's eyes narrowed. "Do you want her to win?"

Jeez. How had he missed it? Now they were getting to the root of his mother's evil purpose.

"It would be nice if she won, but she'd never respect you if you intentionally let her."

Her hand flew to her heart. "Dylan Matthews, what are you suggesting?"

"That you'd lose to make her happy. And if she's happy, you're hoping we get together."

His mother let out a long-suffering sigh. "You know me too well."

"I do. And this…attraction to Kady? It's between her and I. Nothing to do with your machinations of losing the competition. If anything happens with us it's because it's real. Got it?"

His mother grinned. "It is real."

"And you know this how?"

"The few times I've seen you two together the sparks were exploding all over the place."

He had to agree. When he was around Kady his chest ached and his heart soared. He searched for her in a crowded room. Listened for the sound of her laughter. Wanted to tell her all about his life, his job and… Shoot, he sounded like a lovesick poet. "Let's get through today. See if your flowers arrive, because you are entering the contest. Clear?"

"Clear. And at the banquet, maybe you two can sit—"

"Mrs. Lawrence?" Kevin hurried over, holding a cordless phone. "I got a call from the kitchen. Your order has arrived."

She smacked Dylan on the shoulder. "I knew it."

"Yeah. That explains the panic."

"Don't sass me."

"Look, I need to get upstairs. If you—"

"Be in my room in thirty minutes."

His mother bustled off, filling Kevin's ear on the way. Smiling, Dylan realized how much he'd actually enjoyed being at the convention with his mother. It had been a long time since they'd spent time together, and ever since he'd been shot, well, he knew the toll it had taken on her, especially with Dad gone. Now she had her flowers to create a masterpiece and a competition to win. He was happy for her, pleased by the smile on her face.

He'd just exited the elevator on his floor when his cell rang. Agent Turner's name came up on the screen.

"Matthews here."

"We've got eyes on Esposa. I need you here, now."

CHAPTER FOURTEEN

KADY HAD TOSSED and turned all night, so she got up early, took a quick shower, dressed in a professional navy suit with a white blouse and packed up her tools and design drawings to get a jump on the day. She still had the competition bouquet to put together, then had to get it to the hotel for potential clients to view. She made a cup of coffee, not really needing the caffeine, but did so more out of habit. She needed the consistency to steady her nerves.

She arrived at the flower shop fairly early. The alley behind the shop remained dark. The light above the back door had burned out. "I should have listened to Dylan." Changing a bulb wasn't high on her current list of priorities right now. She'd take care of it after the convention ended.

A gust of wind whipped through the alley, blowing loose debris around. Kady juggled a coffee thermos, tote and the extra flowers she'd stored at her apartment. Her hair lifted and tangled in her eyes. She tossed her head in an effort to brush it away, until another gust made her task impossible.

Why hadn't she pulled it back before she left the apartment? She should have thrown on an overcoat, too, but left the house in too much of a hurry. She didn't have time to backtrack, and since she'd be in the hotel all day, it wouldn't matter.

"Focus," she said, reprimanding herself. The day had only just started and her thoughts were all over the place. The competition. Dylan. Losing to Jasmine. Dylan. Worrying that she'd fallen in love with a guy she barely knew. Dylan.

Fallen in love? Yes. With a man who wouldn't give her any details about his life.

Great. Just great.

Her stress turned to surprise when she glimpsed the wholesaler leaning against the delivery van, hands deep in his jacket pockets, a container of flowers at his feet. Was she that far behind already?

"Mr. Ness. What a surprise," she said. After managing to locate the right key on her ring, she unlocked the door and switched on the lights. After punching in the security code for the newly installed alarm, she placed her belongings on the worktable. Ness followed with her special order. Strange. He never made deliveries. In fact, she'd met him only once, many months ago.

She closed the door against the churning wind that continued to blast cold air into the shop. "It's wild out there." Shivering, she ran her hands over her arms.

Ness merely nodded in agreement.

"Is there a problem at the warehouse?" she asked conversationally, the man's muteness getting to her.

"Due to a lack of good help, I'm making your delivery this morning."

"Did something happen to Tommy?" she asked as she moved her belongings aside to make room for the container. "He's the best delivery guy we've ever had. I'd miss him."

The tall, well-built man, with his hair shaved close to his scalp, set the flowers on the work-table. She wrinkled her nose against the body odor he'd unsuccessfully tried to mask with a large dose of cologne. "Tommy? No, he's off today."

"Oh. What about the guy who was shadowing Tommy?"

"Scott. Yes. Turns out he doesn't have what it takes to work for me."

Thankfully, Mr. Ness moved away. She gulped in some fresh air.

"Nothing is done best unless you do it yourself," he remarked in an offhand manner.

Kady wasn't sure how to reply, so she checked over the flowers. Why hadn't Mr. Ness left them in the van until she arrived? How long had they been outside, exposed to the wind? She brought them to her nose and inhaled. Light and sweet, just as she expected them to be. Thankfully, they were fresh and undamaged.

Out of the corner of her eye she watched the man roam the workroom, his gaze moving over every shelf, every surface. What was he doing?

"Um, why don't I sign for the delivery so you can take off? I'm sure you're busy."

Ness leaned against the counter, his hands still in his pockets. His unnerving gaze never left her. "That won't be necessary."

Okay, this was weird. The creepy vibe from Ness kept growing stronger. She hated being here alone, but Christine wouldn't open the shop for a few more hours. Kady was on her own. Her hands trembled slightly as she separated the blooms, but she squared her shoulders against the uneasiness building inside her.

"Well, I can't thank you enough for getting these flowers to me today."

Ness nodded, not moving an inch. Why wouldn't he leave?

"Is there something else you need? I'll be going shortly." Well, soon, anyway. She had to make her bouquet first, but he didn't need to know all the details.

"Why, yes. You have something that belongs to me."

"I do?" she asked with a slight shake of her head.

"My clueless employee left some boxes here the other day. He came back to retrieve them, but they were gone."

"Really? I've been in and out of the shop due to a commitment, but I'm sure Christine would have helped him."

"She was unable to."

"Oh. Well, she's new. Maybe she didn't realize what he wanted."

"Very true. So he came back after business hours to look for himself."

She frowned. That didn't make sense. "After hours? No one would be able to help him then. If there is a problem—"

"There is a problem. The boxes aren't here. We've searched."

"Why would you search? Christine would gladly give you back what belongs—" She stopped when the realization of Ness's words hit her. "You broke into the shop?"

"Not me, personally. My men."

She blinked. His men? When did wholesale flower distributors call employees their men? "I'm sorry, Mr. Ness. I'm confused. What boxes are you talking about?"

"The ones you asked Tommy for. The ones Scott mistakenly left here."

She had to jog her memory. So much had happened in a few short days. "I remember now. I needed empty boxes to carry arrangements in. Tommy always gives me a couple when I run low."

"Except they weren't empty. At least one wasn't."

Kady thought back to the stack of boxes that Tommy—er, Scott—left for her. Christine claimed they were heavy, but after piling all her supplies and the vase into the top box, Kady had attributed the weight to her items, never considering that one of the other boxes might actually be full. Explained why Ness wasn't happy.

She glanced at him, noticing the dangerous gleam in his eyes, the taut way he held his body in check. Lines wrinkled his forehead. He radiated anger. Over a box?

That was when Kady realized she was in trouble.

Clearing the tremor from her voice, she said, "I'm sure we can sort out this mix-up."

"There is no mix-up. Return what is mine."

"As you can see, the boxes aren't here."

A nasty grin curved Ness's lips, making Kady shudder. "But I'm sure you want to tell me where they are."

She could. They were still in her trunk. But whatever he was after must be bad news. Would she give it to him so easily?

"I can see the wheels turning in your head, Ms. Lawrence. Let me assure you, there is only one outcome here. I leave with my possessions. And if you don't give me any problems, maybe I don't hurt you."

Kady swallowed. Hard.

An uncomfortable silence engulfed the room.

She had two options. Give the man what he wanted or somehow call the police. Which wasn't going to be possible since her cell was in her tote and Ness stood next to the shop's phone. Okay, no to the shop's phone. But her cell?

"I think I know what you're talking about, Mr. Ness. My employee carried the boxes to my car trunk the other day. I haven't bothered with them since."

"See. Now you're being reasonable."

With clammy hands she opened her tote. "My keys are in here."

He nodded.

She fished around, found her cell and tried as subtly as possible to punch in 911, hoping Ness wouldn't notice. Then she grabbed her keys, leaving the phone near the opening of the tote in case she needed it. In a loud voice, to cover the dialing sound, she said, "Why don't we go to my car?"

Ness pushed away from the counter. "Wise choice."

Stomach in a hard knot, Kady led the way. They had just reached the door when she heard a faint voice coming from her tote. "Nine-one-one. What is your emergency?"

In blinding-fast speed, Ness shoved her from behind. Bright flashes of light swam before her eyes. She'd hit the back door and crumpled, before feeling something hard jabbed into her side. A gun?

"You did not just call for help," he growled into her ear, shoving her harder. She couldn't answer with her cheek mashed against the door.

He abruptly let go, stalking to the table.

Kady sagged but took a breath and croaked as loud as she could, "The Lavish Lily. Help."

But Ness had already picked up the phone. He threw it to the ground and stomped on it. Lifting a handgun from his side, he pointed it directly at her. "Under different circumstances, I'd be impressed, but your plan didn't work. Now get outside and open the trunk."

Kady forced her shaky legs to move. So much for her options.

She stepped outside. Weak light had begun to filter through the morning shadows, and it was still windy and cold. Kady shrugged her shoulders together, pulling her arms close to her body for warmth. Ness stayed behind her, the gun lodged in her back. She had to get out of this, somehow, someway.

They'd made it only a few feet when a loud voice yelled, "Freeze!"

DYLAN'S HEART NEARLY gave out as he watched Esposa grab Kady around the neck to drag her back into the shop. In the gloomy morning light, he'd barely been able to make out her features, but what he did see was like a punch in the gut.

Once Dylan had met the team of four agents, they'd taken up various positions in the alleyway. Donning bulletproof vests, everyone had a strategic view of the back door. Dylan stayed with Turner, lead agent of the group. They'd called for more reinforcements, but time was their enemy. Dylan hoped to get the situation under control soon, making the need for more manpower unnecessary.

"We have to get inside that store," said Turner, his voice nearly carried away by the building wind. Was a storm approaching?

Dylan knew there were only two ways in. Esposa would be watching the back entrance, keeping watch on the authorities he knew about, which left the front. "Ms. Lawrence's brother has a key."

"Can you get ahold of him?" asked Turner.

"Give me a minute."

Rising from his crouching position in the long alley, Dylan nearly stumbled as the muscle spasm in his thigh took a few seconds to ease. He balanced himself by placing a hand on the scratchy stucco of the building. Cell in hand, he limped a few feet away, out of everyone's sight, and hit the police chief's number.

"What's up, Matthews?"

"Found the suspect I'm after, but we have a problem."

In as few words as possible, he explained the situation.

"I'm sending over backup. Then let me give Will a call and I'll head down there." He paused a moment, his voice careful when he spoke. "Did Kady seem okay?"

Her fear flashed before Dylan's eyes. He'd never forget the look on her face as long as he lived. "Shaken. I really didn't see her for very long."

The chief ended the call. Dylan resumed his position next to Turner. "It's in the works. The chief is on his way."

Turner nodded. "What do you want to do?"

"All we can do is wait for the key. If we can keep Esposa's attention here, then there might be a chance to quietly slip in through the front."

"He's probably thought of that."

"Like I said, we *might* have a chance."

KADY DROPPED HER keys as Ness dragged her inside the shop. He pushed her across the room, where she now huddled by the far wall of the workroom. Through the slightly opened door, he peered out at the alley. What on earth was happening here? With the police, or whoever was outside, Ness wasn't going to let her go.

Thankfully, her family wouldn't be walking in here, unaware. She'd been so happy when her folks had gone on the cruise, and now she was doubly so. The thought of them also held at gunpoint made her heart trip.

Okay, her family was safe. But what about her? Was there something she could do?

"You know they won't just leave," Kady said, unsteadily rising to her feet.

Ness never took his gaze off the alley. "Shut up."

She took a few small steps toward the counter where a pair of scissors stood out in a mixture of pens and pencils.

Ness turned the gun on her. "I wouldn't make any sudden moves. This thing might accidentally go off."

"So…what? You're going to stand there all day hoping they go away?"

He'd gone back to the door, but this time he looked over his shoulder at her. She wished he hadn't. The fury in his dark eyes made her knees tremble. "Not at all. I'm deciding how best to use you as a shield to get away."

At those words, she held the counter to steady herself. She honestly needed the support, but the move also brought her closer to a possible weapon.

Keep him distracted, her mind screamed.

"So, I'm guessing you aren't in the flower industry?"

"My family is. I needed a legit cover for my real business."

"Which is illegal?"

From her angle, she saw a slight grin curve Ness's lips. "Let's say the authorities don't appreciate the entrepreneur I have become."

What did that mean? He spoke as cryptically as Dylan.

"But in all fairness, I must thank you."

"Me? What for?"

"For the use of your corsage boxes."

Confusion reigned again.

"A very neat and easy way to transport my product. No one suspects a florist box to contain…hidden delights."

Hidden? The man was talking in riddles. The tension headache taking up residence in her temples spread.

Something must have caught his attention outside because he changed position, his head moving back and forth as he scanned the alley. Taking advantage of this, Kady eased closer to the scissors, now only mere inches away.

"I don't think you want my guest to get

hurt," he shouted from the doorway. "Back off!" Ness barked.

Taking her chance, Kady grabbed the shears and shoved the hand with her prize behind her back. When Ness glowered at her, she hoped she'd pulled off a blank look.

"I said, quit moving around."

"Right." She stepped away from the counter and squeezed the cold metal in her hand. All she could do now was wait.

"WELL, THAT DIDN'T WORK," Turner muttered.

"I warned you." Dylan had tried to tell the agent that Esposa would keep a close eye, noticing any movement in the alley. The creep hadn't become so successful and difficult to apprehend because he was careless.

"So what do you suggest?"

Dylan was still going with the unlocking-the-front-door theory. Esposa wasn't easy to fool, but he was also focused out back. Since the alarm would have been disengaged when Kady and Esposa entered, he didn't have to worry about making noise as they sneaked in the front. The hallway connecting the retail part of the shop from the workroom might also play to their advantage. The only obstacle they faced, which had his stomach in knots, was how to keep Kady safe if they did storm the shop.

A movement out of the corner of his eye revealed Chief Gardener with Will in tow, both men sporting identical grim expressions. Dylan elbowed Turner and they then met the men halfway up the alley.

Will spoke first, his hair lifting in the wind. The dark worry circles under his eyes matched the purple bruising from the previous night's encounter. "Is my sister still in there?"

"Yes."

"This wouldn't have happened if you'd told her the truth."

"We don't know that. I couldn't predict Esposa would end up here."

"At least she would have had a heads-up."

"Let's focus on the present," the chief ordered. "Situation?"

"Esposa is camped out in the workroom. I'm hoping to use the front door to gain access to the building."

"You're just going to walk in?" Will asked, his tone incredulous.

"Sometimes the obvious works."

Will ran a hand over his jaw and cursed.

"You brought the key?" Dylan pressed. "Time is of the essence."

"I get it." Will fished a key chain from his pocket. "Here."

Dylan took it and stopped for a moment. Will looked as bad as Dylan felt. "Thanks."

Will grabbed Dylan's arm in a fierce hold. "Nothing better happen to Kady."

"I will do everything in my power to protect her." Dylan met the chief's steady gaze. "Back me up?"

"My pleasure." The chief pointed to Main Street as he spoke to Will. "I'm only gonna tell you once. Get a couple blocks away from here."

"But—"

"Now."

Will hesitated, then jogged away in the opposite direction.

"You know he isn't going far," Dylan pointed out.

The chief nodded. "Still, we can't have him on our heels."

Dylan held up the key for Turner to see. The agent gave him a thumbs-up. Dylan and the chief proceeded to the front door, but just before reaching the shop, Dylan heard running behind him. He glanced over his shoulder to see Will.

The chief held his arms out, ready to stop him. "I told you—"

"Something's occurred to me." Will spoke over the chief to Dylan. "There's a bell above the door. It sounds whenever someone enters the shop. They'll hear it in the workroom."

Frustration mounting, Dylan strode over to Will. "How loud is it?"

"Loud enough to alert anyone working in the back that someone's come in the front."

He *was* slipping. He hadn't even considered that. "Let me talk to Turner."

"Make it fast," the chief said and Dylan raced to the agent in charge.

"WHY DON'T YOU let me talk to them," Kady suggested. "You know, convince them to go away."

"Won't work," Ness answered in a tight voice. "I'm a wanted man. Trust me."

"What if I go out, open my trunk and give them whatever you've got boxed up?"

He didn't respond.

"Then let me go as a sign of good faith."

He snickered. "You watch too many cop shows."

"What could you have done to make them want you so badly? C'mon. You just want a box of stuff."

Silence. Then he said, "I shot and killed a cop. Injured another."

Okay. She didn't need a television show to know this was bad.

Retreating into the corner, she tried to ignore the pounding in her chest. How would she get out of this?

For all the jumping around from job to job over the years, why couldn't she have worked at a gym? Picked up a few self-defense moves? She may have scissors, but when would she get to use them?

"So we sit here?"

Ness seemed to be considering what she'd said. Finally he told her, "Bring me the phone."

"What?"

He snapped his fingers. "Phone. Now."

Hiding the scissors beneath a corner of the floor mat, she stood and took a couple of halting steps to make sure her legs could carry her. Crossing the room felt like a million miles instead of a few short feet. As she passed her flowers, lying haphazardly on the worktable, melancholy eclipsed her fear. The competition. She'd forgotten all about it. Would she make it back to the convention? Or would this crazy man take everything from her, including her life?

She retrieved the phone and cautiously held it out to him.

He grabbed it. "Now, get back over there."

As she did so she noticed the keys she'd dropped when he'd dragged her back into the shop. Kicking them under the worktable, she returned to the far corner. Now was not the time to buck this guy by trying to retrieve them. The beads of sweat on his forehead indicated he was more than a little nervous, despite his bravado. Were his jerky movements proof that he was no longer in control? Crouching down, she snatched up the scissors, hoping Ness hasn't seen her. He hadn't.

After dialing a number, Ness waited for someone to answer. Apparently nothing happened because he spit out several choice words and dialed again. This time someone picked up. In brisk terms he carried on a heated conversation and finished with the order, "Get here. And hurry."

He tossed the phone onto the worktable, but missed the mark. Kady cringed when the plastic hit the floor and broke apart, loud as a bomb in the quiet room.

"Now what?" she asked.

"Help is on the way."

Kady imagined there were plenty of cops outside by now. How was his help going to get anywhere near here? If he was so desperate, maybe she could annoy him enough to let her go.

Or kill her.

She had to do something. Sitting in the corner would not bring her freedom.

Scissors securely in hand, she summoned what courage she had left. Probably not the wisest choice of action but she nudged him with her words. "You know you don't have a prayer here."

"Shut up!"

"Why? You're going to shoot me, or if the cops out there decide they've had enough and make a run for you, I'm probably a goner anyway." She silently cringed. "Looks like we're at an impasse."

Ness lowered the gun and aimed soulless eyes at her. "Unless I go with my earlier idea of using you as a shield."

Kady gripped the scissors, waiting for him to make good on his threat.

"WE HAVE A PROBLEM," Dylan told Turner as he hunkered down next to him. The morning had begun to lighten up, giving them a better handle on their surroundings. "There's a bell over the front door. I need a diversion."

"Ideas?"

Dylan looked at his watch. "Give me two minutes to get into position. Then start giving Esposa instructions to surrender. Get him engaged in conversation and make lots of racket so I can get in without him noticing."

"I still say he won't fall for this."

"He knows he's not getting away."

"You really know the guy?"

"I do. And he's sweating up a storm in there."

Turner seemed to be mulling the idea in his head. Dylan wanted to shake him. Finally, Turner said, "We'll go with your plan. As soon as you go in, we won't be far behind."

Dylan nodded in relief.

"Go for it."

Dylan slapped Turner on the back as he rose. "Start timing now."

Rushing back to the chief, Dylan waved. "Follow my lead."

The chief pulled his firearm from his side holster.

Easing up to the door, Dylan fit the key in the lock. Turned ever so gently. The lock clicked. He checked his watch, marking the countdown. Right on schedule, Turner started yelling for Esposa to surrender his position. Before long, ugly words flew back and forth.

With the tiniest pressure, Dylan pushed the door, waiting for the bell to sound and give them away. Taking a bracing breath, he got ready to push and run inside when he heard a gun blast.

KADY COWERED IN the corner. When the yelling had started she'd hoped to use the distraction and maybe run up the hallway. But when Ness took a shot outside, her plan disintegrated. Her mind went blank.

More shouting ensued. Now or never.

She jumped up, ready to flee when Ness intercepted her. In her struggle she thought she'd heard bells. She hadn't hit her head, had she? With scissors at the ready, she blindly lashed out at Ness, hoping to jab him enough to let her go. His body odor overwhelmed her as his grip became tighter, like a band constricting her arms. She cried out as the scissors flew from her grasp and crashed to the floor. Then everything was happening at once.

A tall man burst through the back door. Ness placed her between himself and the gun aimed in their direction. Behind her, footsteps sounded from the hallway, startling her. Could someone have entered from the front? Before she could find out for sure, Esposa propelled her forward. The officer lowered his weapon as she tripped and flailed in his direction. Another shot from Esposa missed its mark as the agent dodged a bullet. She dropped to the floor, hands over her head. Dark shoes moved past her but she stayed still until someone pulled her to her feet.

Chaos reigned. Loud voices shouted out commands as a bunch of officers surrounded Ness. She noticed Chief Gardener in the mix as someone grabbed Ness, who fought with all his might, cursing and yelling. They finally subdued him enough for an officer to yank his arms behind him for the handcuffs. Once captured, Ness spit and the tall man, apparently in charge, ordered him outside. As they led Ness away, he shot a belligerent glance at Kady, before his gaze moved to the person behind her. He scowled, his mouth open to speak, but the officers whisked him away before he could say a word.

When it finally registered that she was safe, she sagged against the person holding her up. Wait—who was behind her? In a panic she jerked free and her gaze tangled with a pair of gunmetal eyes.

CHAPTER FIFTEEN

"DYLAN? WHAT ARE you doing here?"

Due to the roaring in his ears, Dylan found it hard to find his voice. Kady stood before him, in one piece, her features flush with what he figured was surprise. He'd reluctantly let her go when she spun to face him, but now his fingers itched to hold her close. To breathe in the sweet scent so unique to Kady. Only standing here with her made it possible to get his control back. Esposa was gone now, leaving Kady safe.

He couldn't say the same for himself.

Kady's beautiful eyes widened. "Did the chief call you? Because that would explain a lot of things. Like—"

Before she had a chance to finish, Will came rushing up to her.

"Kady." Will pulled his sister into his arms. Over her shoulder Dylan saw her brother close his eyes as he hugged her tight. A few seconds later he opened his eyes and mouthed, "Thank you."

Kady returned the hug and then asked, "Will, how did you know what was going on?"

"The chief called for the key."

"I'm so glad he thought of using the front door to get in."

"Actually, that was Dylan's idea."

She focused on Dylan. He almost smiled at the incredulity glimmering in her eyes. When he opened his mouth to explain, Turner joined them.

"Matthews. A word."

"Just a sec." He held Kady's hand. "Are you okay?"

She blinked, wide-eyed. "Um, yes. Confused, but okay."

"I'll be right back."

He crossed the room in a few brisk strides. "What do you need, Turner?"

"With Esposa in custody, the higher-ups are going to want a report, pronto, and your supervisor requested a call. Everyone wants this arrest by the book so we can put him away for what he did to your partner. To you."

No one wanted it more than Dylan. "Did you get any info out of him?"

"More from the family member who gave

him up. Seems Esposa showed up out of the blue six months ago."

"Right after the shooting."

"He strong-armed his way into the floral business to use as a cover for the drug running. After he shot your partner, none of his contacts would give him any product. With the manhunt on for him, he became persona non grata. He horned in on the local synthetic-drug distribution to stay in the game."

"Explains a lot."

"He tried to lie low for a while but got antsy. He knew we were looking for him."

"I wondered why he got sloppy. Not his usual MO."

Turner shrugged. "Hard times. We got him now."

Dylan held out his hand. "Thanks."

"It's what we do. But we still need to find his stash."

"I have a lead."

Turner left to deal with the investigation. Dylan returned to Kady, who was deep in conversation with her brother.

"But why The Lavish Lily?" Dylan heard her ask Will.

"They used our corsage boxes to deliver the drugs."

"I can't believe the DEA was involved and we didn't know it."

"It's serious, Kady." Will looked up when Dylan joined them.

Kady hadn't noticed him. "Why didn't you call me when you were hurt last night?"

"I—I couldn't."

"Why not?"

Will glanced at Dylan. "It's a long story."

She acknowledged Dylan then.

"And why don't you seem more surprised by the DEA showing up here?"

Will hesitated. "I already knew about their involvement."

"What? How?"

"Christine."

Dylan waited while Will related his story. He told Kady about Christine's brother, their quest to find him, the drug involvement and finally getting roughed up by two thugs. Kady's expression went from surprised to horrified to angry.

"You still should have called me," Kady admonished her brother.

Looking like he wanted to change the subject, Will met Dylan's gaze. "Need something?"

"Actually, yes. The agent in charge needs to talk to Kady about Esposa."

She jerked back, as if realizing for the first time that he knew more about the situation than she did. Holding up a hand, she asked, "Who's Esposa?"

"The man who held you captive."

"No, that's Mr. Ness."

Dylan shook his head. "Clever." No wonder no one around here heard of Esposa.

Turner came forward. "Actually, his real name is Nestor Esposa, and we do need to speak with you now, Ms. Lawrence."

"Okay." She touched her brother's arm. "Stay?"

"I'm not going anywhere."

She nodded, then met Dylan's gaze. Her head dipped and she followed Turner to the other side of the room. As he asked questions, Dylan could see she spoke haltingly at first, and then her confidence built, with Turner taking notes. Dylan wanted that job, to reassure Kady after her ordeal, but left it in the capable hands of his fellow agent.

"She hasn't figured it out yet?" Dylan asked in a quiet voice.

"No. She thinks the chief called you."

Dylan ran a hand over his jaw. "I'll explain after she finishes with Turner."

"There's more than just today's events."

"What're you talking about?"

"Apparently someone was in her apartment. She noticed a few things moved around when she came home last night. Called the chief. He went by to investigate."

"She didn't call you?"

"No. But then, why should she? I haven't exactly been the best big brother."

"Kady is rather independent."

"True, but everyone needs an arm to lean on." Will's gaze roamed to his sister, then back to Dylan. "You know she's going to be angry with you."

Once the adrenaline wore off and he came clean in his role, yeah, she was going to be more than angry.

"They're right here," he heard Kady say as she got down on her knees to reach for something from under the worktable. Standing, she dropped keys in Turner's outstretched hand. "You'll find what you're looking for in my car trunk."

"Kady?" Will asked, his brows drawn.

"Seems I mistakenly took what Ness…Esposa wanted. The drugs are in my trunk."

Will put his arm around her shoulder. "That explains why someone was searching your place."

"I'm just glad it's all over."

But it wasn't. Far from it. Dylan knew there'd be more questions. More reliving the nightmare. And more disappointment when he told her the truth about his part since the wedding reception, where they'd met a mere week ago.

Kady waved at the worktable. "I need to get cracking on my bouquet. I've lost a lot of valuable time, but if I get moving, I can make it to the hotel and hopefully set up my display with time to spare."

"Sis, don't you think that can wait?"

"No. That man took a few years off my life this morning. I won't let him destroy my dreams, too." She pushed her hair from her face, determination written all over her.

Will pulled Dylan aside. "Shouldn't she be more upset?"

"Reality hasn't kicked in yet. Let her work on her project. She needs this right now."

"You're the expert." Will strolled away.

With drug dealers, yeah. Angry women? Not so much.

"Dylan, would you get the tape from the bin on the shelf?"

"Sure."

Turner had gone outside to talk to the chief. The other agents had left with Esposa. Right now, he and Kady were the only two left in the room.

He returned with the tape. Her hand fumbled when she went to take it and the tape fell to the floor. They both ducked to pick it up, bumping heads.

"Ow," Kady said, then laughed. Their eyes met. He saw only trust and safety reflected there. Confidence in the man who had lied to her.

And then it hit him. The truth he'd tried to ignore stared him straight in the face. He loved Kady. Heart and soul. And in a few moments he was going to destroy everything.

Was it possible she loved him in return? There was no debating their quick attraction, the growing respect as he learned more about her. Yes, love had taken him by storm and he realized with every fiber of his being that he wanted to deserve her love, too.

She grabbed hold of the tape first, worked her way to standing. Dylan did the same, tottering as his thigh tightened in a spasm, his gaze never leaving hers. Her cheeks colored and she gazed down. Away from his probing look?

After a few seconds, her head flew back up. The enticing flush from a moment before fled.

She pointed to his waist. Right to the badge he'd attached to his belt.

Busted.

"DYLAN?"

She had to be seeing things, right? Was that a real badge?

"I'm with the DEA," he answered quietly.

"The DEA?" she repeated. "How? Why?"

"Esposa killed my partner. Shot me."

Her eyes rounded. "Oh, Dylan."

"I've been after him for a while. When I heard he was in the area, I decided to stick around."

The revelation jolted her. "The convention?"

"Yes. What better way to be in town and gather information? The convention worked to my benefit."

"I knew you weren't a florist."

He chuckled. "Good guess."

She shook her head, mashing down the stirrings of hurt. "You know how to keep a secret."

"I'm sorry. In order for the ruse to work I couldn't tell you."

"Does your mother know?"

"No. I kept it from her, too."

"I see."

It all made sense now. The florist at a floral

convention who didn't know anything about the business of flowers. Never coming clean about his real job when she questioned him. Suspecting he held something back.

"Were you aware of Christine's brother?"

Dylan shifted. "After I found Will and Christine hanging around the marina while they were searching for him."

"So Will knows who you really are?"

"Yes."

Hurt now mingled with betrayal. "And you didn't feel you could trust me?"

"It had nothing to do with trust, Kady. I wanted to keep you safe."

"Did you suspect my shop was connected to your case?"

"Not at first. After the break-in, I had my suspicions but couldn't prove anything."

"So you kept me in the dark? I could have been hurt, or worse." She shivered at the thought.

"I hated every minute of keeping the truth from you."

"Yet you chose to keep quiet because getting Esposa was more important than me?" She glanced down at the flowers waiting to be turned into a beautiful creation. Touched the delicate bloom of the blush rose. Fragile, just like her heart. "So you used me, then? Because my shop was a lead in your case?"

"No. I explained, Kady. I didn't want you tangled up in all this. Didn't want you hurt."

She almost laughed out loud. Hurt? Ironic. Safe? He'd battered her emotions in his quest to get the bad guy while keeping her out of the loop. Her initial instincts—not to trust him— had been valid, but far off the mark. Here she thought he wanted her bouquet designs, when in reality he was a DEA agent after a criminal. So much worse.

"So the time we spent together?" she ventured. "The kisses? Meant nothing?"

"Of course they did. Kady, I was honest when I told you something special was happening between us. But I needed to find Esposa. Put the past behind me so I could move on with my life. Hopefully with you."

"All this time you lied to me."

"I needed to keep my cover."

He reached out to take her hand. She drew back. Couldn't endure his touch right now.

"And if you had to do it over again, would you still keep the truth from me?"

Dylan ran a hand over his jaw. Right. His silence said it all.

Tension filtered through the room until Dylan spoke again. "Can you forgive me?"

"I understand the undercover part. I do. It was your job. Trying to find the man who had caused a great deal of pain in your life." She stopped. Cleared her throat. "But I can't trust you." Her chest hurt so badly she didn't think she could muster the strength to get the next words out. "You let me fall in love with you while keeping me in the dark. Took advantage of the situation to get revenge and ended up putting me, and my livelihood, in danger. I don't think I can forgive you for that."

"I never meant to hurt you. I love you, Kady."

She blinked back stinging tears. She couldn't bear to hear him talk any longer. The words she'd longed to hear came too late now.

"You should leave," she told him.

"Kady."

"Please. Let me finish my bouquet. Get through the rest of the convention."

"We need to talk about this. About us."

There was no us, but the lump in her throat kept her from telling him so. He finally got the message and went outside.

Leaving her blissfully alone.

Except that was a lie.

As soon as she heard the bell chime over the

front door, hot tears rolled down her cheeks. She'd dared to love and failed. She looked at the flowers, blurry as the tears flowed. Dared to take a chance on a dream. Would she fail there, too?

The bells sounded again. Kady swiped away the tears as Will entered the workroom.

"You okay?"

"You knew," she accused. "How could you and Christine not tell me?"

Will froze. "I wanted to tell you right away, but...there were complications."

Weren't there always? She plucked at the flowers. "Such as?"

Will came right up to her. "I need to tell you something."

She recognized that expression. Nothing good ever came from it.

He took a breath and proceeded to tell her how he'd diverted funds from the business, as well as her folks' personal account, to make more money for the family. How his scheme failed. "I've put a good majority of the money back, but that's no excuse for what I've done."

"No, it's not." Her face grew warm as the anger in her built. "You lied to me, too."

Will nodded. "I never meant—"

"See, that's the problem. No one meant to

hurt anyone. Yet it happened anyway. To me. Mom and Dad. How could you do this, Will?"

"At the time I thought I could make extra money so the shop would thrive and Mom and Dad could retire in style."

She stared at him. "Have you lost your mind? We're all perfectly happy. And with my plans, the shop *will* thrive, allowing our parents to retire any way they want."

"Kady, please. I'm sorry."

The anger fled just as quickly as it came. Totally numb now by all the revelations of the day, she merely accepted her brother's explanation instead of fighting about it. "I understand why you've been so edgy lately."

"I thought I could hide the truth."

"There's a lot of that going around."

He paused. Searched her face. "Dylan told you?"

She nodded.

"He didn't mean to hurt you, either."

"But he did." She met his gaze head-on. "Why couldn't you believe I'd make The Lavish Lily a success?"

"I thought I knew it all. Knew what was best for the business. Turns out I was wrong." He took her hand. "Christine told me about your plans. Showed me the pictures from the weddings you've done. Sold me on your scheme to capture the wedding market. You're good, Kady. Better than I ever imagined."

"You never believed in me."

"I do now. One hundred percent."

Moisture clung to her lashes. So much to take in. Her mind shifted to overload.

"Then let me finish my bouquet. I need to come in first place to get Mom and Dad on board."

Will hugged her, despite her less-than-enthusiastic response. "I have faith in you, Kady."

If only Dylan had. Maybe her heart wouldn't be completely shattered.

She didn't pretend to understand the world Dylan came from. Going undercover was probably a big part of the job. In a sense, she could accept the need for secrecy when going after a suspect. But Dylan had allowed the attraction to build between them. To become something personal. Deeper. Involving her heart.

It was too much to process in her current raw state.

Will left her alone and she focused on her bouquet, pushing the past week's events from her mind. She needed the distraction, the creative outlet. Otherwise she might have to go down to the beach and scream and scream until her voice gave out.

Separating the peonies from the roses, she placed everything she needed to make her creation within arm's reach. Thirty minutes passed as Kady got caught up in the beauty and romance of the bouquet, desperately trying to hold her emotions together when the blooms made her think of Dylan. As she twined the ribbon around the stem, then glued the pearls and, finally, attached the brooch, she stepped back to view her handiwork.

"This is so much better than I imagined," she said to the empty room. Taking the digital camera she kept in the shop to document her work, she snapped a few pictures. These were definitely going in the wedding book. In fact, a copy was going on the cover.

Glancing at the wall clock, Kady realized she had just enough time to get to the hotel and set up her display. She made sure she had plenty of business cards available, threw the binder with photos of her wedding gigs and a decorative bow in her tote, and gingerly placed the bouquet in a special holder so it wouldn't be damaged in transportation. Once she loaded up her car, she was ready for what would come next and it was only ten thirty in the morning.

Carrying her things inside the hotel, she stopped in the foyer. A placard featuring a picture of a wedding-reception arrangement she'd designed leaned against a tall easel, pointing guests in the direction of the banquet room. Nealy must have talked Dane into using the professional photo of her floral design. Upon entering the banquet room, Kady found tables set up in long rows stretching from one end of the room to the other. She waved at the coordinator, who checked her clipboard.

"Kady. Row three. Your space is in the center."

She dodged other florists setting up their displays. The energy in the room buoyed her sagging spirits. All she could think about were the brides entering the lovely-smelling room, ready to get inspiration to make their wedding dreams come true.

To her delight, Melissa was setting up in the spot next to Kady's.

"Hey, girl. Ready to uncover your masterpiece?"

Kady smiled and set down the bouquet. "Thanks for the kind words." Melissa was entered in the table-centerpiece competition, so they weren't vying against each other. "Where's Jasmine?"

"Row one, first space."

"Wow. First crack at the crowd."

"Perks for being last year's winner."

"Which I intend to change." Kady centered the holder. "What do you think?"

Melissa quietly considered the bouquet. Kady bit the inside of her cheek, impatient for a response. "Well?"

Her friend beamed. "This is your best submission ever. Classic. Beautiful. A bride's dream made real."

Tears of relief pricked Kady's eyes. She blinked a few times and puffed out a breath. "Thanks."

"Hey, are you okay?"

No, but her friend didn't need to hear the sad truth. "Nervous."

Melissa took hold of her hand and squeezed. Kady got her calmness back. She looked over Melissa's arrangement of mauve roses and flowering oregano in a deep purple hue, surrounded with lavish greens that complemented the bright blooms. On either side of the vintage vase were votive candles flickering in crystal holders and a place card with the number *1* inked in dark purple calligraphy.

"Awesome," Kady declared. "Table number? Inspired. I love the additional touches."

Melissa fist-bumped Kady. "We are the two to beat this year."

In the short time before the doors opened to the public, Kady hooked the pale pink bow, which she'd fashioned out of lace, onto the table cover. She set out her business cards and opened the wedding photo book for brides-to-be to thumb through.

Once the public arrived, the hours flew by. Kady lost track of the number of brides-to-be and mothers of the bride who stopped to chat about Kady's services. Just as well. Keeping busy stopped her from dwelling on her shattered heart. From dwelling on the man she loved and trusted, who'd been the one doing the shattering. Her face hurt from smiling and her feet ached from standing in pumps for so long, but she wasn't complaining. At least five different women asked to set up consultations.

When the judges arrived to view her bouquet, she tried not to appear worried as they made marks on their clipboards and asked about her inspiration behind the flower choices.

Her hopes all hinged on the success of her creation.

The afternoon eventually wound down. Exhausted from her early start on the day, from the trauma of being Esposa's hostage, to discovering the truth about Dylan, she wondered if she'd have the energy to get through the awards banquet.

Before they left, Kady and Melissa were approached by one of the judges. They were both finalists in their categories. Melissa squealed in delight and Kady felt a bit of the pressure ease from her shoulders. She'd gotten one step closer.

"In a few hours we'll learn the outcome," Melissa said as she blew out the candles in order to pack up.

"Just enough time to get home, change and be back for the event," Kady said.

"I wish my hubby could be here, but he offered to watch the kids."

Kady tried not to think about Dylan. Would he escort his mother to the ceremony tonight? She knew she'd have to see him again, despite the pain she couldn't deny.

"So, we meet back here at seven?"

Kady forced a smile. "Seven."

Nerves, hurt and indecision plagued her. Tonight could not be over soon enough.

"I BLEW IT," Dylan said into the phone.

"Big-time," his brother Derrick agreed.

He'd changed into a powder blue dress shirt and navy dress slacks, looping the silk silver tie between his fingers as he dressed for the banquet. "Thanks for the sympathy."

"Hey, you said it yourself. Kady was going to be upset when she learned the truth."

"I get that. What I didn't expect was to fall in love."

Silence. Then Derrick blew out a long whistle.

"What do I do now?"

"You're seriously asking me?"

"You're older. Wiser."

"And bad at relationships," Derrick retorted.

"So use that experience and tell me what *not* to do."

"No pressure," his brother muttered.

Dylan smiled with grim humor. "I never thought I'd get over what Esposa did. All I could ever see was avenging Eddie. Pursuing the man who had changed my life. I never considered what came next."

"Until Kady."

"Until Kady." Dylan finished the knot on his tie. "I'm starting to feel some closure. I'll always carry what happened to Eddie, but with Kady, it's like the stark reality of the past has finally started to recede. I can actually see a future without the burden of what's happened."

"She really means that much to you?"

"More than I ever expected."

As he waited for some sage brotherly advice, Dylan opened the sliding door to the balcony. A gust of cold wind blew in. He breathed deeply, filling his lungs with the refreshing sea air.

"What does Mom say?" Derrick asked.

"She thinks I'm an idiot."

Derrick barked out a laugh. "I do love that woman."

"She wasn't thrilled with me, either, but she's known about my career a lot longer than Kady. Plus, as her son, I get some slack."

"So, she should have a woman's perspective on the situation."

"She told me to figure it out myself."

Another chuckle from the other end of the phone.

"Stop copping out. What should I do?"

When Derrick spoke, his tone was serious for the first time in the conversation. "Go after her, Dyl. Don't let her get away. You'll kick yourself forever if you don't fight for her with everything you have."

His brother was right. He had to get Kady to give him another chance. He couldn't imagine his future without her.

CHAPTER SIXTEEN

"PLEASE TELL ME you aren't going to wear that old thing," Lilli huffed from her position on the bed.

"It is awful," Nealy agreed.

"When did you two turn into the fashion police?" Kady called from the closet as she picked out another dress.

"Since you have to look perfect tonight. Dane thinks this is your year."

Nealy's boyfriend had an in with the banquet proceedings. Still, his in didn't mean she was the automatic winner. He probably hadn't figured Queen Jasmine into his calculations.

"You could text me the news."

Lilli gasped. "No way. You deserve to be there in person to accept the award."

Kady backed into the room holding a hanger. "Aren't you getting ahead of yourself?"

Nealy waved a hand. "Done deal. And that's not a good color on you."

"Sheesh." She picked a dress that she hadn't

really liked but had found at a clearance sale.
The girls had been shopping, bugging her to
buy something, so she grabbed the first deal that
caught her eye. She held it out for her friends to
view. "What about this one?"

She nearly fell over when Lilli plucked the
hanger from her hand. "Oh, my gosh. Try it
on."

Surprised that Lilli liked it, Kady slipped
out of the current dress and stepped into the
new choice. She stopped in the middle of the
room and twirled. "Well?"

"Stunning."

"Beautiful."

Kady gaped at them. "Are you kidding?"

Nealy grinned. "Perfect for the victor of the
wedding-bouquet competition."

Shaking her head, Kady stood before the
full-length mirror. Was that really the dress
she'd scooped up because of the price? A stunning ice-blue shade, it practically shimmered
in the light. The short, sleeveless style hugged
her curves. Her hair seemed darker against the
cool color. Her eyes turned a richer shade of
honey-brown. Kady barely recognized herself.

"Tell me you have a neutral pair of shoes,"
Nealy demanded.

"Check in the closet."

Her friend jumped off the bed and disappeared for a minute, returning with spiky metallic silver pumps. Lilli clapped her hands.

Kady's brow rose. "Are you sure?"

"Trust me," they responded in unison.

Lilli dragged her into the bathroom. "Give me fifteen minutes to do your hair and makeup and then you're good to go."

As her friend went to work, it was all Kady could do not to fall asleep. Exhaustion hit her hard, but she couldn't sleep just yet. Of course, if Dylan decided to take residence in her thoughts tonight she might not sleep at all, but she'd worry about that later. She was happy Lilli had managed to conceal the dark smudges below her eyes.

Just before she left, Nealy snapped a picture with her cell phone. "Look out, all the single guys."

"Or Dylan," Lilli added.

The moment of lightness faded at the mention of his name. On the most important night of her career, she wouldn't be with the man she loved.

"Hey, what's up? Did I say something wrong?"

Kady sighed. "It's a long story." Her friends were excited for her, so she pasted on a smile, brushed away their questions about the circles under her eyes and promised to fill them in later. She couldn't rehash the week's events one more time.

Thirty minutes later she stood in the periphery of the banquet room. On display were the bouquets, centerpieces, boutonnieres and other floral arrangements of the finalists. Too edgy to do much else, Kady searched for Melissa. She needed support to get through the night. When there was no sign of her, Kady went to the nearest beverage station and ordered a ginger ale. She'd just stepped away when Melissa ran up to her.

"Wow, girl. You look great."

"Thanks. You, too." She noticed a special sparkle in Melissa's eyes.

"Guess what? My hubby decided to surprise me. He's here tonight." Melissa grabbed the arm of the man beside her and pulled him in closer. "Kady, this is Charlie."

Kady shook the man's hand.

"Isn't he the best? He found a sitter and came out just to see how I'd do in the competition." She leaned over and bussed her husband's cheek with a kiss.

A mixture of hurt and jealousy swept through Kady. She took a sip of her soda, but the fizz only made her upset stomach worse.

She didn't begrudge her friend's happiness, but with the prospect of Dylan arriving soon, the pain and humiliation threatened to bubble over any minute.

"Um, please excuse me. I'll meet you at the table."

Melissa noticed her drawn features for the first time. "Are you sick?"

"Just need to visit the restroom. Be right back."

She placed her glass on a table and hurried to the ladies' room. Once inside, she stopped before the mirror, staring at her reflection. So much depended on this night. What if she lost to Jasmine? Again? Would her parents hold true to their threat to sell the shop? Knowing what Will had done might change their minds, but there was always the chance that being away on the cruise might cement their decision to sell anyway.

And what if Dylan wanted to talk? He'd made it clear he expected to at some point. Could she look at him? Meet the strange-colored eyes that not only fascinated her, but also gave her goose bumps.

The headache she'd fought all day slowly crept up her neck to her temples. She opened her small clutch. Lipstick and keys. No pain reliever. Great. Just great.

The door opened and the heavy scent of Coco by Chanel filled the room.

"I take it you haven't forgiven my son?"

Kady glanced in the mirror to see Jasmine walking toward her. "No."

"Not telling you the truth was a rather boneheaded move."

"I'm not going to argue with you."

Jasmine set her small purse on the vanity top. "There's something you have to understand about Dylan," she said as she rooted through the bag. "Out of all my boys, he's got the deepest sense of responsibility. He needs to protect. He's hardwired that way."

Kady sent her a sideways look. "Hardwired?"

Jasmine shrugged. "I hear my boys talk."

"I get your point."

"I don't think you do. Dylan would give his life to save the people he loves. If he could have taken the bullet for his partner, he would have, without hesitation. You aren't the only one he kept in the dark, Kady. I didn't know his real motives here, either."

"Doesn't it bother you? Being lied to?"

Jasmine smoothed on dark berry lipstick, then said, "I don't agree with Dylan's tactics, but I understand him. In his mind, lying to us meant protecting us. He saw it as a means to an end."

"I'm not sure if I can live with that kind of disregard for the truth."

"Then maybe you're the one who shows him there's another way. You don't have to know every single nuance of his job to trust him. He can protect and you can believe in him because you love him."

Kady sent her a flabbergasted look.

"Yes. I can see it written all over the both of you. You love him."

"I do."

"Then work things out."

"I don't know."

Jasmine patted her on the arm. "You'll never know until you try."

Kady met her gaze in the mirror again. Could she? Get over the hurt enough to forgive him?

Jasmine dropped the tube in her purse. "Come along. Dinner should be served soon and then we find out who this year's winner is."

At the prospect of losing to the woman standing beside her, Kady's spirits plummeted even lower.

Jasmine watched her with perceptive eyes,

so Kady pushed away from the vanity. "After you."

As they left the room, Dylan stood sentinel a few feet away. Kady stumbled over her feet. Pain seared her chest. She'd thought she was ready to see him, but obviously not. Maybe she never would be.

Ever the protector, he reached out a hand to steady her, but she dodged him. "I'll see you both later. Good luck, Jasmine."

"You, too, my dear."

Close call. She didn't know what she'd have done if Dylan had touched her. Melted? Hit him? In her exhausted state, she couldn't decide between the two.

She got through the next forty minutes of pushing roasted chicken around her plate and making small talk. She swore she felt Dylan's gaze on her back, but refused to turn and give him the pleasure of knowing she was thinking about him. Once the table was cleared, the award ceremony started. She was so tense she'd snap in half.

The emcee for the night started off by thanking the hotel for hosting the convention and soon the winners of the different categories were being announced. Hands clasped tightly in her lap, Kady waited. The list grew smaller, until the centerpiece category was next. Melissa grabbed her arm and squeezed.

"Please, please, please," her friend repeated like a mantra.

Despite the hurt, Kady smiled. And when Melissa was announced as the winner, everyone at the table jumped up and clapped. Kady, truly happy, watched her friend hurry across the room to receive her award. She caught a glimpse of Melissa's beaming husband and her heart ached all over again.

When the bouquet category was announced, Kady crossed her fingers. Holding her breath, she waited to hear her name. Her heart pounded loudly in the hushed murmurs of the room.

The emcee finally spoke. "And the winner is…Jasmine Matthews."

Kady blinked. Shook her head. Tried to reconcile the truth.

She'd lost. Again.

As the noise level of the room ratcheted up, her hearing dulled. Melissa spoke to her, but she caught only a few muffled words. Was she having an adverse reaction to Jasmine winning? If it wasn't so sad, she could almost start laughing. All her hard work. For nothing. Fourth time was not the charm.

Jasmine gave her speech, but Kady could only wallow in her dismal failure.

No matter what she did, she couldn't seem to accomplish her goals. Her parents wanted to sell the shop. Would they still after learning she lost again? Will was on board now, admitting he admired her work, but would it matter? Too little too late? And Dylan? Well, she couldn't go there. Not now.

She had lots of thinking to do.

And she was never, ever, entering the bouquet competition again.

The ceremony mercifully ended. Folks gathered around to congratulate the winners and say goodbye to friends. As of tomorrow, the convention attendees would be heading home. The Sunshine State Florist Convention would meet again in another year.

Taking hold of her clutch, Kady eased through the crowd to pick up her bouquet. She needed to get out of here. When she neared the table, she found her bouquet next to Jasmine's. What had been the defining factor between the two? Could she have done anything differently? No. As far as she was concerned, her entry was beautiful. And hopefully the brides who had viewed her handiwork during the day would agree and reward her by using her services when they planned their wedding ceremonies.

With a shuttered sigh, she picked up her bouquet. Sniffed the aromatic fragrance. Blinked back hot tears. She would not cry. She would not.

Taking a cleansing breath, she turned to leave, only to find Dylan standing in her way.

"I'm sorry," he said, somber voice matching his expression.

Clutching the bouquet in front of her, it didn't escape her notice that she held the piece just like a bride would, standing before her groom. Only this wasn't a wedding and Dylan was far from her groom.

She shrugged. "Not in the cards, I guess."

"You did a beautiful job."

"Yet your mother won again."

"If it makes you feel better, she feels bad about it."

"No. It doesn't help." She lowered the bouquet. "If you'll excuse me, I'm leaving now."

Dylan reached out to stop her, then dropped his hand. "Can we go somewhere to talk?"

"I don't have anything to say."

"But I do."

She stared at him, heartbroken. Why did it have to end like this?

Mistaking her silence for an opportunity to speak, Dylan took her elbow and steered her through the open patio doors. So empty and unsure of herself, Kady let him lead her to a quiet spot. The cold night sent shivers over her skin, but she ignored the discomfort. In the dim lighting, Dylan's gaze, resolute and unyielding, met hers.

"We have something good going, Kady. From the moment we met there was this spark of attraction, which has grown every day since. Yes, I lied to you, but knowing why, can't we come to some sort of understanding? I love you. I've never told that to another woman because I vowed to myself that when I did someday say those words, I'd mean them from the depths of my heart."

Kady swallowed hard. Tears burned the backs of her eyelids. She believed him; she did. But her world was falling apart around her.

"I love you, too, Dylan. But I need some time. Space. To figure out my jumbled emotions. Can you understand?"

"Yes. I'm not giving up on you. On us. After I was shot I never imagined I'd have much of a future, but now, all I can think about is us, together through the long haul. No secrets, no lies, no regrets. Consider that when you make your decision."

After his speech, Dylan leaned down and gently brushed his lips over hers. Her traitorous body reacted like she always did when he kissed her. She melted beneath his touch and knew that was never going to change.

Dylan broke contact. Stepped back. His open expression hid whatever emotion was brewing inside him.

"It's up to you, Kady."

As he walked away, tears streamed unchecked down her face. He'd laid it on the line. Now she had to decide what step to take next.

TWO WEEKS HAD passed since the disaster Kady would always remember as the convention debacle. She'd had time to think, time to see events from Dylan's perspective. Forgive him, even. He hadn't planned to lie to her. Things had spiraled out of control and they'd all been sucked up in the vortex. True to his word, he'd kept his distance. Was he back at work? Still bothered by his leg injury? She wanted answers, but held off calling him.

"I like this arrangement," Lilli said, holding the sample book up for Max to see. "What do you think?"

"You have until the end of the month to get your wedding plans completed because I'm marrying you with or without all the festivities."

Lilli giggled. "I love a strong man."

The couple had finally scheduled an appointment to finalize the floral choices for their wedding. Over the chatter in Cuppa Joe, they'd discussed their options. Kady had hoped to set up an area in the shop for just this purpose, but her parents hadn't decided a direction for The Lavish Lily yet.

They hadn't been happy when they learned the shop had been the scene of a drug bust. Even less happy that Kady had gotten involved with a DEA agent and didn't have a clue as to what had gone on right under her nose. Although curiosity brought in new customers, Kady acknowledged the events during the convention would have a role in her folks' verdict.

As much as they were disappointed in Kady, they were blindsided by Will's confession. The boy wonder had screwed up in such a big way they were clueless as to how to proceed in their relationship with him. The only bright spot was that their mother was thrilled that he and Christine were a couple.

Kady sympathized with him, knowing how

it felt to be the object of their parents' displeasure. No one in the Lawrence family was coping very well these days. But in spite of the trouble, she and Will had made time to sit down for a long, overdue talk. They were able to patch things up and move on. Kady had her big brother back.

Once she finished her discussion with her friends, she had a meeting with her family. Her stomach twisted, a chronic condition if the past two weeks were any indication. Today she'd find out her fate and that of the shop.

Kady jotted down Lilli and Max's choices. Everyone rose. Lilli hugged her. "Thanks. You've been so patient and I appreciate it."

"It's what I do," Kady said, knowing her big fake smile wasn't fooling her friend.

Max's troubled eyes focused on her. "Have you talked to Dylan?"

She stopped placing her belongings in the tote. She knew Max and Dylan had become friends during his stay in Cypress Pointe. "No."

"He went back to Miami."

Her breath caught. She fussed with the objects in her bag to cover her reaction. "I guess he had to tie up the case."

Max nodded. "He'll be back, you know."

Lilli elbowed Max. "Why don't we change the subject?"

"Why? He's crazy about Kady. She should know."

Oh, she did. His parting kiss confirmed his love and so much more. Would she be able to get over the hurt and lack of trust? Even though she truly loved him?

"Thanks for the news flash, Max."

He grinned, knowing exactly that she was yanking his chain.

Looping the tote strap over her shoulder, Kady headed for the door. "On that note, I have another meeting."

Lilli frowned. "Will you be okay?"

"Yes," Kady answered, straightening her shoulders. "Yes. I will."

The walk down Main Street took only minutes. The beginning of February had warmed up. Perfect tourist weather. She loved this town. Loved the people. Hoped her parents opted for the shop to stay in the family.

Before long she was in the back room of The Lavish Lily. She and Will on one side of the worktable, her parents on the other. Christine manned the front counter so the meeting would not be disturbed by customers.

Her father cleared his voice. "Your mother and I have had much to think about."

Kady tried not to cringe at the censure in his tone.

"Kady. We understand that the circumstances surrounding events at The Lavish Lily were not within your control. As was the outcome of the competition. It was wrong of us to put undue pressure on you."

Some of that undue pressure eased from her chest. So far, so good.

"Your brother came by the house last night," her mother continued. "We had a good talk. While we aren't happy with his actions, we understand his motives. Seems both of our children have been surprises lately. Good and bad."

"What do you mean?"

"Your ideas have a great deal of merit, Kady. Will explained your plans and how they affect the bottom line."

"But I explained all of that to you."

"You did," her father said. "But more from the angle of how you would run the shop. Not the business." Her father drew a heavy breath. "Now, the other news. Your mother and I have an opportunity to sell our shares of the shop."

She sneaked a look at Will. His impassive features gave nothing away.

"To Will?"

"No."

Her heart sank. "To whom, then?"

Her parents exchanged glances. "We've had an offer from a serious buyer. We'd like you to meet the person and make the final decision."

"But—"

"We think this is a positive change," her mother interrupted. "For everyone. Will can continue with the finances and you can continue with the creative side. A new partner will also add a fresh outlook."

Disbelief spread through her. "I don't... So what happens next?"

"You meet the new part owner. Tell us what you think."

"You really trust me to make this decision?"

Her parents looked at each other, then at her. "We do," her mother answered.

Wow. Okay. "When do I meet this person?"

Her mother rounded the table. "Today." She cupped Kady's face with her hands. "Kady, our decision to sell is not a reflection on what happened here while we were gone. You handled the situation quite well, in spite of not having all the facts." She frowned at Will. "Your father and I want to travel. Do things we never had time for before. I do trust you'll do The Lavish Lily proud."

Apparently not enough to give Kady full control.

She then hooked arms with her husband and son. "We'll send the potential buyer back so you two can meet."

Kady rubbed her forehead. "Fine."

Her mother chuckled. "And get ready for another wedding. It seems your brother and Christine are headed down the aisle."

Kady gaped at her brother.

His lips lifted at the corners. "We'll fill you in later."

"You bet you will."

As her family left, nerves took up residence in her stomach. Unlike the last meeting, this time her folks wanted her opinion. But what if she disagreed with her parents' choice? As much as she was humbled by their newfound belief in her, what if she made the wrong decision? How could she be so happy and so panicked at the same time?

Kady played with a daisy left over from an arrangement her mother had been putting together on the worktable. She lifted the stem, ran her fingers over the delicate bud. With one sweeping motion she could yank off the white petals, destroying the beautiful creation. It might make her feel better, but it wouldn't change the circumstances. She would have to work with a partner.

"Kady?"

She dropped the flower and twirled. Her eyes grew wide. "Dylan."

He stood in the threshold of the hallway. "I just got back from Miami and needed to see you."

"This isn't a good time…" She stopped, stammered over her words. How was it possible he was standing here now? She'd thought about what she'd say when she saw him again, what she'd do. But this hadn't been in any of those scenarios. "My parents are considering selling their shares of the business. My potential new partner will be here soon."

Dylan slowly walked to her. "He's already here."

"How could you possibly—" The realization became clear. "You?"

He moved a few steps closer. "I'm getting too old for the crime business. It's time for something new." He stood directly before her. "This way I get to be by your side on the journey of transforming The Lavish Lily into the best wedding flower shop in Florida."

He wanted to be part of her journey? Her pulse raced. Her parents finally trusted her. It meant the world to her. Couldn't she do the same with Dylan? He hadn't set out to intentionally hurt her, just as she hadn't set out to fall in love with him. But both happened and the earth still kept spinning.

"I… We… Oh, the heck with it." She launched at him. He staggered back, but his arms surrounded her quickly, like they were always meant to protect her. "You're crazy."

"About you," he said. Then he proceeded to kiss her until she lost her breath. She gulped some air and resumed the kiss at a much slower pace. Once she got her fill, she pulled away.

"How? Why?"

"Will called me when your folks made their decision. Asked if I was interested in investing in your future. With your approval, of course."

He was offering her an olive branch here. "You don't have to buy into the shop."

"I know, but I want you to see how serious I am about spending my life with you. How this could be the first step for us."

"Dylan, I don't know what to say."

"Say you need a delivery guy? How about making boutonnieres? I think I passed that class. Nope. I've got it. I'll spy on my mother so she doesn't win next year."

Kady laughed, so carefree it surprised her. "You don't have to do any of those things."

"Then how about you forgive me?"

She ran a finger over his bristly cheek. "I do. I was going to tell you when I saw you." She trailed her hand down to rest over his heart.

"So why do I detect a *but*?"

"Well, I was going to insist you never keep anything else from me, but you've shown up here out of the blue, so that won't fly."

"You knew I'd be back."

Her tone softened. "I knew."

"I didn't keep my interest in the sale from you on purpose," Dylan assured her. "I wanted to surprise you."

"Your plan worked."

"So, are we going to crush the floral world?"

She grimaced at that description, then took a step back, tapping a finger on her chin. "On two conditions."

"So soon?" A brow rose over one gunmetal eye. "Derrick warned me about this."

She ignored him. "One, you get your mother to promise she won't enter the wedding-bouquet competition at the convention next year. I need to see if I can win without her legacy getting in the way."

"I can do that. Next?"

"Any chance she might want to come work for her son?"

"Wait. You *want* to work with my mother?"

"She's an awesome designer. We could really grab a big chunk of the wedding industry if she's on board."

"I... Well, I'm sure she'll be honored when I ask her. She's been hinting about moving here since she and my aunt have started planning trips together." He smiled slowly. "If she moved to town, they could make my uncle crazy for a while."

Kady circled her arms around Dylan's waist. "And lastly—"

"You didn't mention a third condition."

"You should stay in law enforcement."

His gaze grew serious. "I figured getting out was best for us."

"No. You putting bad guys away is best for us. For everyone."

He grinned. "A transfer was discussed when I went back to my field office. Tampa, as I recall."

"Then I think we've just decided our future together, Mr. Matthews."

"I wouldn't have it any other way, Ms. Lawrence."

* * * * *

More books are available in
THE BUSINESS OF WEDDINGS
miniseries from USA TODAY
bestselling author Tara Randel!
Visit www.harlequin.com today!

LARGER-PRINT BOOKS!

GET 2 FREE
LARGER-PRINT NOVELS
PLUS 2 FREE
MYSTERY GIFTS

Love Inspired®

Larger-print novels are now available...

LILP15

LARGER-PRINT BOOKS!

GET 2 FREE LARGER-PRINT NOVELS PLUS 2 FREE MYSTERY GIFTS

Love Inspired®
SUSPENSE
RIVETING INSPIRATIONAL ROMANCE

Larger-print novels are now available...

WESTERN WP PROMISES

YES! Please send me **The Western Promises Collection** in Larger Print. This collection begins with 3 FREE books and 2 FREE gifts (gifts valued at approx. $14.00 retail) in the first shipment, along with the other first 4 books from the collection! If I do not cancel, I will receive 8 monthly shipments until I have the entire 51-book Western Promises collection. I will receive 2 or 3 FREE books in each shipment and I will pay just $4.99 US/ $5.89 CDN for each of the other four books in each shipment, plus $2.99 for shipping and handling per shipment. *If I decide to keep the entire collection, I'll have paid for only 32 books, because 19 books are FREE! I understand that accepting the 3 free books and gifts places me under no obligation to buy anything. I can always return a shipment and cancel at any time. My free books and gifts are mine to keep no matter what I decide.

272 HCN 3070 472 HCN 3070

Name	(PLEASE PRINT)	
Address		Apt. #
City	State/Prov.	Zip/Postal Code

Signature (if under 18, a parent or guardian must sign)

Mail to the **Reader Service:**
IN U.S.A.: P.O. Box 1867, Buffalo, NY 14240-1867
IN CANADA: P.O. Box 609, Fort Erie, Ontario L2A 5X3

* Terms and prices subject to change without notice. Prices do not include applicable taxes. Sales tax applicable in N.Y. Canadian residents will be charged applicable taxes. This offer is limited to one order per household. All orders subject to approval. Credit or debit balances in a customer's account(s) may be offset by any other outstanding balance owed by or to the customer. Please allow 4 to 6 weeks for delivery. Offer available while quantities last. Offer not available to Quebec residents.

WPBPA16R

LARGER-PRINT BOOKS!
GET 2 FREE LARGER-PRINT NOVELS PLUS
2 FREE GIFTS!

HARLEQUIN®

super romance®

More Story...More Romance

REQUEST YOUR FREE BOOKS!
2 FREE WHOLESOME ROMANCE NOVELS IN LARGER PRINT
PLUS 2
FREE
MYSTERY GIFTS

🌟🌟🌟🌟🌟🌟🌟🌟🌟🌟🌟🌟🌟🌟🌟🌟🌟🌟🌟🌟

HEARTWARMING™

🌟🌟🌟🌟🌟🌟🌟🌟🌟🌟🌟🌟🌟🌟🌟🌟🌟🌟🌟🌟

Wholesome, tender romances

YES! Please send me 2 FREE Harlequin® Heartwarming Larger-Print novels and my 2 FREE mystery gifts (gifts worth about $10). After receiving them, if I don't wish to receive any more books, I can return the shipping statement marked "cancel." If I don't cancel, I will receive 4 brand-new larger-print novels every month and be billed just $5.24 per book in the U.S. or $5.99 per book in Canada. That's a savings of at least 19% off the cover price. It's quite a bargain! Shipping and handling is just 50¢ per book in the U.S. and 75¢ per book in Canada.* I understand that accepting the 2 free books and gifts places me under no obligation to buy anything. I can always return a shipment and cancel at any time. Even if I never buy another book, the two free books and gifts are mine to keep forever.

161/361 IDN GHX2

Name	(PLEASE PRINT)	
Address		Apt. #
City	State/Prov.	Zip/Postal Code

Signature (if under 18, a parent or guardian must sign)

Mail to the **Reader Service:**
IN U.S.A.: P.O. Box 1867, Buffalo, NY 14240-1867
IN CANADA: P.O. Box 609, Fort Erie, Ontario L2A 5X3

* Terms and prices subject to change without notice. Prices do not include applicable taxes. Sales tax applicable in N.Y. Canadian residents will be charged applicable taxes. Offer not valid in Quebec. This offer is limited to one order per household. Not valid for current subscribers to Harlequin Heartwarming larger-print books. All orders subject to credit approval. Credit or debit balances in a customer's account(s) may be offset by any other outstanding balance owed by or to the customer. Please allow 4 to 6 weeks for delivery. Offer available while quantities last.

Your Privacy—The Reader Service is committed to protecting your privacy. Our Privacy Policy is available online at www.ReaderService.com or upon request from the Reader Service.

We make a portion of our mailing list available to reputable third parties that offer products we believe may interest you. If you prefer that we not exchange your name with third parties, or if you wish to clarify or modify your communication preferences, please visit us at www.ReaderService.com/consumerschoice or write to us at Reader Service Preference Service, P.O. Box 9062, Buffalo, NY 14240-9062. Include your complete name and address.

HW15